US

"You've lost a lot, Ket," Blake said, cupping her chin in his hand.

"I don't need your sympathy." Ket tried to turn aside, but he turned her face back to his. Compelled by his probing gaze, she searched the depths of his blue eyes, unable to quell the fascination that swirled inside. Even as she hated him, she felt drawn to him.

"Since the beginning of time, men have been fighting and killing themselves over land, Ket." He was so close that his breath blew hot and sweet against her face when he spoke. "That's war. It's been going on forever." As tenderly as though he touched a babe, he cupped her cheeks in his palms. His fingers spread up her temples and into her hair. "We may not like it," he continued, "but it happens. It doesn't have anything to do with us, not if we don't let it."

"With us?" Her mouth was dry and the word came out like a sigh.

"Us." He repeated the word like a love song and followed it with his lips. They spread over hers, wet and hot and demanding . . .

It was a kiss like nothing she had ever experienced. Deep and sensual, it seemed like the headspring of a river. He clasped her face in his hands again and kissed her tenderly, almost chastely. "This is what I meant, Ket . . . *us*."

BOOK YOUR PLACE ON OUR WEBSITE AND MAKE THE READING CONNECTION!

We've created a customized website just for our very special readers, where you can get the inside scoop on everything that's going on with Zebra, Pinnacle and Kensington books.

When you come online, you'll have the exciting opportunity to:

- View covers of upcoming books

- Read sample chapters

- Learn about our future publishing schedule (listed by publication month *and author*)

- Find out when your favorite authors will be visiting a city near you

- Search for and order backlist books from our online catalog

- Check out author bios and background information

- Send e-mail to your favorite authors

- Meet the Kensington staff online

- Join us in weekly chats with authors, readers and other guests

- Get writing guidelines

- AND MUCH MORE!

**Visit our website at
http://www.zebrabooks.com**

CATCH A WILD HEART

Vivian Vaughan

Zebra Books
Kensington Publishing Corp.

http://www.zebrabooks.com

ZEBRA BOOKS are published by

Kensington Publishing Corp.
850 Third Avenue
New York, NY 10022

Zebra and the Z logo Reg. U.S. Pat. & TM Off.

First Printing: March, 2000
10 9 8 7 6 5 4 3 2 1

Printed in the United States of America

Chapter One

Texas, West of the Pecos—1880

It should have been a simple task, Keturah Tremayne thought impatiently. *Find two runaway boys.* Now look where it had gotten her.

"Nothing involving white eyes is ever simple," she muttered to herself. Huddled in a rocky crevice a hundred yards or so above the valley the Comancheros had chosen for their camp, Ket rubbed her cramped leg.

"Nothing," she repeated. She had no liking for what she was about to do, but that didn't change the fact that she had to do it. She had given Lena her word.

True, the promise had been made before either she or Lena knew the boys had been kidnapped by Comancheros—a major obstacle, no doubt about it. But the fact remained—Ket had given her word. And she had to keep it, regardless that she would now be required to sneak into a camp of three dozen or more armed and dangerous men.

Absently drying wet palms on her soft deerskin britches, Ket watched the men secure camp for evening. She studied every aspect of the layout, knowing they would not be foolish enough to let down their guard, not for a single second. Within a day's ride of the Río Grande, where they would find sanctuary across the river in Mexico, they could be counted on to remain armed and alert.

With each passing hour doubts about her ability to pull off such a difficult rescue increased. Who was she to think she could slip into that camp, free two dimwitted white-eyes boys, and get them all three out alive?

"You're our only hope," Lena had written.

Some hope, Ket thought now, awaiting nightfall. Her stomach filled with dread in direct relationship to the descent of the afternoon sun. From her perch high in the rugged cliffs of *Puerto del Piasano,* she watched the fiery golden disk disappear behind the serrated peaks of the High Mountains further west. The effect was startling. Alternate bands of gold, red, and darker shadows striated the valley. Campfires sparkled like brilliant jewels.

Below her the riding stock had been watered in nearby Piasano Springs and staked for the night. A hush had begun to fall, as darkness encroached. She had spent the last few hours huddled here between two outcroppings, watching, waiting, biding her time.

Now the Comancheros, many stumbling from drunkenness, had begun to settle on the ground for the night. Soon their bedrolls would spill from the mouth of the canyon out onto the cactus-strewn desert plain.

Her hours of observation paid off, for she had located the missing boys, then observed as the Comancheros bound and deposited them along with other booty in the center of the camp near the largest bonfire.

The fires would burn through the night, surrounded, of course, by the sprawling mass of armed men. The boys she had come to rescue wouldn't have been more securely imprisoned inside a white man's jail.

Ket watched carefully, more distressed than she would have imagined herself being over the plight of two white-eyes boys.

They seemed in good health, if weary from their weeklong ordeal. She'd been trailing them three days when their tracks merged with those of a single man; not half a day later, the three pairs of tracks had been overrun by a party of thirty-odd armed men and double that number of pack animals. A herd of domesticated horses, probably stolen from ranches along the Comanche Trail, were loose-herded on the far side of the camp.

She could tell nothing about the single man the boys had taken up with, but it hadn't taken her long to identify the captors as Comancheros.

Their retinue gave them away—their tracks a mixture of shod and unshod ponies and heavily laden pack animals. Their haste and direction confirmed this conclusion. Making a beeline for the Mexican border, they traveled at double the expected speed for a party their size.

It was, after all, late fall. The air was already cool and crisp. Winter fast approached. Normally Comancheros wrapped up their raiding activities and headed for Mexico before this time, not wishing to be caught in the vicinity of the major military outposts of Davis and Bliss by an early snowstorm.

Their location for this camp further proved the point to Ket and added to her urgency. Equidistant between Fort Davis and the privately owned Fort Leaton, this site would be an overnight stop, at best. When pushed, Comancheros were known to camp a few hours, then push forward into the night.

Time was short; the situation, desperate. Night guards would be especially alert. Secreted within the dark shelter, surrounded by her weapons, Ket dried her palms again as two men ascended the hills to either side of her. First watch. Large-brimmed sombreros covered their faces. More to the point, each wore two pistols and crossed bandoleers of bullets for their rifles. She must assume they also carried knives.

Still she waited. Outmanned and outarmed, she must lay her plans with care and choose her time equally well. Impatience could mean death for the boys, death for herself. Let the darkness deepen and the men below fall asleep . . .

Keturah's dilemma had begun with a call for help she could not ignore. It couldn't have come at a worse time. But wasn't that the way with white eyes? Their intrusion into her life and the lives of her people had not been limited to this request to find two runaway boys.

On the other hand, these weren't just any runaway boys. Luke Tremayne was Ket's half-brother, born to her white-eyes father and his flame-haired wife. Tres Robles, eleven, was the son of the only white eyes Ket trusted in this whole world, Nick Bourbon and his wife Lena.

It was Lena who sent word to the Apachería that the boys had gone off to seek the old Tremayne home place, Apache Wells, and had not returned.

"Your father and Nick are up in the Delawares," Lena's message explained. "They've taken most of the cowhands to help drive cattle down for the winter. Sabrina's delivery date is near. You are our only hope to find the boys, Ket. We've no one else to turn to."

As skilled at tracking and as knowledgeable of the country as her father and as competent with weapons as any of Victorio's warriors, Keturah Tremayne was the obvious choice for so difficult a task. Branded a half-breed by the white community and an orphan at the Apachería after her Apache mother had been murdered by white soldiers, Ket had forged her own individual lifestyle. There were those in both communities who said she had patterned her life after her father, whose vast wilderness skills were renowned in this wild country. She cynically denied such claims, even to herself. Especially to herself.

Adding to Ket's present dilemma, Lena and Nick had come to her aid more than once in her tumultuous twenty years. No, she could not ignore Lena's request. She could only hope the Apaches holed up in the Diablo Mountains wouldn't decide to raid Fort Davis before she found the two dimwitted boys and returned them to their mothers.

The dozen or so warriors left at the Apachería, those who for whatever reason hadn't followed Victorio to Mexico, had been gathered in war council for two weeks trying to talk themselves into raiding Fort Davis.

"We need not ride all the way to Mexico to fight with Victorio," Ket had heard them reason. "We can die as honorably and without that long ride right here at home."

Most of their women and many of the old men hoped the young warriors would eventually decide to go to Mexico to be with their great leader, Victorio. Most had remained behind with their sons, husbands, fathers. All would follow their men to Mexico. Though none spoke aloud of it, no one among them doubted that the time of the Chiricahua, indeed of all free Apaches, was nearing its final days. Whether the end came here in the Diablo Mountains or in Mexico mattered little to the haggard, haunted, and hunted vestiges of a once proud people. Perhaps they should all be together.

Ket intended to follow her people to Mexico. Her decision had been reinforced recently when her cousin, called Emily by the white-eyes colonel and his wife who adopted and raised her, returned to the Apachería to be with her blood people at the end.

Ket didn't fear the dying. She had always known—they all had always known—that the People were born to die. She would be proud to die with them. They were, after all, half of her heritage, the only half she claimed. Having her cousin beside her would be appropriate and welcome.

Beyond that she resisted analyzing her innermost heart. She knew her decision to leave this land was prompted by anger at the white-eyes soldiers who murdered her mother; anger at Sabrina, the flame-haired woman who had stolen her father; anger at her father for abandoning her to a life of virtual nonexistence.

Although it didn't matter to Ket whether the warriors raided Fort Davis, it did matter to Emily. After ten years with the white eyes, the fourteen-year-old was more white than Apache. But not to everyone. Ten years with the white eyes and Emily was suddenly not good enough to be courted by the young officer she fancied herself falling in love with. He had chosen a blond-haired, blue-eyed girl to court.

"Love?" Ket had scoffed. To her, Emily's claim was yet another example of the white man's definition of love—betrayal.

"She only wanted to love you," Ket's father had said the day Sabrina left the Apachería for good. Next thing Ket knew, her father had married the flame-haired woman.

"Sabrina and I are in love," he had tried to explain later. "One day you will understand."

Ten years later here Emily was, barely fourteen years of age, claiming to love a white-eyes soldier. Reba Applebee, Emily's adoptive mother, had tried to soothe Emily, but it hadn't worked, and Emily returned to the Apachería.

"She doesn't think I'm old enough to fall in love," Emily told Ket with tears flowing down her cheeks. "She thinks I'm still a child, too young to know what love is."

Ket held her tongue. She didn't tell Emily the truth, that Reba Applebee's concept of love was surely the same as her own father's had been.

"I know I would have to wait a few years, Ket, but . . . Apache women marry at a younger age than I am now," Emily had cried. "I'm not too young to know what I want. I've known white girls to marry at thirteen."

"It's over, Emily," Ket had said. "You will forget." But Ket wouldn't forget. To her this was the sort of treatment one should expect from all white eyes—betrayal.

Betrayal. That's what they meant by love. She couldn't tell Emily that. Emily, broken-hearted that her dream would never come true, may have returned to her blood people, but she had not yet learned to hate the white eyes.

"Please persuade them not to raid the fort," she had pled with Ket.

"You know little of our ways, girl. I am not Apache enough to speak my mind. Certainly not and have it heard."

"But you must try, Ket. I couldn't stand for my . . . my other family to be murdered by my blood people. Or the other way . . ."

Strangely, Emily had remained dear to Ket, when everyone else had abandoned and disappointed her. Without delving into the meaning, Ket knew it had something to do with the symbolic connection she felt with Emily, who shared a similarity with Ket's own disparate situation. Half Apache, half white, Keturah Tremayne was all nothing.

"I will try," she promised. Then, while talk of war escalated, Lena's urgent message arrived.

Lena and Nick were Ket's one link with the white world, which she had shunned since her mother's death when she was a small child. Through Lena and Nick, she had kept up with Emily, even visited her at the Bourbons' ranch, to which Emily had finally come for help in returning to the Apachería.

Through Lena and Nick, Ket had also kept up with the comings and goings of her father, Tremayne, and his hated wife, Sabrina. Through Lena and Nick, she had come to know her half-brother Luke. Lena and Nick were as solid a foundation in Ket's life as the red volcanic bedrock was to the Davis Mountains.

So when Lena's message arrived, she felt obligated to

respond. Lena worried about the boys being alone in the mountains with the Ramériz brothers loose; they still threatened revenge against Tremayne for their father's murder.

Ket feared that a worse fate could befall the boys if warriors from the Apachería decided to attack the fort. What better way to provoke the citizens of Fort Davis than by killing the sons of the area's leading ranchers?

Not that she cared what happened to Luke Tremayne, but she couldn't let Lena and Nick's son cross paths with a band of warriors who were itching for revenge.

Not that she cared what happened to Luke, Ket insisted. Yet, she did care. She didn't actually *like* the boy, this half-brother, but for some unexplored reason, he fascinated her.

Looking at him she saw vexing similarities. True, his complexion was fairer; but the eyes that shone from his boy-soft, sun-kissed white face were the same eyes that shone from her tawny face. Tremayne green eyes. She hated them. Yet, looking Luke in the eye always brought a queasy feeling to her stomach.

And his hair, though not as dark as her own, was nevertheless dark enough, and wavy.

Green eyes. Dark wavy hair. The two characteristics she could never hide. On her otherwise pure Apache face they became her nemeses, proclaiming her an outsider in every man's world, a person who belonged nowhere, to no one.

Unless to the Tremaynes, who did not want her.

Chilled by the night and by her own ghosts, Ket reached to chafe her arms and felt the cold steel bullets in her bandoleers. The agony of her unrequited past faded into the reality that awaited her.

Time to move. Time to rescue the boys and return to the Apachería before her two worlds collided.

In the valley below, the bonfires had died to embers.

Forms of sleeping Comancheros and their captives mounded across the plain like so many anthills.

Tonight Ket wished that Luke had inherited his mother's flaming hair; Luke's mother, Sabrina, the hated soldier's daughter who had stolen her father, had hair so red it must have been colored by spirits of the Underworld. Hair that red would glow in the firelight, lighting her way even as the stars above threatened to sabotage her mission.

To avert immediate failure, Ket knew she must disarm the night guard who had taken position directly above her. Soundlessly, she removed her crossed bandoleers and placed them beside her rifle to retrieve later. She stretched her scarred leg, burned in a ceremonial fire when she was ten, loosening it for the climb ahead, then slipped out of her hiding place.

The guard never heard a sound. An arm around his throat, a strategic chop to his windpipe, and he was unconscious. She bound his hands and feet with leather straps she carried on her belt for such purpose, then tethered him to a stunted shinoak. His own bandanna proved a suitable gag.

In less than three minutes Ket left the unconscious guard behind, stopped for her rifle and bandoleers, and headed down the mountain wearing his serape and sombrero over her deerskin britches and calico shirt. Her knee-high Apache moccasins made no sound when she reached the outskirts of the camp and threaded her way among the sleeping Comancheros. If any awakened, they would think her one of them, returning from a call of nature.

Arousing the boys would be more difficult. One false move or sound from either and all would be lost. Tres Robles, levelheaded and mature for a white-eyes boy of his age, might react more sensibly.

Luke was the first she came to. Stretching out beside him, as though she were lying down to sleep, she felt his wakefulness. Uncertain what he might do, fearing the worst, she brought her lips close to his ear and whispered, "It's Keturah. Do as I say and don't make a sound."

"Ket!" He didn't yell the word. She only heard it that way.

No sooner had she slit his bonds than he threw his arms around her neck, catching her off guard. "I knew you'd come, Ket."

Again the words made no more sound than a slight breeze blown directly into her ear, but she froze in terror that they would draw attention. After a moment she repeated, "Do exactly what I say."

This time he simply nodded.

"Pull your hat down over your face, get up, and walk away. Slowly. Stay behind those far trees, enter that canyon directly beneath the rising moon, and wait."

He was gone before she finished speaking, and she curled up in his place, where she waited impatiently, listening for trouble. Her heart thrashed so loudly she knew it could surely be heard to the furthest reaches of this camp of miscreants. She had never felt such anxiety. Not for her own safety, but for the life of this boy. She told herself it was because he was a stupid, inept white eyes. An Apache boy ten years old would have been able to pull off the assignment in a minute. But a white eyes . . .

What if he were caught? What would her father say?

The thought came unbidden and unwanted, and the resulting anger fueled Ket's resolve to complete this job and return to her suffering people. Focusing on the stars overhead, she counted time by their movement.

Half an hour later, Tres Robles, as she had expected, followed her instructions to the letter. Again she watched the stars and waited, allowing time for any Comancheros who might have been aroused by the boys' passing to return to sleep.

Now for her own escape. Stealthily she rose to her knees—

A man grabbed her arm. Her heart stopped. She thought only to keep him from sounding the alarm.

Quickly, she clamped one hand over his mouth and, with the weight of her body, wrestled him to the ground. Deftly withdrawing her knife, she thrust the razor-sharp point to his throat. "A thousand Apache warriors wait in those hills to take your scalp," she whispered. "One sound and I'll beat them to it."

"*¡Silencio!*" growled another Comanchero, this one from down the line.

"Ugh!" Ket's attacker gasped when she squeezed her elbow around his throat, cutting off his breath. He slumped back, and she slipped away, fearful that at any moment he would rouse and call his compadres to arms.

The cry that came was not from a Comanchero but from her half-brother Luke. No sooner had Ket stepped into the mouth of the canyon than Luke threw his arms around her neck for the second time tonight.

"You came for us, Ket! I knew you would." Then he took her by surprise. "We gotta go back down there."

"What?" She could feel his trembling. Indeed, her own breathing was still hard, not as much from exertion as from the anxiety of moving through thirty-odd sleeping Comancheros, expecting any one of them to sound the alarm at any moment. They weren't free and clear, yet.

"For Blake," Luke explained. "We gotta go back for Blake."

Ket stared at him, dumbfounded. Why had she thought rescuing these two boys would be simple? Nothing involving white eyes was ever simple. How could she have expected this to be different?

"What we have to do is get up this canyon and away from here," she whispered roughly. They were still too close to the camp to risk conversing, much less arguing. "They'll be changing guard soon. We have to get away before then. Our horses are at the head of *Puerto del*—"

But Luke, for all the fact that his voice still rasped with fright, refused to give up. "We can't leave without Blake."

She had no idea who Blake was. Lena had mentioned only the two boys. "We can and we will." She took each boy by an arm and shoved them both up the canyon. "I brought two extra horses. They're—"

"Luke's right, Ket." Tres Robles was generally the level-headed one. "We can't leave Blake behind to fend for himself."

"He's a greenhorn, Ket," Luke added. "A surveyor. He's only been out here a few weeks. He'll never make it on his own."

Suddenly she recalled the single set of tracks that had merged with the boys' tracks the day before they were overtaken by Comancheros.

"We can't leave him," Tres repeated. "The fellow spoke up for us more than once."

"Then he can speak up for himself." She gave each boy an extra shove from behind, but Luke dug in his heels.

"If you won't go back, then we'll go by ourselves. Come on, Tres."

White eyes! When Ket sought a tighter grip on Luke's arm, he pulled away.

"Luke's right, Ket." Tres Robles had dug in his heels, too.

She was sure they were both right. No greenhorn surveyor who had been in the country only a few weeks would be able to survive capture by Comancheros, no matter how well he *talked*. Few seasoned warriors could survive alone with that rabble.

"I understand what you're saying," she conceded. "But this is no time for compassion. You both know how lucky we were to get out of there. We can't go into that camp a second time tonight without getting caught. You know that."

But Luke was a Tremayne through and through. He

ground his heels into the hard rock trail. "I'm not going home without Blake. You can't make me."

"Don't bet on it," she retorted. Although she couldn't see his expression in the heavy darkness, she felt Luke's defiance and recognized it as yet another trait that proved her kinship to this boy.

"We all know you're as tough as a warrior," he challenged, "but that doesn't mean you can stop me from doing what's right."

"What's right is that I get you back to the fort before you find out how tough warriors really are."

"Not without Blake."

Ket heard the resoluteness in the boy's voice and given the overwhelming odds against anyone, even one of her own expertise, sneaking into a Comanchero camp and getting out alive not once but twice in one night, she had to admire his courage. Misplaced though it was.

Luke, however, was serious. "If we leave Blake to those Comancheros, you'll have to take me to the Apachería. I couldn't go off and leave a man to die and ever face our father again."

The boy might as well have socked her in the gullet. The only sound she heard was the intake of her own breath. She tried to tell herself she had gasped out of frustration with this white-eyes boy. But this white-eyes boy was her half-brother, and he had just admitted it.

Precious moments passed while the words *our father* hovered in the chilled air. Here in the darkness she couldn't see those green eyes, but she felt the connection. The words made it. It was the only time in the ten years since her father married Luke's mother that she had heard a Tremayne acknowledge the relationship.

Our father.

For a second time, Keturah Tremayne accepted a challenge she could not ignore. "Go straight to the horses," she told them. "Wait for me there . . . unless I don't come back by daylight. Or unless you hear gunshots. Either way, head for the fort. Your mothers are there."

"Our mothers are at the fort?" Tres questioned.

"I sent them there," she replied. No time to tell them about the threatened attack. To be truthful, she didn't even think about Apache warriors. Her mind still wandered around the edges of the connection Luke had made.

The full impact of her acquiescence didn't strike her until she turned back toward the circle of sleeping outlaws. That's when her cousin Emily's profession of love for her adopted white family popped into Ket's head.

Love? Was she so desperate for her father's love that the thought of displeasing him caused her to go soft in the head? Disgusted, she tried to turn around, but for some unexplainable reason she couldn't. *Love?*

Love had nothing to do with it. Her promise had been to Lena, not to her father. And her promise to Lena had been fulfilled, or it would be when the boys arrived safely at the fort. That in itself was reason enough to turn around.

Still, she didn't. Disgust became aggravation, then confusion. Lena had said nothing about a greenhorn white-eyes surveyor. Not one word. Ket had no reason to put her life in jeopardy for this stranger.

Not one good reason! She had no obligation, absolutely no obligation to this surveyor.

So why didn't she turn around . . . ?

"Be careful, Ket," Luke whispered behind her.

Blake Carmichael returned to consciousness slowly. He grabbed his throat, knowing that most of his pain was mental—anguish, distress, fear. He had recognized Keturah; the boys had spoken of her endlessly.

"Ket will come," the boy called by the strange name of Tres Robles assured him. "Mama will get word to her."

"Keturah? Isn't that a girl's name?"

"She's not like any girl you ever saw," Luke said. "Ket's the best. She'll make mince pie of these ol' Comancheros."

"Ket'll rescue us," Tres Robles vowed.

And she had, although thinking on it now, Blake wasn't certain why he had allowed himself the fantasy that she would rescue him along with the boys. Keturah Tremayne didn't know him from Adam's uncle.

It hadn't taken Blake long to realize what was happening beside him. First Luke left, then Tres Robles. Ket had come for them. Waiting his turn, he had torn skin off his hands slipping his bonds. And for what? To have a knife thrust in his throat and the breath squeezed out of him.

Ket had taken him for a Comanchero. Looking back on it, that was the reasonable thing for her to have thought. She had gotten the boys out, he assumed. If they'd been caught, the commotion would surely have brought him out of his haze. Now he was on his own.

Blake was a realist. He had never entertained the illusion that these highwaymen—he still wasn't certain what the term Comanchero meant—intended to allow him to live his life to a natural end. He'd known from the moment they were captured that his only chance for a long life would be to take charge of it himself. He'd been biding his time, awaiting the opportunity.

Now the wait was over. The choice had been taken out of his hands.

Closing his eyes, he forced his breathing to steady, cleared his mind, and tried to plan. He had to make his move tonight. He would give Ket and the boys a head start, then he must try to escape. One thing was certain—come morning when these murderers found the boys gone, they would take it out on him.

Besides, the country was becoming increasingly rugged. From maps he had studied, he knew they were traveling toward the Río Grande, across which they would arrive in Mexico.

Yes, the time was now. But which way to go? He didn't want to head out in the direction the band would take come daylight, but since the Río Grande made more crooks and turns than a lady's hairpin, he couldn't begin to guess which way the Comancheros might take.

Blake was pragmatic enough not to put a percentage on his chance of escaping these murderers; he figured it would be too discouraging. But it wasn't impossible. The boys considered him a greenhorn, and in many ways he was. In more ways, however, he was well trained to take care of himself—given decent odds. Which, he had to admit, these were certainly not.

Not to be deterred, however, he checked his pockets for the two round stones he had stashed to use for weapons, then slowly, cautiously, his lungs filled with a suffocating sense of trepidation, he began to rise. He had just attained a partial sitting position when he sensed movement beside him. He froze in place, instantly alert. Then, by some indefinable process, he recognized her.

Keturah. His senses heightened by her presence, his heart set up a clatter. She had returned for him. He wasn't alone. He wouldn't die at the hands of these . . .

Euphoria overwhelmed him as she crept into place beside him. Instantly the forlornness of struggling through life alone, a feeling Blake had battled in one form or another all his life, disappeared. Help had arrived.

And in what form! If ever an angel wore buckskin, this was she!

Ket drew a deep breath and held it a moment to steady her heart rhythm. The sense of imminent doom she had carried like a pack on her back while she wound her way through the scattered forms of sleeping men lifted somewhat when she slipped into the vacant place Tres Robles had occupied next to the greenhorn they called Blake.

But her relief was short-lived, for she had barely eased herself to the ground when he moved toward her again. *Just like a greenhorn.*

To stave off the inevitable commotion, she reached quickly to reassure him. Covering his mouth with a hand, she started to whisper an introduction directly into his ear when he grabbed her unexpectedly and kissed her hard and full on the lips. Her eyes met his in the starlight. He seemed as startled as she.

A reflexive action, spontaneous and not at all thought out, it caught her entirely off guard. His lips slashed over hers, hard and open and demanding. As a kiss it was almost violent in nature, but then she didn't have much to compare it with—an irrational thought in that initial stupefying moment. All senses seemed to have left her.

Where seconds before her thoughts had been ordered and precise, at the touch of his lips her brain began to swirl. Her thoughts skittered like waterbugs, dancing here and there but never lighting on anything of consequence. It was a feeling more than anything else, no substance to it. Lips and skin and wetness combined into some unnamed but deeply sensual emotion, like the tug of a familiar dream . . .

It lasted only a fraction of a second. Then reality surfaced. Fury chased fear through her returning consciousness. In a desperate attempt to gather her wits, she shoved him away and slapped him hard against the side of the face. Again their gazes met in the starlight.

The sound of her hand hitting his face startled her. Starlight, which she had feared would spell defeat for her mission, glittered in Blake's eyes and revealed his own panic-stricken expression.

"Watch out!" he called sharply, if softly, just as someone grabbed her shoulder from behind.

Swirling into action, Ket followed her momentum with a right-handed punch to the attacker's windpipe. Blake stepped around her, relieved the fallen man of his sombrero, crammed it on his own head, and reached for the man's serape.

Pandemonium erupted. Comancheros, awakened by the sound of a fight, came to their feet. Ket heard grunts and groans and guns being unsheathed.

Without another second lost, the greenhorn Blake aborted his attempt to relieve the fallen man of his serape. Grabbing Ket's hand, he pulled her through the melee.

"Stoop over," he instructed in a loud whisper. "Get beneath them, and they won't recognize us."

Stupefied, she obeyed. By the time they wended their way through the aroused Comancheros, she came to her senses.

What was she doing following a greenhorn? She jerked her hand from his, caught his arm, and brought him to a halt.

"Wrong way," she hissed, half in anger, half simply gasping for breath.

"Lead on."

His amicable response further dumbfounded her. Who was this man? For a greenhorn he had unusually sharp instincts. Fortunately, he had the sense to acquiesce to her better judgment.

By now the camp had been alerted to the disappearance of the captives. Pistols discharged around them. Shouts were raised. *"¡Los niños!" "¡El gringo!"*

Their roles reversed, Ket pulled a willing Blake toward the canyon where she had left the boys. It was by now the darkest part of night, that time just before daybreak when the moon pales and stars begin to fade. For that she was grateful.

Preoccupied with escape, she didn't immediately identify the light that raced toward them. A man carrying a torch. And yelling.

"¡Emboscada! ¡Emboscada!"

The night guard! How had he gotten free so quickly? The answer followed him, in the person of the second guard, who had very likely set him free.

"Oh, no! Not him." Time had run out. "We didn't make it."

"You know these men?" Blake questioned beside her.

The first guard thrust the torch in Ket's face.

"*¡Mi sombrero!*" He jerked his hat off her head and peered closer. "*¡Mi serape! ¡Es tú!*" Then to the angry mob, "*¡Aquí, aquí!* Come over here!"

Before Ket could aim her pistol, much less answer Blake's question, Blake had grabbed the torch from the guard's hand and backslapped him across the head with it. Then, waving the flaming torch in a circle above his head for momentum, he tossed it into the crowd.

Ket took the moment to shed her stolen serape.

"Let's get out of here." Blake grabbed her by the arm. "We'll talk direction later."

A few minutes later, he pushed her behind the nearest shelter of boulders, then dropped her arm. "Now, ma'am, you may lead me to freedom."

She glared his way, wondering what kind of fool the boys had taken up with, wondering against her will what he would look like in full daylight. Saying they were both still alive when the sun came up.

"No need to thank me for rescuing you from that unholy mob of cutthroats and thieves." Following her higher up the narrow gorge, he continued to babble.

He might as well have been speaking a foreign language. The boys said he had *talked* the Comancheros into not killing them on the spot. Likely those murdering Comancheros had been as dumbfounded by this greenhorn's nonsense as she was. She resisted the temptation to remind him that it was he who should be thanking her. He continued.

"Lead on, Ket. We'd better find those boys before those Comancheros or Comanches or whoever they are do."

"Comancheros."

"I've been wondering what's the difference."

Greenhorn, no doubt about it. "Pray you never find out the difference."

At the head of the rock-strewn draw they found two of the three horses gone. "They obeyed me," she commented, relieved. Her palomino stallion, a gift from Nick and Lena, stood bareback, patiently cropping grass.

"We'll have to double," she told the greenhorn.

"No saddle?"

Her glare was designed to put him in his place and might have succeeded in broad daylight. On the other hand, she couldn't keep her eyes from searching the shadows that still cast his features in darkness, wondering what those large hot wet lips looked like. She couldn't shake the feeling they had triggered inside her—like a dream or . . .

Angered, she retorted, "If you can't ride without a saddle, white eyes, you'd better get started walking." She wished he would. She wished she had the courage to leave him here, but the boys would set up another fuss. And he would argue. She didn't have time to argue with a white-eyes greenhorn surveyor.

"No thanks, ma'am. I have no objection to this mode of travel. Absolutely none whatsoever."

There it was again, his infernal wordiness. Even more disconcerting, though, was the way he seemed to be looking at her when he spoke. Was he really focusing on her lips, or was that her imagination?

Keturah Tremayne was not given to flights of fancy. Life was too harsh, reality always present. Who was this white eyes? A sorcerer or something? She should leave him right here in the middle of the *Puerto del Piasano* with Comancheros swarming below. Let him walk, talk, run, fight it out or hide, as he chose. But the boys had pled with her.

"Don't press your luck," she advised him after they both sat astride the palomino's back, Ket in front, Blake behind, much too close behind. At least with him behind her, she didn't have to worry about staring at those lips.

In a moment of panic, she realized that his lips might not be the only threatening part of this man. The intimate way his body wrapped around hers caused that dream to flutter in her stomach again. How had she managed to get herself into such a predicament? She should strangle Luke and Tres Robles!

"You owe your life to those boys," she told Blake, determined to make sure he understood his precarious situation. "I wouldn't have turned a finger to go back into that camp for a white eyes like you."

"Don't reckon you are," he mused. When he reached around her to take the rawhide reins in his hands, she slapped him away.

"I will direct this horse," she told him, tight-lipped. Unable to resist, however, she questioned, "I'm not what?"

"Ready to thank me for saving your life."

Stupidity was one of many white-eyes traits she detested. "You're as dimwitted as those boys. I shouldn't have bothered."

Moments passed in silence before he asked, "Why did you, Ket?"

Unlike his previous bantering, this question was voiced in a serious tone that confounded her further. "The boys begged—"

"Don't lay it off on the boys," he challenged. "A woman of your independence, you could have stood up to two fairly small boys."

Although the air was chilled, she flushed from his nearness, both to her body and to her thoughts. Before she could decide how to put him in his place, he brought his face around close to hers. His breath blew hotly in her ear when he spoke.

"Why'd you do it, Ket?"

Her father's image sprang instantly to mind, betraying her, even as her body betrayed her at the nearness of this man. She wondered what the boys had told him. More accurately, she *feared* what the boys might have told him. She didn't want to know. Yet, she already knew this white-eyes gringo surveyor well enough to realize that if he decided to, he would tell her anything and everything he knew, whether she wanted to know it or not.

"Listen, white eyes. You've only been out here two weeks, so don't start thinking you know everything, or even *anything* about me or this country."

His only answer was a chuckle that reverberated through her back, straight to some softly fluttering spot inside her. Until tonight she had not known that spot existed. Rather, she corrected upon feeling another tug of that old dream, until tonight she had not *felt* it. She pressed her lips together, unable to forget the feel of his. Her weakness confused her.

Although their ride through the awakening dawn had begun in discord, it soon settled into a semblance of harmony. Blake was the first to notice this, and he attributed it to their shared goal to escape and the imminent threat to that goal.

While he bantered with Ket, his senses were trained on his back, specifically on the space between his shoulder blades where bullets could be expected to strike first, should the murdering thieves overtake them.

Once they topped the hill at the head of the canyon, the rising sun painted the sky with unexpected brilliance. They rode through the pink and gold dawn, escape foremost in both their minds; daylight would make tracking them more feasible for the Comancheros.

"They're late leaving the area this year," Ket explained

once, turning her head slightly so he could hear her words, a motion ripe with intimacy. "They won't waste much time looking for us."

"They won't need much time with us riding double."

"You doubt my horse?"

Although she hadn't spoken in jest—he doubted the cynical Miss Keturah Tremayne would know how to jest— her tone hadn't carried the heavy cynicism of earlier.

"I would never doubt your horse," he replied sagely. Then he couldn't resist adding, "Although wouldn't a mustang have surer feet in these mountains than this pure-blooded riding horse?"

Again she surprised him by not taking offense. "This horse doesn't know he's a thoroughbred. He was bred on Nick Bourbon's ranch north of Fort Davis."

"What's his name?"

"Nick's?"

"The horse's."

"Name a horse?" Her disdain returned in full force. "Do you name your shoes? Or your—what do you call them—buggies?"

She had a point, so he shut up.

As escape appeared more possible, Blake became conscious of other things, namely the woman he sat behind. Or around, which more aptly described their position. Without so much as a saddle for a barrier, his body enveloped hers.

Although he hadn't had a glimpse of her face in daylight, he knew intimately how she was shaped. Her firm, supple buttocks settled against him, thighs to thighs, bright hot spot to bright hot spot.

With the dawn she picked up the boys' trail as quickly as any hunting dog he'd ever known and followed it over mountain ledge and down the rocky draws.

Just when Blake had decided she was right, the Comancheros wouldn't take the time and trouble to track them

down, Ket drew rein without warning. Blake's erotic imag-
inings came to an abrupt halt, too, when his arms flew
around her, crossing not over warm soft breasts but cold,
hard bandoleers. She didn't appear to notice.

"Those dimwitted boys," she muttered.

Blake came alert. "What?"

"They've changed course."

"Changed direction? To where?"

When she inhaled, the outer edges of her breasts swelled
against his inner arms. But with death staring them in the
face, or in the back as the case might be, he had no trouble
focusing on the trouble they faced.

Without responding to his question, Ket nudged the
palomino forward. Not quickly this time, but slowly, step
by step, while she concentrated on the rocky ground. When
she stopped again, it was to throw her right leg across the
palomino's mane in front of her and slide gracefully to
the ground.

Blake had just entertained the idea that she was the most
graceful woman he had ever seen, when she crouched on
the ground and sifted her fingers through a pile of horse
droppings. Lifting those same fingers to her nose, she
sniffed, then wiped horse dung off her hand on a rock.
She stared vacantly into the distance ahead of them.

But as Blake was beginning to learn, Ket's mind was
never vacant. She turned, and her one word was enough
to dampen his anticipation at finally seeing her face in
broad daylight.

"Apaches," she said simply.

He sat the horse, stunned, while the sight of her mesmerized his beleaguered senses.

Before him stood a breathtakingly beautiful woman.
Broad forehead, high rounded cheekbones, and thick
black eyebrows framed liquid green eyes as if they were a
fine painting. She looked like a portrait one might find
in the National Gallery of Art. Wisps of black waves had

come loose from her single braid and tumbled about her tawny face, playing over an image of exquisite beauty: finely formed nose, small chin, and lips . . . those lips he had kissed so recklessly taunted him now in the relentless light of this fall morning.

Forget your troubles, they invited. *Let me show you the way.*

"Apaches?" he asked, feeling the fool she thought him to be. Half Apache, half white, the boys had described her. What did that mean? Half civilized, half savage?

"Apaches," she confirmed. She seemed as mesmerized as he. Or was it his imagination? What did she see? A tired and dirty, disheveled, hungry man who was too white, too civilized for her?

"Comancheros behind, Apaches in front," he quipped, a half-hearted attempt to break the spell. "Friends?" he inquired finally.

"Not of yours, white eyes." Remounting, she guided the palomino westward. Her disdain for him was as arousing as a full-fledged toss in the hay with any lady he had yet known.

Chapter Two

Blake Carmichael could come up with no rational explanation for the way Keturah Tremayne affected him. Nor could he find one good reason for feeling attraction to any woman at a time like this. Yes, she had rescued him from an unnatural death at the hands of Comancheros—so far, at least.

Yes, she had been skilled and alert enough to read the sign of an Apache raiding party headed for Fort Davis. Both of which should have aroused enough fear inside any normal man to erase all erotic thoughts. It certainly wasn't that Blake was braver than most men; indeed, he could not recall ever having been more frightened for his life during his entire thirty years on this earth.

But that, the fear, was on the periphery, while the heat emanated from the very core of him.

They rode through the rough mountain country, up one canyon wall, down a crevice, then up another sheer wall. Ket had been right about the palomino. The animal's footing never faltered, nor did he seem particularly winded taking the steep, narrow passes or sprinting across the occasional plain, even though she drove him like the devil chased them.

Dual devils, Blake corrected.

It was mid-morning when she drew up in a wide space on the steep rocky trail. "A *tinaja,*" she explained. "If you want a drink today, you'd better get one now. It's filled with runoff—"

"I know what a *tinaja* is," he countered, coming toward where she squatted before the basin-like depression made in the stone by centuries of runoff. Filled by the infrequent rains, *tinajas* provided scarce drinking water for animals and travelers, although he doubted that many of the latter passed this way.

Blake, however, did not dwell on *tinajas* or ancient travelers for long. For this was only his second chance to view Ket full-faced, and as on the first time, the sight of her captivated him.

By now more lengths of dark, wavy hair had come loose from her once-thick braid. They wisped about her face, which was more oval than he had realized. Her lips were fuller, too, and evoked memories of that one brash kiss, causing his pulse to quicken. But here in the clear light of this crisp fall day, her eyes held him enthralled. They were green, like Luke's. Except Ket's were a deep feral green.

Her insolent gaze held him in place, even after she had summoned him to drink at the *tinaja,* for in the depths of those fierce green eyes he saw acknowledgment of his own erotic urgency, and not acknowledgment only, but reciprocation. She felt it, too, this extraordinary attraction of opposites.

Even as the want for her thrummed through his veins, he realized that there couldn't have been two more opposite people on God's good earth. Nothing Luke and Tres Robles said about her had prepared him for this woman.

Half Apache, half white, the boys had said, and Blake had imagined her. But his imagination had been limited by his own experiences, which until this moment he hadn't considered all that limited. He'd known women. A number of them, with different backgrounds, from different social classes. Half Apache, half white couldn't be all that different.

Now he wondered what he had expected. Half civilized, half wild? Had he expected her to put on petticoat and corset when he showed up? He doubted that the woman before him knew the existence of those items.

Half Apache, half white. Six of one, half a dozen of another did not apply in this case. Keturah Tremayne was not half of anything. She was all wild—wild to the bone.

Wild to the soul. And Blake was drawn to her—or to this wildness—as he had never been drawn to anyone or anything in his life. His body trembled with the insidious sense of expectancy; his mind hummed with a startling curiosity that bordered on fascination. In a few brief hours, this woman had become the center of every physical need he had ever experienced.

Fortunately, he retained the presence of mind to drink of the stale rainwater. Afterward Ket took her hat off her head and dipped it in the stagnant pool and gave the palomino a drink and they headed on. It was high noon by the time they stopped again. By then Blake had learned enough about the imminent peril that threatened them that the hair stood up on the back of his neck.

Yet his desire for this woman continued to burn like a live coal deep inside him. It didn't make a tinker's damn worth of sense.

High noon found them sitting the palomino atop a high mountain ledge that overlooked the most beautiful miniature valley Blake had seen since arriving in this land west of the Pecos River. Steep red-rock walls enclosed a space of no more than a few acres. Even now in late fall the grass was green; a small creek angled across one corner; a huge cottonwood shaded an ancient rock cabin; and in the middle of it all stood a rock well. Tranquility emanated upward from this place. He was captivated by a sense of homecoming. That live coal in the pit of his belly continued to burn hot and bright.

The entire valley could be viewed with one turn of the head. In the wooded areas he spotted wild sumac, a piñion tree, a wild cherry, and desert willow. Several species of cacti dotted the open spaces in and around the scattering of red rocks.

The quietness became palpable. He imagined that were he to listen hard, he could hear the trickle of the creek. Had not the cabin and well stood as testament, he would have been convinced that no human had intruded upon these grounds.

Ket sat motionless, except for her heartbeat, which Blake could feel through her back. He decided she must be searching for a trail that led down.

"What is this place?" he asked in a hushed tone.

"Apache Wells."

Blake caught his breath. *Apache Wells?* The name stunned him. "This is where the boys were headed when I ran into them." He searched the small expanse again. "I've heard others speak of this place. There's something spiritual here, someth—"

"*If* spirits reside down there, they're from the Underworld." Ket spoke in a tone of utter loathing. Unnecessarily she added, "I hate this place."

He didn't doubt it for an instant. The sad truth was, there didn't seem to be anyone or anything Keturah Tremayne did not hate . . . or profess to hate.

"If this is an example of Hades," he challenged, "it's no wonder so many folks are attracted to sinful living."

She didn't respond, and he realized that, strangely, he was becoming used to her silences. Following her line of vision, he spotted the boys. The valley had only looked deserted. Ket must have seen them at the same time, for her body relaxed against him at that moment.

Even her disdainful "There they are" didn't disguise her relief.

The setting that had moments before appeared ethereal now became bizarre. As though oblivious to earthly dangers—Comancheros and warring Apaches were a couple that popped to mind—the boys raced from behind the well, leaping into the air and clapping their hands over their heads in the way of children the world over. Frolicking, Blake's mother would have called it. Their shirtless torsos glistened in the noonday sun.

"What are they doing?" Blake was tempted to share Ket's assertion that spirits of the Underworld were at work here. "Have they forgotten that the Comancheros and Apaches are after us?"

Ket's guttural grunt told him her scorn had resurfaced. Before he could grab a tight hold, she had kicked the palomino in the flanks. The horse responded with lightning speed, plunging down a hillside Blake would have considered impassable.

But that was only his opinion, and as Ket had said, he was new to this country and didn't know a hill of beans about it or its native inhabitants.

Well, perhaps he wasn't totally ignorant about its inhabitants. In his hasty search for a hold to keep from falling off the horse's back, he found and grabbed the most feminine waist he had touched in possibly forever. Unable to resist, he pulled Ket back against him.

Strangely, she allowed it, settling into him as if she belonged right there next to his heart. Of course, her mind, he knew—or rather hoped at this stage—was on guiding their fleet-of-foot steed safely to the valley floor below them.

While Blake, unable to control anything about this downward plunge, held onto the one soothing sensation in the overwhelming sense of doom that engulfed him.

Finally the world stopped falling and he realized they had reached the bottom. A second later his head settled down, too, when he suddenly realized that his arms were empty. Keturah of the effortless grace had stopped the horse and slid to the ground.

Blake was left holding an armful of empty air in the most surreal setting this side of a fairy tale. By the time he cleared the cobwebs from his brain, Ket had taken charge.

"What do you mean, showing yourselves like this? You saw those Apache tracks—"

"Aw, Ket, don't go getting' het up," Luke interrupted. "They've already gone."

"We ran 'em off!" Tres Robles lifted a rusty bucket above his head. "We're the kings of Apache Wells!"

"The chiefs," Luke corrected.

While Blake watched trying to decipher the strange conversation, water that resembled blood too closely not to elicit a shudder dripped over Tres's bare torso. Dense red water—that was what had been glistening, Blake realized. Both boys were covered with it. It dripped from their hair and ran in rivulets over their chests. Their britches were soaked in it.

"It was ol' Mangas Che himself," Tres Robles told her, a broad grin on his stained face. "He just sat his painted pony and stared down at us. After a while he called the others off and they went on their way."

"He knew he couldn't touch us in this valley." Luke caught the bucket Tres tossed him. Jubilation lit both their young faces. "We're the chiefs of Apache Wells!"

Blake listened in confusion. Half his brain was focused on the Comancheros who at this point might or might not be following them; the other half on a band of Apache warriors who, according to Ket, were headed for Fort Davis to wage war on the white eyes—black-skinned soldiers and their white officers.

Those Apaches had been here, and they knew exactly where these boys were. They had come and gone, to hear the boys tell it. But would they stay gone? Or would they draw up somewhere out of sight and reconsider? Hadn't Ket claimed that killing two boys, especially these two, would add substance to their *coup d'état*?

"The Tremayne name must stand for nearly as much as folks around here claim," he commented, seeking reassurance that at least one group of their pursuers was no longer a threat.

"It wasn't the Tremayne name that ran Mangas off," Tres Robles told him. "It was the legend."

"Yeah!" Luke enthused. "We're the chiefs of Apache Wells. He wouldn't dare bother us."

"The legend?" Blake asked dubiously.

"The legend of Apache Wells," Luke explained, as if Blake had just stepped off the stage. In effect, he had. "Anyone who can drink this water and not die on the spot is chief of Apache Wells."

"You drank it?"

"You bet we did." Luke wrinkled his nose. "It was bitter, hot, awful—but a great idea, wasn't it?"

Luke was still proud of himself. Blake was still dubious, and Ket . . . well, she was still her sweet scornful self.

"Not all Apaches believe that nonsense. You're lucky the clever ones went to Mexico with Victorio."

Blake couldn't help but ask, "Do you think this Mangas Che fellow will reconsider?"

"No," Ket replied. "But not because he believes in spirits concocted by the white eyes. He has a more important raid in mind."

"What more important raid?" Luke wanted to know.

"They're headed for the fort."

Both boys' eyes widened. Their concern was obvious.

"Fort Davis? That's where you sent Mama." Luke's comment was not so much an accusation as a statement. Blake wondered how Ket would take it.

"And my mother, too." Tres Robles turned toward the rock cabin as he spoke. "Let's get going, Luke."

"Nobody is leaving Apache Wells until we know the Comancheros aren't coming," Ket informed them.

Tres Robles had already entered the old cabin. When he exited, he led two horses. "We stabled them in there so's not to tempt ol' Mangas. A couple of fine horses might considerably weaken his belief in the legend."

"Or make it worth his while to challenge it," Luke added. When he reached for the reins of one of the horses, Ket stopped him.

"No one is leaving, Luke. We're all staying right here until tomorrow morning."

"But our mothers . . ." the boys cried in unison.

"I promised to return you to them in good health, and I intend to do it. We'll wait until we're sure about the Comancheros and until Mangas and his warriors have had a chance to accomplish their ill-fated scheme."

"Ill-fated?" Blake figured if Ket explained the situation a bit further, the boys might settle down. "How do you know it'll turn out that way?"

"Those warriors are trying to get themselves killed, and they're sure to succeed." When the boys showed no signs of relenting, she added, "Your mothers will be safe at the fort. A handful of rebel warriors won't be any trouble for a fort full of soldiers."

"But—"

"On the other hand," Blake put in, following Ket's line of thinking, "the warriors would spell big trouble for the four of us."

Luke and Tres Robles turned to him, defiance in their eyes.

Yes, he thought, *I am the outsider here.* Could that mean he had more sense?

"Ket's half Apache," Luke reminded him. "They wouldn't attack us. She's one of them."

Ket glared at her half-brother. "I'm not one of anyone." Abruptly, she turned on her moccasined heel and headed off up the rocky hillside afoot.

"Where're you going?" Blake called to her retreating back. She either didn't hear him or simply refused to respond. Were he a betting man, he would wager on the latter. Her gait was determined, her stance rigid. She defied anyone to follow her.

He watched until she was out of earshot. Her shoulders had relaxed by then, and she climbed the rest of the way to the summit with the same easy grace she exhibited in dismounting a horse. His attention fastened on the sway of her rounded behind, while his libido ran amuck.

When the boys started clamoring behind him, he turned to them. "Where's she going?"

"To lookout for those danged Comancheros," Tres Robles explained in the same tone Luke had used earlier, the one that suggested Blake had just ridden in on the stage.

"You an' Ket see any sign of 'em?" Luke asked.

Blake shook his head. He was feeling out of his depth and not liking it. Grateful for being rescued, he was not so happy about having relinquished control over his own fate to two runaway boys and a woman who more nearly resembled a savage than any fictional character he had ever encountered in books about the West. From the sound of things, he didn't stand to regain the upper hand anytime soon.

"Bet your ribs are sticking to your stomach," Luke observed.

Blake nodded absently. "What'd you have to eat?"

"Tins of things. Mama and Papa lived here when they first married. Before they got the ranch started."

Hungry as he was, Blake was tempted to refuse the offer. "Those tins would be what . . . nine, ten years old?"

"Nah. We come here time to time. Hunting or just to get away."

Blake glanced around. An ethereal place, Apache Wells, small and secluded, surrounded on all sides by the same kind of volcanic columns of red rock that surrounded Fort Davis. They reminded him of sentinels standing guard. A secure feeling in this land of Comancheros and warring Apaches.

But the sentinels here were guarding a legend, and from the sound of things they did it very well.

Staring up the hill, he could just make out Ket where she sat on top of one of those ancient flows of hardened red lava, legs crossed, rifle over her lap. If he hadn't known exactly where to look, he would never have suspected she was there. "I'll go relieve Ket. She needs to eat worse than I do."

"I wouldn't do that," Luke warned.

Blake eyed him, waiting for an explanation.

"Ket's got her own food."

Blake doubted that.

"Didn't you notice that bag around her neck?"

"Bag?" Actually, he hadn't. He'd been too busy noticing everything else about her. "What could she carry in a bag around her neck?"

"Dried meat, roots, stuff like that. She never eats with us," Tres Robles explained. "Always brings her own stuff."

Wild, Blake had thought her. Keturah Tremayne was wild to the core. Even his stomach protested that she would eat something she had carried in a bag around her neck. It made him want to run. Or at least to take charge of his own life. How could he be drawn to a woman like that? Still, undeniably, he was.

"I'll go relieve her."

"I wouldn't." This time the warning came from Tres Robles. "We generally let her do things her way. She's a tad touchy."

"Touchy?" Blake grinned. An understatement if he'd ever heard one.

"Let 'er be," Luke advised. "Ket's better left alone."

"I'm beginning to see what you mean." While the boys brought out tins and proceeded to open them with the point of a penknife, Blake studied this valley. He knew enough geology to know that these red cliffs, like those at Fort Davis, had been formed centuries earlier when lava cooled before it stopped flowing. They reminded him of raspberry icing his mother used to push through a tube to decorate a cake.

Some of the vegetation he recognized—desert willow, evergreen sumac, and that wild cherry tree, along with the usual cholla, agave, and several species of prickly pear. Others, like the woman who hated this place and the boys who believed the legend, intrigued him.

"Tell me about the legend," he quizzed, accepting the offered tin of something labeled "roast mutton." It looked inedible, but he was hungry enough that he decided not to give it too much thought. With Comancheros and Apaches about, who was he to worry about food poisoning?

"Ket called it a white-man's legend. Who made it up?"

"Aw, she was just talking," Luke replied. "It's an old Apache legend. They put a lot of stock in it. That's why Mangas Che turned away. Ket just doesn't want to admit it."

Blake didn't pursue that line of thought. He considered it unlikely that these boys had Ket figured out much better than he did. "That legend sounds pretty important."

"It's important, all right," Luke admitted.

"That the reason your pa didn't sell Apache Wells to Senator Carmichael when he sold the surrounding acreage?'' Blake figured the question was innocent enough not to give himself away. By asking it he hoped to learn something about a subject that had baffled him much of his life—his father's reason for spending the larger part of his career out here west of the Pecos River. He immediately regretted his misjudgment.

''Carmichael!'' Luke spoke, but both boys stuck out their tongues and made gagging motions. Finally Luke eyed Blake soberly. ''How'd you know ol' SOB Carmichael owns all this land?''

Taken off guard by their disparaging response to his father's name—and his own, for that matter—Blake offered a true but perhaps feeble excuse. ''I'm a surveyor. It's my business to know every parcel of land around here and who owns what.''

''He works for the railroad,'' Tres Robles reminded Luke.

''Not exactly,'' Blake objected and immediately felt like a Judas.

''An' ol' SOB owns the railroad.'' Luke responded to Tres, as if they hadn't been disputed.

''*Senator* Carmichael doesn't own the railroad,'' Blake objected.

''Don't tell *him* that,'' Tres replied with more sarcasm than Blake would have thought possible coming from an eleven-year-old boy. Sarcasm directed at Blake's own father, albeit the boys didn't realize that, of course.

''The Second Transcontinental Railroad is a major accomplishment for Senator Carmichael and for this country,'' he explained to the boys. ''The senator played a large role in getting the rails through here. He dedicated most of his career, his life, to the project. He has a right to be proud.''

''Take up for him if you want,'' Tres Robles said, ''but proud isn't what folks around here call that man.''

Blake was dismayed. He'd realized that his father was

not universally liked. What successful man was? On the way to the top, enemies were made by the most discreet. Which was one of the reasons he had not given his last name after he and the boys were taken captive by those Comancheros. He hadn't wanted to bring the wrong kind of attention to his father. Now he was relieved the boys hadn't thought to ask beforehand.

It wasn't all that unusual. Single names were not uncommon in this part of the world. Ket and Luke's father was a prime example. Even after he married and produced children, the patriarch continued to go by the single name Tremayne.

Yes, Blake was relieved that he'd had the presence of mind to withhold his own name. At the time he had feared embarrassing his father—now he learned that his father's good name wasn't considered all that good in these parts. He would have expected as much from Ket—she disliked everyone with white skin—but these boys had seemed open-minded. Disillusioned, he realized that they were surely parroting opinions heard at home.

Feeling the traitorous son, Blake vowed to change the subject at the earliest opportunity. Which didn't come soon, for the boys had warmed to their subject like a maiden lady takes to gossip. And gossip it surely was. They seemed determined to share every accusation and aspersion that could have ever been hurled at a man Blake had been reared to revere and respect.

"Your father is a great man, Blake," his mother preached. "You must strive to grow up and be just like him." That chant had become his mother's mantra, and Blake had followed her direction, even though striving to emulate a man who was never present had been difficult.

Now Blake set his empty tin aside and rose to his feet. "Think I'll mosey around, look things over," he told the boys. Perhaps by the time he'd walked around the valley, they would have found something else to occupy their minds.

Later, he realized he didn't know boys very well. These two acted like chatty schoolgirls. He had barely reached the creek when they caught up.

He knelt to drink of the cool water. They knelt to either side.

"If ol' SOB doesn't own the railroad, then how do you know him?" Luke wanted to know after Blake had started off downstream. Like horseflies nipping at his heels, the boys kept pace.

Blake felt trapped by their probing questions. "I grew up in Washington, D.C.," he offered. "I'd been surveying around the area since graduating university. Last year Senator Carmichael hired me to survey commercial sites along the future tracks."

"How'd he know you?"

"Washington is a small place. Mutual friends knew my reputation."

"You mean folks there *like* him?" The emphasis on the word *like,* spoken as though it couldn't possibly be true, took Blake's mind off the string of lies that was quickly growing into a bramble bush. What did these kids know about the esteemed senator?

"A lot of people like him," Blake replied. "He's been elected to the United States Senate every term since he first ran at twenty-eight." The longevity of his father's record of service didn't impress these boys.

"It's a good thing folks out here couldn't vote for him," Tres Robles commented sagely. "He'd never've been elected dog catcher."

"Dog catcher?" Luke mocked. "What's that?"

"Somebody who goes around gathering up dogs."

"Why would anybody wanta do that?"

"I dunno, but my father says every city has to have a dog catcher to keep the streets safe for pedestrians."

"Well, Fort Davis doesn't have one, not that I've ever heard about."

"Me neither," Tres replied. "Fact is, though, ol' SOB wouldn't have been elected if he'd run in this country."

They had reached the north end of the valley. Blake stroked a hand over one of the red-rock columns that ringed Apache Wells like gigantic ancient centurions. They lent a majesty to the place that surpassed any rock formations he had ever seen. When the boys continued to disparage the senator, he decided to put a stop to it.

"You boys are being unfair. This is the kind of gossip political leaders continually have to fight from uneducated, illiterate electorate back home. Everyone out here couldn't feel the same way about Senator Carmichael, else why would he have spent most of his life here?" *Away from his wife and son,* he wanted to add.

The inequity of it made Blake sick. His mother had lived an extremely lonely life. Time and again she tried to persuade her husband to allow her to come west and bring their son.

But J. J. Carmichael was a man dedicated to more than the cause at hand. He wanted his son, an only child born to them late in life, to have the best upbringing and education his position and power could provide. His son must be reared in the East, educated in the East. So both wife and son were left to a solitary life of loneliness, at times feeling more abandoned than special.

Blake wanted to say all these things and vowed that he would as soon as they reached the fort. He wouldn't do his father any good if he got himself thrown out into this vast wasteland without so much as a horse.

"You wouldn't be so quick to take up for him if you knew the truth," Tres Robles vowed.

"I doubt either of you know the truth about Senator Carmichael."

"He stole Papa's land," Luke said bluntly.

"What Luke means," Tres explained, "is that his father didn't sell any of that land. It was stolen."

"Stolen? If the folks in this country have nothing better to do than sully a man's good name, a man who has given his life to serving this country, then they're not the open-minded folks they've been made out to be."

"Don't reckon you'll find many to agree that Carmichael's a good name. Out here the name Carmichael stands for an ol' wore-out womanizer and a drunk."

When he had thought it impossible to be more stunned, Blake was. How could his father's reputation have become so denigrated? If this gossip should turn out to be the prevailing attitude, why had the senator spent much of his life here? If he'd had to fight local gossip all these years to ensure that the Southern Route of the Second Transcontinental Railroad would be routed through this country, was he a hero or just plain stupid?

Stupid, Blake thought. He could have been home with a family who loved him, who needed him, but he chose to have his name printed in history books.

Surely these boys had it all wrong. But the accusations stung. Stealing land? His father? A United States Senator? Blake vowed to learn the truth.

"Frankly, Senator Carmichael is far too intelligent to steal land, even good land. Why, this valley is the only piece of hospitable land for miles around, and it's still in Tremayne hands."

"Ol' SOB wouldn't touch Apache Wells." This from Luke. "He thinks it's haunted."

"Haunted?"

"Yep," Tres Robles concurred. "My father says when they found Rosa's husband's body draped over the well here, ol' SOB wouldn't come down off that mountaintop up there to help remove it."

"Rosa's husband's body . . . ?" The story was becoming more bizarre by the moment, and Blake suddenly realized what these boys were up to. It was the oldest trick in the West. Pulling the leg of a newcomer. A greenhorn, he'd been called more times than he could count the past couple of weeks.

"It's called payin' your dues, son," Edward Bolton who ran the mercantile in Chihuahua had told him. "Hang in there. Once you prove your worth, they'll give up."

"But that's not the worst of it," Tres added to the story. There was no stopping them now. "Bet you haven't heard about Neeta."

"Neeta?" Blake instantly regretted the question.

"She's ol' SOB's daughter."

Blake wasn't sure he had heard right, then again he knew he had. "Don't your mothers ever wash your mouths out with soap?" he challenged. "I've never heard two boys go to so much pains to overuse an expletive."

"What's an expletive?" Luke wanted to know.

"A swear word," Tres explained. "If you're talking about SOB, it's just initials. He goes by those initials J. J., whatever they mean. Folks out here thought they'd give him a set that fit better."

"James Jefferson." Struggling to contain his temper, Blake spoke between clenched teeth. "I don't think either of you know the senator well enough to call him anything but Mister." But the chastisement sounded weak, and the words that rang in Blake's ears were the ones most abhorrent to him.

Could these boys be right? Could his father have a daughter? If so, she would be his own sister. My God, could his father have a whole other family? Was that what had kept him away from Washington most of Blake's life? Not the railroad, but another family?

Was Blake the victim of horseplay by these boys or of a father who abandoned him and his mother for another woman and other children? "You mean the senator has a . . . family out . . . here?"

"He didn't marry Rosa Raméríz," Tres explained. "He raped her."

Raped? Blake felt physically sick. Horseplay or not, this charade had gone far enough. "Rape is a heinous crime. Nothing to be joked about."

"It's no joke. Ever'body says so."

"What everybody says can be a far cry from the truth." But he couldn't keep from asking, "Does . . . does the senator confirm this?"

"You mean does he claim Neeta? Nah, 'course not."

"But you said . . . ?"

"I said he raped Rosa Raméríz. That's a fact. Luke's mama knows."

"Besides, Neeta's got ol' SOB's blue eyes."

Blake stared across the valley. The air swam before his eyes, as if there were heat waves. But this was fall. The air was chilled. Nothing heated about it, even though inside he felt like a thousand bonfires had been lit. "A lot of people have blue eyes."

"Like you," Luke observed.

It wasn't an accusation, Blake just heard it that way.

"I've got Papa's green eyes," Luke continued. "So does Ket."

Turning toward the center of the valley, Blake struck out for the well, determined to put this despicable conversation to rest. The boys, of course, followed him like two dogs worrying a bone. When he stopped at the well, they stopped, too.

"So, why's the well considered haunted?" he asked, knowing by now that he would get a detailed explanation. The only difference this time was that it would have nothing to do with his father. At least, he could hope so.

"Not haunted," Luke corrected. "A spirit lives inside it. A guardian."

"A guardian?" Blake mentally prepared himself for another round of horseplay, one that was far enough removed from his own history to be appreciated or at least endured. "Whose guardian?"

"Whoever hears her laughter," Luke said.

If anyone ever needed to hear laughter, Blake decided, it was this crowd, who had nothing good to say about anybody. "A laughing guardian? Where'd she come from?"

"Mama says she's my grandmother. Papa's mother. She was murdered here." Luke looked around as if searching for the spot. "Somewhere right here."

"You're into ghost stories, huh?"

"You wouldn't doubt it if you'd heard the laughter," Luke chastised. "My mama did. Mama says the laughter was what made her marry Papa."

"How's that?"

"The laughter confirmed that their love was true."

Blake almost laughed at Tres Robles's solemn assessment. The boy was far too young to know what true love was. Another attempt to pull Blake's leg? Probably, he decided.

"Some guardian you've got here. Protects folks from Apache warriors and confirms true love. It's a wonder this place isn't overrun with folks seeking her services."

"She's *our* guardian," Luke protested. "The Tremaynes' guardian. No one else's."

Blake looked askance at Tres Robles. "What about friends? Didn't she protect Tres Robles from what's his name, Mangas Che?"

"I didn't drink the water," Tres protested. "I didn't dare. If anyone who isn't a Tremayne drinks the water, he will die on the spot."

"Yeah," Luke confirmed. "That's what the legend says. By drinking the water in front of Mangas Che, I proved I was protected."

"So what would have happened if he hadn't believed in the legend?"

"He'd be consumed by fire."

"Fire? That so?"

"If anyone brings harm to the chiefs, they'll be consumed by fire," Tres Robles explained.

"You don't have to believe it," Luke offered graciously, "but I wouldn't suggest you test it, either."

Blake grinned. "Wouldn't think of it, boys. But what about that part of pouring it all over yourselves? What does that protect you from?"

He missed the gleam in the boys' eyes. Luke explained in solemn tones.

"The legend says that to find true love, you have to bathe in the water. And believe me, you'd better want to find true love. That water is scalding hot."

"Hot, huh?" Still, he missed the boys' baiting, but for good reason now. The image that had sprung instantly to mind was of Ket, her eloquently lovely, perpetually sad face. No need to wonder whether she believed in the redeeming power of that red-hot water. Hell, she probably didn't even believe in love. To tell the truth, he didn't, either. He'd like to ask her, though. Thinking about it, there were a lot of things he'd like to ask her.

Why was she so angry at the world? Why did she hate her stepmother? Why did the mere thought of Ket bring his blood to boiling?

He'd like to ask her these things and more, but he wouldn't. There wasn't a chance on earth she'd give him anything but hell.

"Hey, Blake." Tres Robles called him out of his trance. "You ever been in love?"

"Several times," he responded, truthfully or not, depending on one's definition of love. Later, he regretted not paying more attention to these boys.

Before he realized they had set a trap, they sprung it. Luke heaved the bucket shoulder high and tossed its contents straight at him. They'd been right about one thing: the red water was hot and bitter as ragweed.

He spat quickly, not because he feared the legend, he told himself, but because it was the bitterest gall that had ever entered his mouth, liquid or solid.

Meanwhile, the boys whooped it up. "Next time it'll take," Luke explained gleefully.

"Now that you've bathed in the water of Apache Wells," Tres added, "you'll find love everlasting."

It didn't take Ket but a couple of hours to decide the Comancheros had bigger things on their mind than chasing after two white-eyes boys and a greenhorn gringo. Not that she gave up her watch. She wasn't the greenhorn in this crowd.

But as time passed, her attention was drawn more and more from their back trail to the valley below her. She had a bird's-eye view of the surveyor called Blake and the two boys who followed him around the valley talking him to death or very nearly.

She nibbled on a piece of dried mescal and wondered at the curious attraction she felt for that man—a white eyes. She, who had never been seriously attracted to a man of any race before.

Finally she came to the conclusion that it didn't matter what caused her attraction or whether she felt it or not. She certainly would never act upon it, so what harm did it do to watch from afar? Nevertheless, while she watched, she couldn't keep from analyzing her feelings—or trying to.

She found him physically attractive, which in itself bewildered her. She had never been able to look at the sickly white skin of those who resembled the soldiers who murdered her mother too close for comfort.

But for whatever reason, this man called Blake was attractive to her. Although she was unusually tall for a woman, he was taller than she was by half a foot. Rather than threatening, however, he struck her as sheltering.

True, his white skin was sun-darkened, the exposed parts. But when she tried to suppress the attraction by visualizing the unexposed parts, how sickly white they would be by contrast, she was unable to find anything remotely disgusting in the image.

Blake unclothed was a fascinating image, enthralling, even though it was pure imagination.

The reality, however, was equally inviting—a strong face covered by a week's growth of brown stubble. She didn't like facial hair, didn't believe she would like it even if she hadn't grown up in the Apachería where facial hair was nonexistent. Rather than repulse her, Blake's unshaven face presented a curious exercise in imagining him without it.

Then there was his greenhorn status. If his white skin didn't disgust her, or his stubble of beard, his lack of manly prowess should have.

But as hard as she tried, she couldn't find anything lacking in his physique. Indeed, his extraordinary frame— somewhere around her father's height, she realized suddenly, which again failed to quell her fascination—was well proportioned, harmonious, pleasing to the eye. He'd been right to worry about his added weight on her palomino's back. Blake was a big man, broad of shoulder, narrow of hip . . .

She was the one dim in the head, Ket chastised. She rubbed the old scar on her leg and tried to concentrate on her hatred for Apache Wells, while below Luke and Tres Robles raced around from cabin to creek to well, showing Blake the sights, she supposed.

He was too far away for her to see his expressions, but

she began to feel, to sense, perhaps, his emotions. The valley fascinated him, she could tell that much. For he examined the rocks and vegetation with the absorption of a man studying a trail. Yes, this valley which she hated fascinated him, while he fascinated her.

Unaccustomed to any display of emotion, she watched enthralled while by his stance Blake displayed an ever-changing inventory of feelings. She saw his shoulders straighten in defiance, then slump in frustration. She watched his stride lengthen, as if to outdistance those pestering boys. No telling what pranks those two were pulling on the greenhorn, she thought with glee.

At the well, he listened attentively, certainly to the legend. When she saw Luke lift the bucket of well water behind Blake, she knew what they were about. He jumped aside when the water splashed across his broad shoulders, staining his dirty denim jacket and soaking his already tight denim britches.

The boys doubled over with laughter and Blake shook his head, showering them with hot red water. But it was Ket who felt those heated droplets. While she watched the scene below, the dream that had tugged at her ever since she met Blake flashed through her mind.

Rain. It was raining in the dream—but it wasn't a dream. Suddenly she saw it more clearly and realized that it was a memory of something that had actually happened. Exactly what, she wasn't sure, but she recalled hiding in rocks somewhere and rain and a woman with long black hair.

In her mind's eye the hair and the rain combined to form a curtain that became a barrier to the memory. Whatever it was, though, it was sensual. She might not be able to see the images, but she felt the insidious flame leap to life deep in her belly.

While she sat mesmerized by this veiled memory, Blake

glanced up the hill. Their gazes seemed to hold, even though the distance was too great for that to really happen.

She could almost see his mind change course. Of a sudden he turned on his heel and headed for the creek, where he splashed cold, clean water over the hot red from the well. She felt the change of temperature as surely as if he had splashed her from the icy mountain stream.

When he stood again, his first act was to locate her. She almost tumbled off the rock where she sat when their eyes made contact. Again, the distance was too great for her to actually see the color of his eyes, but the result was the same.

Or so she told herself. When he disappeared between two enormous rock pillars, she knew where he was headed. Her first thought was one of pride. He possessed a sure sense of direction. The path between the pillars led directly to where she sat, although she would never have credited a white-eyes greenhorn with knowing that.

Then he came into view and he was much closer and that insidious sense of expectancy grew unbearable. Still, it never occurred to her to turn away.

"They were initiating me," he observed of the boys, coming closer. The trail was steep, straight up, and he wasn't even breathing heavily.

Again pride swelled inside her, but something tied her tongue. Mesmerized, she watched him run splayed fingers through his hair. Droplets of fresh creek water fell enticingly over his shoulders. Reaching her, he offered an old tin cup for her to take.

"Figured your thirst might need quenching by now." His voice was different from what she'd recalled. Deep and husky, it held her spellbound.

"Thought you might be thirsty," he rephrased. This time she heard something like amusement in his tone.

When she took the cup she was surprised to see her hands tremble. Rarely had anyone offered her a kindness; on the other hand, she rarely offered kindness of her own. She simply wasn't that close to anyone. The water tasted cool and good.

"Thank you," she said simply, allowing the cold water to mingle with the heat in her stomach.

Without waiting to be invited, he sat beside her. "Any sign of our erstwhile compadres?"

"Who?"

"The Comancheros?"

She shook her head. Her unexpected and certainly unwelcome fascination with this man made her uncomfortable. He sat too close, yet she was unable to move away. She tried to think of something to say, but small talk was not a thing she knew. In desperation, she tried. "I see the boys showed you around."

"Ran me around," he corrected.

"I didn't see you run."

"Not literally, figuratively. They were bent on telling me every tall tale they've ever heard and some I'm sure they made up on the spot."

In spite of her determination to remain detached, she smiled and was immediately engulfed by an awkward sense of giddiness.

"Thought maybe you'd like to come down for a while," he said, another kindness. It left her wondering even more why she sat here. "I can actually be trusted to keep watch."

That was something she understood. "Aren't you the one who got himself and those boys caught by Comancheros?"

"Ouch! That hurts. Who told you it was my fault?"

"No one had to." After a time, she felt obliged to add, "You were quick on your feet back there in that camp."

"I had a choice?"

She didn't know exactly what he meant, but for some reason she felt it necessary to talk. That almost amused her. She often went days without talking to a single person. "You surprised me. I didn't expect a white-eyes greenhorn to respond so quickly."

"Not just the greenhorn in me, huh?"

She sensed he didn't expect an answer, so she remained quiet. When he spoke again, however, his tone had changed. She had aggravated him.

"Tell me, Ket, does any white eyes measure up in your books?"

"Against what?" If he could be aggravated, so could she.

"You tell me."

Again he spoke in such a harsh tone, she felt like he had struck her unexpectedly. She didn't know what to say, so she remained silent.

"Against those fellows we crossed paths with earlier today, for starters."

"The warriors?" She frowned quizzically. His eyes were as blue as the sky above them. They didn't look nearly as intimidating as his voice sounded. This confused her further. "They are desperate men. They have no way out."

"Their desperation excuses them? On a whim, they ride off and kill innocent men, but they're desperate, so they're excused?"

"Innocent? The soldiers who hunt and kill people who want only to be left alone are not innocent."

"Therefore you hate all white eyes?"

"I don't hate all white eyes."

"Ah? I must have missed someone somewhere."

How could she have thought this man fascinating? Rather, he was infuriating. And stupid. He understood nothing. "I respect Tres Robles's parents."

"Why?"

Why? She was tempted to tell him the truth, that it was none of his business. His probing into her life, his questions aggravated her. She felt exposed, as though he had crossed some barrier and stumbled into her world. Well, he certainly didn't belong there.

On the other hand, she realized that he had opened an area of her life she had never allowed herself to think about. Why should she respect Nick and Lena when she had nothing but hatred for other white eyes?

"Nick is different," she replied finally. "He has never been with the soldiers."

"Your father was a soldier?"

"He scouted for them."

"And that makes him unworthy?"

"Unworthy?"

"Of your respect? Of your devotion?"

His words struck her like a barbed arrow, aimed straight at her heart. She was angry now, but not in any sense she had ever experienced. Perhaps it wasn't anger; perhaps it was hurt. Jumping to her feet, she tried to move away, but he was quick, too. He caught her loosely around one wrist and held her in place.

Irrationally, tears stung her eyes. She couldn't recall the last time she had felt like crying. "Why don't you ask my father that question? He was the one who left *me.*"

They stood close, touching only by his hand encircling her wrist like a band hot from the fire. The first sound she was conscious of hearing was the thrumming of his heart. Then he spoke.

"I'm sorry, Ket." His voice was low and soft. He sounded sincere. "Sit down . . . I didn't mean—"

Her heart seemed to stop beating. She heard no sounds, thought no thoughts. "You don't understand anything. You could never understand."

When he tugged on her wrist again, she sat—something else she didn't understand. A lengthy silence followed, during which she became more and more perplexed about her own conduct. She never cried. She never talked about personal things. It made no sense. White eyes had a way of doing that to a person, making them act in irrational ways.

She turned to him, furious. "Didn't I tell you you're new out here? You don't know anything, not anything."

Then he took her by surprise again. While she waited for him to respond, wondering how he would, she smiled.

"Hey, Ket, I'm sorry. Really. Truce?"

Ket had lived for twenty years a virtual loner. She knew little of the interactions between people and had always shunned conversations with white eyes. This man both intimidated and infuriated her. Yet, she was unable to gather enough wits to leave him sitting here on the mountain.

"The boys said you spent a lot of time in that cabin."

"They talk too much."

"Yeah, well, I figured that out on my own. They said you were badly burned when you were a child, and that Luke's mother nursed you back to health."

Reflexively, Ket massaged her scarred leg beneath the deerskin britches. She didn't want to discuss her injury, certainly not with this . . . this white eyes.

"They said you—"

"You spent your hours down there discussing me?" she asked angrily.

"Not all of them. Those boys are plumb full of knowledge. They filled me in on quite a few folks. Senator Carmichael for one—"

"Whatever they said about Carmichael, I agree with."

"I don't doubt it. He's a white eyes, after all."

"The worst of the lot." Although she had never discussed this with another soul, she jumped at the chance to change the topic from her own family.

"I hate Carmichael for a reason they probably didn't tell you. Carmichael got Lon Jasper off a murder charge."

"Murder?"

"Jasper gave the order that murdered my mother and other women and children. Carmichael got the bastard off."

"General Lon Jasper, commander of the fort?"

"He was a captain back then. Look at him now. Commanding a post. Not just any post, either, but this one, where everyone has to live with the reminder."

"Why would the senator do such a thing?"

"Get Jasper off a murder charge? You're asking the wrong person. I don't know the answers to any of your questions. If you want to meddle in people's business, you'll have to ask them."

"In this country a United States Senator's business is everyone's business. Believe me, Ket, I intend to ask Senator Carmichael a bunch of questions."

"Don't expect him to tell you anything you can believe. The man's evil to the bone."

"So I heard." When Blake turned to her, his deep-set blue eyes were fierce beneath the slash of brow. She didn't have to hear his voice or his words to know that he, too, was angry.

"Funny, isn't it? Carmichael is everybody's demon right now, but wait until the railroad comes in and folks turn a profit. Then he'll be the savior of this country."

"Not for my people."

If their vision had been physical they would have been locked in heated conflict. Blake broke it first. "Which people, Ket?"

She turned her head away so sharply her neck felt the pain. Bitterly she glared down into the valley, at the cabin, at the creek, and finally at the hated well.

After a while, he said lightly, "They threw that water on me."

Even as angry as she was, mention of the scene she had witnessed earlier washed her with heat. That old memory flashed to mind again, veiled still, but brimming with sensuality. Stunned by her reaction, Ket held her breath, lest he notice.

"They said next time I fall in love it will last forever," he told her matter-of-factly.

Next time? The phrase ignited the flame in her belly. Her arms went weak. Questions assailed her, but she hadn't the courage to speak them. She didn't want to know anything about this man, she argued.

"Did you ever hear the laughter?" he asked suddenly.

It was a simple question, simply voiced. Had she heard the laughter? A simple reply was all that was necessary, but it was impossible, for there was nothing simple about sitting here beside this white eyes while he discussed falling in love and spiritual laughter and . . . forever. She believed in none of it, forever least of all.

"Luke said his mother heard it," Blake continued. "Said it convinced her to marry your father."

The memory vanished, burned away by the stupidity of this white eyes. "If Sabrina heard the laughter, that proves the guardian is from the Underworld." Before her words had died in the cool mountain air, she added, "I was wrong a while ago. Carmichael isn't the worst of the lot, Sabrina is."

Before she could disgrace herself further, Ket jumped to her feet and raced for the top of the mountain. Blake caught her shoulders from behind.

Humiliated, she jerked to free herself. "Let me go."

The harder she struggled, the tighter he held her. Although her own strength was renowned, his was greater. Or was it his determination that was greater? The thought startled her. Confused, she thought again that nothing involving white eyes was ever simple. Why did she allow herself to become tangled in their lives?

While she struggled not only to free herself, but also to understand her predicament, Blake slowly drew her back against his chest and encircled her with his arms and sheltered her in the cradle of his great shoulders.

When he brought his lips so close to her ear that she felt his heated breath against her skin, she couldn't suppress a shudder.

"What say we start over, Ket?"

Chapter Three

"Damnit, Ket, you can't run away from life."

Keturah stared down the trail ahead of them, refusing to respond to Blake's barrage of verbal prodding.

They had left Apache Wells earlier that morning, headed for Fort Davis. It was now nearing high noon, and Blake had talked the entire time. Or so it seemed to her.

She had yet to respond. Until they reached the fort, where they could go their separate ways, silence was her only weapon against this man. Certainly, she couldn't use words. Her limited experience with the English language was no match for his facile tongue. She had a difficult enough time understanding most of what he said, much less defending herself against thoughts that were almost as foreign as his words.

Dismally she knew that were she to open her mouth, it would be to reveal her innermost forbidden feelings for this white eyes. The compelling fascination he aroused within her left her stunned and short of breath. Even if she found words to reply to him, they would surely tremble from her throat.

"What say we start over, Ket?" he had asked the day before—an innocent enough suggestion, or so she had thought. She had been hard on him, and to be truthful about it, he hadn't deserved it. He was actually a nice person, for a white eyes. But that was before she realized what he meant by starting over.

No sooner had the words left his mouth than he had turned her in his arms and lowered his lips. He must have seen the alarm in her eyes, for just before his lips touched hers he mumbled, "Don't be afraid of me, Ket."

She wasn't afraid of him. She was afraid of herself, of her own startling attraction to this man who had somehow managed to penetrate the ten-year-old barrier she had erected around her emotions. Not since her encounter with Sabrina and the subsequent betrayal by her father had Ket allowed herself to *feel*. Oh, she got angry, afraid, and sad for her people, but not for herself.

She was close to no one. She loved Emily, but Emily was not a real part of her life, so closeness had never been a problem. She respected Nick and Lena, but they had never demanded a close relationship. And she avoided her father. In the past ten years, she could count on one hand the number of times she had seen him. Even then she had not exchanged over a handful of words with him. She couldn't remember the last time she had touched him, or he her.

Truth known, closeness was the thing Ket feared most. Closeness like she had felt with her mother, who had been killed; closeness like she had felt with her father, who abandoned her. Opening oneself to closeness with another human being could result in only one thing—betrayal. And Ket figured she had experienced enough betrayal for a lifetime.

But from the moment Blake's lips touched hers on the

hillside that day all sane thoughts had fled. She realized what was happening, and it was—or should have been—frightening. If ever there were a cause to fear disaster, that kiss would have been it.

As unlike the first kiss Blake had surprised her with at the Comanchero camp as winter was from summer, the second kiss had been soft and gentle. Instead of spur-of-the-moment, quick and unintentional, the second kiss had been deliberately slow, and possibly the most amazing thing she had ever experienced.

She hadn't even thought about resisting. More frightening still, that kiss called forth feelings she had heretofore only dreamed about. Since that kiss, the old memory that had nagged at her since she first met this man now absorbed her. It still consisted of feelings, rather than images. Standing on the side of the mountain overlooking Apache Wells with Blake's arms around her and his mouth moving across hers, images of that memory were as intangible as the guardian of the well.

The images finally began to come to her later that night, when she curled up under the cottonwood tree and dreamed of Emily's parents.

Emily's long-dead parents. In the softly falling rain.

"It was just a kiss, Ket," Blake called now. "That's all it was, just a kiss."

Just a kiss? If that was all it had been, a kiss went way beyond the touching of two people's lips, beyond the heat and the wetness and the sizzling tingles that radiated from some central core deep inside her to the most extreme regions of her body.

Remembering it left her weak in the stomach, even though she rode separately from him, the boys having doubled on the third horse. She hadn't touched Blake in almost a whole day, which made his claim that they had exchanged *just a kiss* even more difficult to accept.

He made it sound like a passing thing. Yet, it lingered

still. With the memory of it creating such an insidious urgency inside her, she couldn't help but wonder what kissing him again would do. Absorbed in that frustrating image, his next words brought her back to reality.

"Way you're acting, I took unwanted liberties. Hell, you'd think I ripped off your clothes in broad open daylight in the middle of Main Street or some such travesty."

Ket wasn't sure what a travesty was, but the idea of standing completely nude in front of this man, whether on Main Street or in the middle of the Apachería or in some private shaded glen, was one of the most unnerving images she had ever envisioned—her massive, disfiguring scar uncovered for his eyes to see. She would never bare her leg for anyone to see.

But when she turned to look at him, her shame vanished, and her fear reignited, for the fiery heat that burned in Blake's eyes seared away the image of her leg and told her he was envisioning other parts of her, unclothed and unblemished. The tingles began . . .

Yes, the only way to handle this alarming situation would be to ignore him until they reached the fort. Then she would never have to see him again.

The boys, who had been riding off in first one direction, then another ever since the four of them left Apache Wells, had for whatever reason returned to dog Ket's and Blake's trail.

"Hey, Ket," Luke called, "did you know we doused ol' Blake with well water?"

The image of falling red raindrops flashed through her mind again. When she tried to admonish Luke, she found her throat too dry to speak, so she settled for an awkward nod.

"Know what that means?" Tres Robles pressed.

Of course she knew what it meant. She also knew the boys were baiting her. Unaccustomed to exchanging such banter, however, she had no idea how to stop them.

"Means ol' Blake here's lookin' for everlasting love."

Ket blanched. Without the slightest intention whatsoever, she turned to Blake in time to see a broad streak of red sear his near cheek. This time he didn't have a word to reply. Thankfully.

By late afternoon they approached the fort. The haze of the late fall day had returned, and she felt that it protected her from the glare of the new and unwelcome feelings this white-eyes surveyor stirred inside her.

Blake was too white for her. Too . . . civilized. Although the negative connotation she had always placed on that word seemed to have been reduced to a mild distaste, civilized was still the most frightening word she knew.

Even so, the urgency that simmered in her belly continued to expand insidiously. Her pulse skittered. Time and again her eyes sought his, only to find his rapt attention on her. It was as though she had known he would be looking at her but she had looked at him anyway—not just looked, but held his gaze until their mutual attraction had been acknowledged.

It was as though she had lost all control over her senses—she, who prided herself on self-control, on self-denial. They couldn't reach Fort Davis soon enough.

A sudden cry from Luke jolted Ket back to reality.

"Phew!" he called. "What's that smell?"

They approached Sleeping Lion Mountain from the west. Around the promontory and at the moment out of sight lay Fort Davis. The boys raced ahead.

"It's a dead horse," Tres Robles yelled back.

"And another—" Luke began.

The raid! Gripped by the pain of comprehension, Ket didn't have to be told what the boys' discovery signaled. She drew rein. Even before she reached the bloated carcass of the painted war pony, she knew what she would find.

Ignoring the stench, she dismounted and stared dumbly around the area. Then she started walking through the dried mesquite grass, stumbling over rocks. She followed a trail of dead horses and discarded Apache weapons.

"Hey, Tres," came Luke's voice from somewhere ahead of her. "Ain't that the painted pony ol' Mangas was riding yesterday?"

As though she moved through a world of her own, Ket looked ahead to Mangas Che's war pony. Her toe stumped on something else—

Choking back a burning surge of bile, she glanced down at another pony. *Delgado's.* She recognized it by the rawhide pannier many Apaches carried over their horses' withers. Fashioned of rawhide with cutouts backed with red flannel, the sight of it brought a surge of tears to her eyes. Furiously she fought them back. She would not cry. No white eyes would ever make her cry again.

Yet the loss of this one warrior, foolish though he had been, represented much more than just the loss of one man.

"Ket . . . ?"

When Blake took her shoulders, she slumped back against his chest. Hot tears stung her eyes.

"You recognize this . . . ?"

"Delgado. My cousin Emily is promised to him." When she tasted her own salty tears, a fierceness swept over her. She jerked away and began to tug at the fringed pannier, thinking only that she must save it.

"Ket, darling, let it go . . ."

With her elbows, she shoved Blake away and kept pulling at the rawhide. It was a futile task, for a good half of the three-foot length was caught beneath the dead horse.

"Here, let me help."

When Blake lifted the neck of the horse, Ket was able to pull most of the pannier free. Several inches of fringe tore off, but she hardly noticed. Burying her face in the soft leather, she forced herself not to cry. Slowly, gradually, her anger won out.

When she looked up, it was into the troubled blue eyes of a white eyes. His name, Blake, flashed through her distress, then fell to the coldest part of her heart, the place to where she banished all white eyes.

Jumping to her feet, she strode toward the hated white-eyes fort with Delgado's rawhide pannier thrown over her shoulder. She felt wounded herself, as though she had been ripped apart by the violent life in which she found herself trapped and by the futility of that existence and the hopelessness of ever escaping.

She stumbled over the rocky red plain and through golden dried winter grass, and the voices of the warriors came to her again.

"Better to die here, in this place we call home . . ."

"Better here, where we can leave dead white eyes behind."

Courageous words, foolish words. Wasted deaths and wasted lives. She prayed these brave and desperate warriors had taken white eyes with them on their journey of death.

It had taken Blake several moments to grasp the situation, then a few seconds longer to comprehend the significance to Keturah. He might have been more observant, he suspected, if he hadn't been embroiled in a heated argument with his better senses. When should he tell Ket who he was—his name, who his father was? He didn't want her to hear it from someone else, yet he had never faced a task with such a doomed sense of dread.

He finally decided he could wait until after they reached Fort Davis, since his father rarely visited the fort, and then only to visit Commander Jasper. His father rarely even used his house in the small town of Chihuahua, located just west of the fort. Enmeshed in details for joining the rails by the first day of spring the following year, the senator spent the majority of his time at the old stage station at

Van Horn's Wells, which had been outfitted for an office and sleeping quarters.

More than once recently Blake had had to force himself not to take offense at his father's constant supervision. If the senator intended to attend to every detail himself, why had he hired Blake?

Although Blake's assignment was to survey sites along the railhead, which his father had sold to businessmen, he was also charged with surreptitiously keeping an eye on progress of the rail work. That his father looked over his shoulder, questioning every minute decision, did not mean the senator regretted his decision to hire his only son and heir, yet . . .

Luke Tremayne's cry cleared Blake's mind of all thoughts of the railroad and his father.

"Hey, Tres, ain't that the painted pony ol' Mangas was riding yesterday?"

When the Apache's name registered in Blake's brain, he snapped back to the present. Before him, Ket stumbled from one fallen horse to another. Dismounting, he scooped up her dropped reins and led both of their mounts. He had just reached her when she fell to her knees and began to keen. Ever so much softer than a shriek but with the same eerie overtones, the sorrowful notes curdled his blood.

In two lengthy strides he was kneeling beside her.

"Ket." He took her shoulders, felt her tremble. His heart jumped to his throat when she began to tug at a bloodstained strip of rawhide, the use of which he could not guess.

"Ket, darling . . ." Suddenly he was without words. Soundlessly he drew her back against his chest and held her while she lay against him. He felt her body tense with the struggle to contain her pain—or her rage—or both. Something totally foreign to his nature overwhelmed him. He experienced a compelling need to nurture this woman.

The thought was at once ludicrous and exhilarating. It left him bewildered.

He helped her dislodge the strip of rawhide, which he soon realized was a flat bag of some sort. Freed, she clutched it to her heart, an act that wrenched at his own.

Then she looked up at him. Even though her green eyes glistened with unshed tears, they were rock hard. For an instant, she didn't seem to recognize him. Puzzled, he watched her jump to her feet and walk away. Swept by a strange sense of loss, he again took both sets of reins and followed her toward Sleeping Lion Mountain, beyond which lay the fort grounds.

Even the boys were silent. As eager as they had been to arrive, they held back now, subdued by the reality of death.

A horseshoe-shaped formation of towering red columnar mountains formed the perimeter walls of Fort Davis. Built flush against the mouth of Hospital Canyon, the open side of the post was protected by the San Antonio to El Paso Road and a front guard of quartermaster storehouses and cavalry stables.

Sentries could now be seen atop Sleeping Lion. Several men, military and civilian mixed, came up the road from the fort. They walked hastily in a cluster, rifles held at their shoulders, fingers on triggers, ready to drop into action at a moment's notice.

Blake recognized one of the civilians, a man called Joshua, who ran the mercantile for Edward Bolton.

Joshua stopped in the roadway long enough to exchange greetings. "Yawl best git yourselves into the post," the man advised solemnly.

Blake nodded. "Where're you headed?"

"Chihuahua. Gotta see what those red savages left for us, if anything."

Blake hurried on, but the man wasn't finished.

"Saw your father up at the fort," Joshua called back. "He's safe. Got in ahead of them redskins."

A quick glance to Ket assured Blake she hadn't heard the man's remarks. With the death and dying on her mind, she wouldn't be interested in his parentage. The piercing, distant look she had given him earlier warned him she might never be interested.

Then the question became moot, for they rounded Sleeping Lion and ran smack-dab into a sentry who blocked their path.

"Halt right there or I'll shoot you dead in your tracks." The soldier didn't recognize any of them. Blake had visited the fort only a couple of times, but he had assumed Ket and the boys were well known.

"Can't have no more trouble like with Injun Emily," the sentry added.

Ket, who had shown little sign that she was aware of anything around her until now, snapped to attention. "What happened to Emily?"

"Can't be divulgin' no information to the enemy."

Enemy? In two steps Blake had moved between Ket and the sentry. He glared into the young man's serious black face. "Enemy, hell. This is Keturah Tremayne. These boys are sons of Tremayne and Nick Bourbon, and I am . . ." Blake's words fizzled into the cool mountain air when he realized what he had been about to say. "I'm a surveyor. And we've had about all the trouble we're going to take—"

"They're okay, Johnny." The words were spoken by a sergeant who had stepped into the road, unnoticed by Blake. "Go ahead an' pass, yawl. Johnny here's new. He was just obeying orders; gotta keep things peaceful 'round here."

But Ket didn't budge. She, too, glared at the soldier called Johnny who was having trouble lowering his weapon. "What about my cousin Emily?"

"Ah . . . ah, I don't rightly know . . . ah, ma'am."

Johnny was openly flustered by Ket's appearance. The

thing about her, Blake realized suddenly, the angrier she got, the more she looked full Apache.

"You said another incident ... ?" She turned to the sergeant. "What did he mean, Phil?"

"Well, Miss Ket, it's like this." The sergeant scuffed his toe in the red earth. "Miss Emily's been injured. She's up to hospital with Miz Breena."

"Mama's in the hospital?" Luke inquired. The boys, who still rode double, kicked their mount.

"Where're you going?" Blake called.

"To the hospital. Come on."

By now the only possible speed was a slow walk. A few paces inside the fort grounds a crowd of people milled like a herd of uneasy cattle. Military and civilian—men, women, and children. No one seemed to move with a purpose; rather, they seemed to be waiting for someone to take charge.

Blake caught up with Ket. "Where'd all these people come from?"

"Chihuahua. Outlying ranches. They've come to escape the *savages.*"

Her cynicism was clear and understandable, Blake thought. He couldn't begin to understand how it would feel to be mistaken for an enemy. The only time anyone he knew had ever been considered an enemy had been during the war when they *were* enemies.

Again he was overwhelmed by a desperate need to hold Ket, to protect her from the cruelties of her dual world. To have her mistaken for a warring savage was inconceivable and at the same time entirely believable. She looked Apache. She dressed Apache. Hell, she even seemed to walk Apache. He wouldn't have been surprised to hear the Apache language come from her mouth.

But Ket spoke no more, not even to greet those who recognized her and called her name. She shouldered forward single-mindedly, leaving Blake to follow with the horses.

Men gathered all about, some on horseback, most afoot; huddled in groups, talking quietly, others shouted and pointed, attempting to be heard above the din. Just when Blake decided they had seen the last of the boys, they came barreling back, afoot themselves now.

Confusion reigned. Out of it a plump woman rushed forward. She stopped just short of throwing her arms around Ket's neck. Ket wasn't the hugging kind. Even Blake knew that.

"Mrs. Jordan?" Ket asked, wary.

Blake wasn't sure which surprised him more—that a white-eyes woman knew Ket well enough to consider hugging her or that Ket knew the woman by name.

"Yes, my dear. Alice Jordan. I just wanted to say . . . uh, I'm sorry about your cousin Emily, dear. It was the most awful, awful mistake."

Blake watched Ket recoil. "What happened?" she finally asked in a tight voice.

"You don't know?" Mrs. Jordan clapped chubby hands to equally chubby cheeks. "Oh, my dear, I shouldn't be the one to tell—"

"What happened?" Ket's voice was low, tight.

Detecting her fervor, Blake moved closer. They were being jostled on all sides. He couldn't decide where everyone was headed, for each person seemed to move in a different direction. Like an eddy at the bottom of a waterfall, the bodies of humans and horses, civilians and soldiers, men, women, and children surged to and fro with no semblance of order or destination.

"Well, I . . ." The flustered woman obviously found herself in an untenable quandary. "I would have thought you'd known."

"Known what?" Ket demanded.

"That Emily had come to warn us about the attack."

Blake watched Ket's chest heave with a swift intake of breath. When Mrs. Jordan continued, it was with a defensive edge to her voice.

"We have a whole new battalion," she explained. "They arrived since Emily left the post. The sentry, he didn't recognize her and . . ."

Mrs. Jordan couldn't finish the sentence, but her meaning was clear. Without so much as a glance backward, Ket dove into the crowd, leaving Blake to catch up as best he could, again leading both horses.

By the time he caught up again, she had already passed the row of officers' houses and was halfway across the clearing that separated the fort proper from the post hospital and the munitions magazine.

The layout of the fort had been designed originally in 1854 by Lieutenant Colonel Washington Seawell, who from the beginning considered the location too vulnerable to attack. After the Civil War the pine and slab buildings had fallen to ruin and were replaced by the present stone structures.

When Ket stopped suddenly in front of him, Blake ran into her. His hands grasped her waist, but his initial pleasurable sensations were interrupted by the sobbing of a child.

Before he had time to analyze further, Ket had gone down on her knees to embrace the little girl. Blake knelt, too.

"What's wrong, Neeta?" Ket crooned. "Lost your mother?"

When the name Ket spoke registered, Blake's heart came to an abrupt standstill. *Neeta?* Could this be the child Luke and Tres Robles spoke of? The child rumored to be his father's daughter?

Ket held the little girl's head back. Tears ran down her dark face, leaving muddy trails, but it was immediately obvious that she was very pretty. She wore a tattered calico dress and was barefoot. Her straight black hair needed a comb. Tenderly Ket swept strands off her face.

"Come with me, Neeta. Maybe Rosa is at the hospital."

The child wailed louder. "No. It's those . . . mean ol' McCabe boys . . . They're . . ." Neeta covered her face with dirty little hands. Her words were accompanied by bitter sobs. "I'm going to put a curse on them."

With the child in her arms, Ket stood as gracefully as a mother gazelle Blake had watched for an hour or more one day at the Washington Zoo. In a moment set apart, he stood absorbed in the woman holding the child. The sight did queasy things to his stomach.

"What did those McCabe boys do?" Ket was asking.

Neeta's response was to turn her head and point toward the road that ran between Sleeping Lion Mountain and the fort proper. "They're roasting Carlos."

"They're doing what?" Blake glanced in the direction the child pointed and saw a plume of smoke rise above the crowd. Ket was already headed that way carrying Neeta.

Seconds later Blake caught up again. By now the smell of smoke had reached him. He pushed through the gathered crowd to where Ket knelt, still holding Neeta in her arms. Hardly a sound could be heard, except the sobbing of the child.

"Who's Carlos?" he asked around the dread that filled his throat.

"Neeta's pet goat," Ket replied.

Greatly relieved, Blake squinted through the smoke to focus on a bonfire, which had already drawn a crowd. A crude spit fashioned from stripped branches held a small animal carcass above the flames. Two brawny boys, each twice the size of either Luke or Tres Robles, stood guard at either end of the spit.

"The Tremaynes always give Neeta a goat for her birthday," Ket was saying. "She has a small herd out at their ranch, but she always carries the youngest one around with her. A lot of the unruly children tease her. They call her Goat Girl.''

Blake felt his fists double when Neeta looked around at him. Recognition rocked him on his heels. Her blue eyes were the same shade he saw in the looking glass every morning when he shaved. Gripped by myriad emotions that ranged from denial to anger to an astonishing sense of protectiveness, Blake swiped strands of hair back from the petite face.

"Hi," he said awkwardly. "I'm Blake."

"They killed Carlos," Neeta sobbed in a small little-girl voice. A bit shy, he thought her, the way she ducked her head into the crook of her neck, the way he had done when he was a boy.

Which proved absolutely nothing, he argued.

A guttural exclamation from Ket drew his attention back to the fire, where chaos had erupted. Luke and Tres Robles had come from out of nowhere to tackle the two bullies. Blake glanced from side to side.

"Where are those boys' parents?" Although he shouted loudly enough to be heard all the way to Headquarters, no one answered him. Nor did anyone move to break up the fight.

In three giant strides, he reached the two nearest boys, Luke and one of the McCabes. Grabbing each by a collar, he pulled them apart.

"Hey, this ain't your fight, mister."

"And that wasn't your goat," he told the instigator. "Go on, Luke, Tres," he called toward the other. "Give it up. You boys run and find your mothers. We'll take care of these ruffians."

"Ah, Blake—"

"Go on, I said." To Blake's amazement, Luke and Tres Robles moved away from the bullies.

"Don't think you're getting away with anything, Jeff McCabe," Luke told the nearest bully.

"You neither, Jack," Tres Robles told the other. "Blake here's a fair man. He'll see you pay for your sins."

"Sins, hell," grumbled the boy called Jeff. "Ain't no sin taking food. Goat Girl don't need all them goats, an' we're hungry."

"This has nothing to do with hunger," Blake responded. "That goat did not belong to you. You took it illegally and you will have to pay for it. Where are your parents?"

When he glanced at the crowd, hoping to see someone step forth to claim the boys, his gaze fell on Ket who still held Neeta in her arms. Something swift and hot and dangerous flushed through him.

"I'll take her to the hospital with me," she told Blake. "Maybe someone there will know where Rosa is."

Rosa. Yes, that was the name the boys called Neeta's mother.

With each culprit gripped tightly by a collar, Blake shoved the boys ahead of him. "I'll come with you. Maybe we'll find someone up there to take charge of these ruffians. A night in the guardhouse—"

"You cain't do that, mister. We're just kids."

"Yeah, and civilians, too."

"And hungry—"

"You'll get fed," he promised them. "And it won't be—"

"Blake!"

The call stopped Blake in his tracks as surely as an arrow would have stopped a deer in mid-stride. *His father. Why had he chosen this moment to appear?*

Instantly Blake regretted such a disloyal thought. His father had called to him rarely. In fact, he couldn't remember a single other time in all his thirty years when he had been in a crowd and heard his father call his name.

Nevertheless, Blake ignored the call. If he could get Ket and the boys to the hospital before . . . A glance told him she was too preoccupied with her own immediate concerns to have heard the call. Almost certainly she would not have recognized the voice as belonging to the senator. The next voice, however, was an entirely different matter.

"Blake Carmichael! Hold up."

Ket's head jerked around. Turning from the two men who approached with lengthened strides, Blake stared at her, watched shock tighten her features. Before his very eyes her shock turned to disgust, which quickly became something infinitely more powerful, like hatred, when she saw the two men who approached them.

"Carmichael?" Her voice was strained, but her lips spoke his name and she glared at him with those hard green eyes, leaving him colder than when she had looked at him earlier over Delgado's dead horse, condemning him along with all white eyes. Now her condemnation was for Blake alone.

"Ket, I would have told you, just as soon as . . ."

She just stood there, looking at him. He watched the truth penetrate, saw it mix with the anger and hurt she already felt over the plight of the warriors and the uncertainty about her cousin Emily. Another white eyes had betrayed her. He felt her anguish, and he had never felt as miserable.

The two bullies jerked at their collars, but Blake only held them tighter.

"Hey, mister, ya don't hafta choke us."

"Ket, I intended to tell you. Just as soon as—"

"Son!" Carmichael's voice boomed like the bass drum in the post band. Involuntarily Blake heard his mother's voice of disapproval.

"Sh, James, you are speaking loud enough to rattle the chandeliers."

When Blake glanced behind him, his father bore down on them. "Where the hell have you been, boy? Those red-devil Apaches attacked the railroad camp. We thought sure those savages got you."

One of the boys kicked Blake in the shin, but he was so

preoccupied that he hardly noticed. Like a horse swatting flies, he shook them by their collars. His mind was not on wayward boys.

"Ket, believe me, I would have—" But when he turned back to the spot where she had stood, she was gone. Ket of the few words had said nothing. Ket of the deep anger had fled. Like a wild horse, she had bolted without giving him a chance to explain.

Yet, how would he have explained? What could he have said? Here came his father, approaching with outstretched arms, welcoming him, worried about him. His father, the man Blake had always wanted, no, *needed,* to know. Blake had come west for that purpose—to get to know his father.

Ket felt abandoned by her father. Well, Blake *had* been abandoned by his—for a higher purpose, his mother had always assured him. Now Blake wondered.

Not that he believed the gossip he'd heard from Ket and the boys. Whatever the reason for his father's absence, however, was there a higher purpose than family? Gossip of a physical relationship notwithstanding, his father had lived without the emotional closeness of his family. And what of his family? Blake and his mother had had no voice in the arrangement.

"Son." Carmichael clapped huge hands to Blake's shoulders. His blue eyes pierced Blake's. He looked anxious, sounded anxious. "I've been worried about you, son."

At sixty Senator Carmichael was still a man of impressive proportions. As tall as Blake, with the same broad shoulders, the senator had always been fleshier. Indeed, his belly heralded a man of great appetites—for food, for spirits, for life. Blake cringed as the rumors refused to remain in the back of his mind. When the senator stepped back, Commander Jasper reached for Blake's hand. He frowned at the boys.

"What's this?"

Welcoming the opportunity, Blake shoved the boys

toward the commander. "You're in charge of civilian welfare around here, aren't you, sir?"

"That's right."

"Then take these boys and do something with them. They stole . . ." Since hearing the rumor, Blake hesitated speaking the name of the innocent child who was rumored to be his father's daughter. "They stole a goat and roasted it. Plenty of witnesses to back me up."

"Well, I ordinarily concern myself with—"

"You better take care of 'em." Luke spoke from behind Blake. Then Tres Robles added to the confusion.

"They roasted Neeta's pet goat. Don't you let 'em get away with it."

Obviously disconcerted, Jasper stepped back. "I'll handle it." But the commander's mind seemed to be somewhere else. Blake followed his line of vision to the hospital, catching a glimpse of Ket as she stepped from the wide veranda into an adjacent hallway.

When the commander looked back at Blake, his brown gaze was hard. "Isn't that Tremayne's half-breed daughter?"

Instantly Blake thought of Ket's claim that Jasper had been responsible for her mother's death.

"What?" his father sputtered. "What were you doing with that half-breed?"

Blake's first instinct was to strike someone. *His father.* Good God, what had he become? What had they all become? "*Keturah* Tremayne rescued me from a band of Comancheros."

"Comancheros?"

"They overtook us south of Van Horn's Wells."

"Us?"

"Ket's half-brother Luke, Tres Robles Bourbon, and me. The Comancheros took us; Ket rescued us."

"Well," the senator blustered, "stay away from that half-breed. She'd as soon knife you in the back as look at you. You're new out here, son. One drop of red-devil blood is too much for civilized folk like us. Can't trust 'em. Not a single drop . . .''

Dismayed by everything that occurred in the last few minutes, Blake listened to the tirade and tried to decipher his father's meaning. Did capture by Comancheros matter less than who rescued you?

The rumors about his father nipped at his mind like flies on the carcass of Delgado's beautifully painted horse. Dismally Blake wondered how he would ever banish them.

Ket found Rosa Raméríz sitting on a gray wooden bench in the breezeway that separated the officers' ward from the hospital offices and mess hall. Her breathing was labored, and Ket wondered if she was sick.

She handed over Neeta, explaining the ordeal with the child's goat.

"Pobrocita," Rosa mumbled, taking her daughter. *"Gracias, Keturah."* At Ket's question, she directed her down the hall. "Emily is in the civilian ward."

Ket found Emily in the room's first bed. A screen separated her from the other occupants, but Ket wasn't interested in anyone but her cousin. Her heart was in her throat.

"Emily, why?"

"Mangas Che finally persuaded the others to raid," the injured girl replied. Her black eyes were dim and her voice was weak. Hugging her, Ket found her forehead hot.

"She came to warn us." The voice belonged to a woman whom Ket had not seen until she spoke. Reba Applebee, Emily's adopted mother, rose to wipe the girl's head with a damp cloth. Neither the tenderness of her gestures, the tears in her eyes, nor the pain in her voice escaped Ket's notice now.

"But why would the soldiers . . . ?"

"We have a new battalion, new since Emily returned to the Apachería," Reba explained, as had Mrs. Jordan before her. "The sentry didn't recognize Emily." The woman leaned over her adopted daughter and kissed her tenderly on the cheek. "My poor, poor baby. She came in such haste, she didn't take time to change into post clothing."

Post clothing, Ket realized, was Reba's way of saying Emily had returned wearing an Apache dress. Glancing around, she saw the deerskin dress on top of a chest, neatly folded. Moccasins and a headband lay beside it. The dress was bloody.

Ket dropped the fancy rawhide pannier she had taken from Delgado's horse to the vacant chair, hoping Emily hadn't seen it. No use borrowing trouble, there was trouble enough in this room.

"How bad is it?" she asked Reba.

Reba responded by pressing her lips together so tightly they turned a sickly shade of white.

Emily stared at Ket wide-eyed. "They say I won't live."

"Then they're wrong!" For the second time today, tears welled in Ket's eyes. What had happened to her emotions? She'd held them back so long; now she seemed to have lost all control. Already today had been one of the saddest of her life. And it wasn't even over.

Of its own accord, her mind returned to Blake. *Blake Carmichael.* The name sliced like a new knife into her heart, creating a wound that hurt worse than the burn on her leg had.

But when she glanced down at Emily, she felt ashamed. How could she think about a man, a white-eyes man no less, when Emily lay dying? The answer that sprang instantly to mind was simple. One dastardly word.

Betrayal. White eyes and their talk of friendship and love could never be trusted. Betrayal. It was as easy for them as drinking from a cool spring, as running through a meadow when the grass was spring-soft.

Blake had treated her with kindness and compassion,

gaining her trust, all the while deceiving her. How easy it had been for him to break her heart.

The thought was absurd. No white eyes could ever break her heart again, not since Sabrina . . .

As though she had spoken aloud, Emily squeezed her hand. The girl's pain was etched in lines on her smooth, youthful face. "Sabrina ran out onto the field and carried me in."

So what? Ket wanted to ask.

"Be kind to her, Ket. For my sake. She has always been good to me."

That much was true. Sabrina had had a great deal to do with Emily's adjustment after she'd been brought to the post as an orphan. Sabrina had also had a great deal to do with Ket's and Emily's reunion; Ket had learned that from the Bourbons years after the first time they brought Emily to the ranch to visit her.

What a glorious day that had been. "Remember the first time we saw each other after you came to live at the post?" Ket asked her cousin now.

Emily smiled. "Sabrina and your father took me to the ranch. I didn't know what was happening. They said it was a surprise." Emily looked up to include Reba Applebee. "Did you know Ket then?"

Reba returned the smile, although Ket could tell it was with difficulty. The pain on the woman's face was familiar, for Ket had seen countless women lose their children in battle—Apache mothers, Apache children.

"I felt like I knew her," Reba told Emily. Then to Ket, "Sabrina had spoken of you so often."

The claim was made with such sincerity that any attempt Ket made to dispute Sabrina's motives would have disrupted the visit. Emily, after all, was Ket's central concern—Emily's recovery, Emily's sacrifice.

Old Doc Henry came in once, greeted Ket, and paused to explain Emily's wounds.

"She got hit twice." He pointed to the bandage that bound Emily's left shoulder. "This one's fine. Bullet went in here and came out there. The other one . . . well, the other dad-blamed bullet's still in there someplace."

At Ket's request for further information, he smiled wanly. "I've sent word to the surgeon at Fort Bliss," he said. "Till he arrives, keep her still. We don't want that bullet to take off in the wrong direction."

Doc Henry's hands were palsied and he was old, far too old to practice medicine. He had retired from military service years ago, but since he had stayed on in the vicinity of Fort Davis, he remained the chosen physician for many of the old-timers.

When he stepped beyond the screen, she heard him greet the room's other patient.

"Sabrina, my dear, how are you doing?"

Disconcerted, Ket chastised herself. Why hadn't she realized that Sabrina would be the other patient in this room? Alice Jordan said Sabrina was at the hospital. Ket hadn't realized she meant as a patient.

White eyes, she thought. They always tangled her in their lives.

Eager to escape further entanglement in her stepmother's life, she was nevertheless reluctant to leave Emily's side. "I should go somewhere and change clothes," she confided in a whisper. "I've been in these same clothes far too long."

"Sabrina carried me back to the fort," Emily whispered. "She is in danger of losing the babe." Her grasp tightened on Ket's hand. "Tell me about the boys. Are they well?" She had helped decide how to search for them.

"By the time I caught up with them," she told Emily, self-conscious now that she knew Sabrina was on the other side of the screen, "they had gotten themselves captured by Comancheros." She finished the account quickly.

"Who's Blake?" Emily wanted to know.

Ket hadn't intended to mention him. "J. J. Carmichael's son."

"Such a nice young man," Reba interjected. "I met him shortly after he arrived out here. He seems to be nothing like that blustering father of his, I'm happy to report."

Ket's myriad emotions surged in conflict. "He's with his father and Commander Jasper now. The Carmichaels and Lon Jasper are thick—"

Emily shushed Ket with a finger to her lips. "Remember Sabrina," she whispered.

Ket glanced toward the screen; rather, she decided later, she must have glared at it, for as weak as Emily was, she gripped Ket's hand tighter. "Be kind to her," Emily said. "She had a rough time back then. She has a rough road ahead now."

Ket couldn't believe her ears. Emily was the one the doctor expected to die. Emily was the one whose road was rough.

"I could use some fresh water, Ket," she said sweetly. "Why don't you fetch some for me . . . and for Sabrina, too."

There really wasn't any way out of it, short of refusing Emily's request. So she fetched a pitcher of water from the cistern and picked up two glasses from the mess hall. She would ask Reba Applebee to take Sabrina the water.

But when she returned, the screen that separated the patients had been folded and set aside. Sabrina was in full view, although, instead of looking into the room, she stared out the window. Watching for Luke, Ket thought. Where were those boys? They'd been so worried about their mothers, now they were caught up in the excitement outside.

The excitement of having destroyed those red-devil Apaches. Blake was a Carmichael.

She had never felt so betrayed . . . except by the woman lying here beside Emily.

Ket studied her now, this woman she had hated for so

long. She hadn't seen Sabrina in years and was surprised at how much she had aged. Maybe it was just her weakened state, but that fiery red hair seemed paler than Ket remembered. Here in this bed, Sabrina looked weak. She bore no resemblance to the demon Ket had always imagined her. But demon she was. Ket seethed, recalling everything this woman had taken from her. Foremost being her father and the home she could have had with him.

Quickly, before Sabrina returned her attention to the sparsely furnished room, Ket turned to Emily with a glass of water. Emily, however, seemed determined to change the world in one way or another before she left it. After a couple of sips, she mouthed, "Go ahead, Ket. Take Sabrina some water."

Feeling trapped again, Ket gritted her teeth, poured a glass from the pitcher, and stepped to her stepmother's bedside.

Sabrina turned and smiled. It wasn't a really bright smile, which would have seemed faked. "Keturah," she said in a voice Ket did not recall, "how lovely. Thank you." After several swallows, she handed the glass back to Ket. This time she looked Ket squarely in the face. "Thank you most of all for finding the boys."

"They're . . . uh . . ." Ket stood stiffly, poised to bolt at the first possible moment. "They should be here any minute now. They're probably making sure Bla . . . uh, that surveyor honors his promise to see the McCabe boys pay for roasting Neeta's goat."

"Poor dear little Neeta. And Rosa, too. She has contracted consumption, you know. One would think that family had suffered enough. Where is Neeta?"

"Rosa was on the porch," Ket answered simply, thinking only of escape.

Sabrina seemed lost in a moment of sadness. "I don't know what will become of Neeta." Then she brightened.

"I wasn't eavesdropping," Sabrina said, "but, well, that screen is thin. Did I hear something about Comancheros?"

"Luke and Tres and a surveyor, Blake Carmichael . . ." Ket stopped short after speaking the name. Bitterness laved her tongue. "Luke and Tres met up with him outside the railroad camp, and the three continued on to Apache Wells. But Comancheros captured them before they got there, and I . . ." She shrugged, self-conscious again.

"Were any of you hurt?" Sabrina wanted to know.

Ket shook her head. "We were lucky."

"*I* was lucky," Sabrina said. "Lena sent for exactly the right person. No one but you or your father could have brought our boys home to us."

Fidgeting under compliments she had no intention of accepting, Ket felt obliged to ask, "How are you?"

"I'll be fine. Bored, but fine. Doc Henry says I must stay in bed until the baby comes."

The thought of Sabrina bearing another child, another half-sibling for Ket herself, added to Ket's distress. While she tried to find a graceful excuse to leave and wondered why it mattered how she left, Sabrina gave her one.

"Lena is over at Reba's house, Ket. Would you mind going to tell her the boys are safe? I know she's anxious."

Irritated that Sabrina had managed to read her mind, Ket bristled. With a curt nod, she turned to leave, but stopped at the foot of Emily's bed.

"I won't be long."

"Take your time, my dear," Reba insisted. "You look exhausted. Draw some water and refresh yourself. Emily has clothes in the wardrobe. They should fit."

Anxiety surged inside Ket like a wild animal struggling to escape. She felt trapped inside this room with these white-eyes women trying to manipulate her. Crossing to the head of the bed, she kissed her cousin on the cheek. "I won't be long." Feeling the parched heat of Emily's forehead, Ket was again ashamed. These women had loved and befriended her cousin. How could she hate them?

At that moment her hatred seemed small-minded and weak. She felt it slip to the back of her mind, where it became hidden beneath the other doubts and fears she had experienced this day.

All except her hatred for the white-eyes surveyor who had betrayed her last. She doubted that anything could ever cloud the hatred she felt for Blake Carmichael.

Chapter Four

"She's a human being!" Blake held the razor poised above his right cheek. His father had followed him home, sans Commander Jasper, thank heavens, and found him finishing a bath in cold water drawn from the well behind the small adobe house. He stared at the reflection in the mirror he had propped against the water bucket and studied the carmine tint to his father's face.

"An ol' wore-out drunk . . . " the boys had called him. The phrase had tormented Blake, as had the fact that he couldn't forget it. But his father made it difficult. He had driven his buggy into the backyard of the little house in Chihuahua and pulled up in a swirl of red dust at Blake's feet.

The senator was irate. "How dare you take up with that half-breed?"

Overwhelmed by encountering his father in the presence of Keturah and by his own inability to ignore the gossip he had heard about the esteemed senator, Blake had fled to Chihuahua where his father kept a small adobe house.

Apache renegades be damned, he had to get away. So he'd followed the small crowd of men returning to their businesses.

He had felt dirty, had never felt dirtier in his life. Nor had he ever felt as disillusioned. Questions swarmed through his mind like angry bees, initiated he knew by the accusations against his father. His meeting with Neeta proved nothing, yet it, too, had provoked unwanted and unanswered questions.

Perhaps it was the cold water, but by the time the senator arrived, Blake had convinced himself that if given the opportunity, his father could explain away the gossip. His expectations were short-lived, however, when J. J.'s first words condemned Ket as being subhuman.

"A man of your stature can afford to be tolerant," Blake responded.

"Don't lecture me about tolerance, young man. You were downright rude to Commander Jasper, rushing off like that. Your licentious nature is understandable, although how you can find a filthy savage attractive is beyond me."

The charge was abominable and brought to mind the question of Neeta's parentage, but rape and abandonment were a whole different topic. Finished shaving, Blake folded the razor deliberately and stowed it in his traveling case.

"You were the one who was rude," he told his father.

"Don't come out here judgin' me." J. J. huffed a moment longer, then conceded, "You haven't been in this country long enough to know what those red devils are capable of."

Where have I heard that before? The accusation, though possibly true, struck Blake all the harder because it echoed what Ket had said. "Keturah is only half Apache."

"Trust me, son, that woman is all savage. Wait'll you meet that father of hers. You'll have a new understanding of what the word savage means."

Having never met the man, Blake couldn't deny that Ket's father might be exactly what his own father claimed. On the other hand . . .

"From the earful I got these last few days, the Tremaynes feel much the same way about you."

J. J.'s carmine-colored face turned dark. "What'd those goddamned savages say against me?" His blue eyes narrowed. "You wouldn't believe them over your own father, your own flesh and blood?"

"I didn't say I believed them. Some of their claims were pretty farfetched. I'd hoped we could discuss them."

J. J. glared silently.

"They claim you stole their father's land."

"Buying up warranty deeds to land that has lain unclaimed and untaxed for years is not stealing."

Blake knew that for the truth; still, the rumors nagged. "Why didn't you buy all of it?"

"All of it?" his father demanded. "You mean that useless little valley, the one they say is haunted?"

"Useless for making money," Blake acknowledged. Apache Wells was hardly useless as a valued piece of property. It was the most ethereal place Blake had ever seen.

"Apache Wells isn't haunted," he explained. "To the Apache, it's sacred. To the Tremaynes, too." He might have thrown a match into the post magazine, the way his father exploded.

"By God, they did turn you against me." J. J. waved a tight fist in Blake's face. "Just like that, those damned red devils turned you against me."

I didn't meet any devils, red or otherwise, Blake wanted to say. "No one turned me against you. The Tremaynes opened questions."

"Questions from the likes of them don't count."

"Luke Tremayne doesn't have a drop of Apache blood. Nick Bourbon's son was along, too. They're just kids, I know, but the way I understand it, Nick Bourbon and Tremayne are respected ranchers."

"Well, you understand wrong. Get that through your head right now. Nick Bourbon is a foreigner," the senator dismissed. "Unlike myself, who has devoted the best years of my life to this country."

At last the senator had made a charge Blake could agree with. "I'm one person you don't have to remind of that, Father."

"Ah, I see what this is. Not only do you have the hots for that filthy half-breed, but you hold it against me for performing a service to our country."

"To our country? Or to yourself?" Blake regretted the questions as soon as they left his mouth. "I'm sorry, Father. I was out of line. I—"

"You'd better be careful, boy. I brought you out here hoping we could work together. I can send you back just as quick."

Blake didn't doubt that for a minute. Thing was, he might beat his father to it. Nowhere was it written that a son—a full-grown son—had to stick around and listen to the abuse the esteemed senator heaped upon others— and others heaped upon him. The senator continued his harangue.

"You stay away from that half-breed, hear me? No kin of mine's going to be contaminated by red-devil blood."

Again Blake was reminded of Neeta, but again he held his tongue, for the topic was too serious to discuss without a lot of forethought. His father was right. He was new out here. Judgments came easy, and judgments that came this easy usually proved wrong, or at best, shallow. Still, even if his father was innocent of wrongdoing, Blake hated his attitude.

"Doesn't it count for something that she saved my life?"

"Damn right, it counts. Means you can get back out there and see that my railroad's finished by deadline."

"I'm on my way." But Blake couldn't leave town without apologizing to Ket.

Emily had clearly left only her white-eyes clothing behind, which Ket had no desire to wear. On the other hand, she was clean for the first time in two long weeks, and she did not relish putting grimy deerskin on her clean body. At length, she settled on a white blouse and loosely gathered black skirt, such as the Mexican ladies in the area wore.

"Ah, you look like you feel better," Lena complimented on Ket's return to the Applebees' parlor. She draped a black woolen *rebozo* around Ket's shoulders. "It's chilly out today."

If anyone had asked Ket the definition of a lady, she would have named Lena Bourbon. Always kind, gracious, and eager to assist, Lena never judged, never meddled, never tried to manipulate or change a person in the way of most white eyes of Ket's experience. Somewhere between the age of thirty and forty, Lena was still beautiful and vibrant. A perfect compliment to each other, Lena and Nick possessed the perfect marriage. To one less cynical than Ket, theirs would have been confirmation that not all white eyes were despicable.

But Ket *was* cynical. She had seen the truth—about white eyes, about love, about life. Still, Lena remained a rock of support, which was why Ket had felt obligated to charge a Comanchero camp to save her son.

Although Lena was undoubtedly eager to rush out to find Tres Robles, her only child, she had graciously insisted that she wait while Ket bathed and dressed, helping carry water and choose clothing.

Ket quickly plaited her still-wet hair and slung the single

braid over her shoulder. "Come on. Let's find Tres. I know he's anxious to see you."

No sooner had they set out for the hospital, however, walking briskly in the cool autumn air, than a call came from across the clearing.

"Ket!"

Blake! As if lightning had struck near the same spot twice today, the call rooted Ket's feet to the red earth. She wanted to run back to the safety of the Applebees' house on Officers' Row, but she was unable to move.

"Ket!" he called again. "Wait up."

Mesmerized with dread, she watched him lope across the clearing toward them. Thankfully, before he arrived, she regained her mobility and resumed her march toward the hospital. This time it was Lena who stopped her with a restraining hand to her arm.

"Shouldn't we wait, dear?"

Ket's response was to grab Lena's arm and pull her toward the hospital. "That's Senator Carmichael's son."

Lena stiffened momentarily, then skipped to catch up. "Isn't he the man you rescued along with the boys?"

Escape was impossible, for Blake was already near enough to hear Lena's question. When he reached them, he fell in step. "Depends on whose story you believe," he told Lena as if the two were the best of friends. "Some might say I rescued *her.*"

His good nature discomposed Ket. Fury singed a path all the way to her toes. Did he expect her to act as if he had never deceived her, never betrayed her? When she tried to outdistance him, he blocked her path. Strangely, though, he ignored her and focused on Lena.

"I'm Blake Carmichael, ma'am. I assume you are Mrs. Bourbon. Your son Tres is a fine young man."

Anger vied with sheer and utter distress. Ket knew she had to get away from this man before she embarrassed herself in front of him . . . and in front of Lena.

"We have nothing to say to you." But when she took Lena's arm and tried to move away, Blake called her back in an earnest tone.

"Ket, please, just stop and listen." He glanced at Lena. "My apologies, ma'am, but I have some explaining to do to Ket, and I'd like to do it in private."

Lena came to a complete halt at Blake's blatant admission. She turned wide black eyes on Ket.

"You owe me nothing," Ket told him. To her utter fury, he turned his charm on Lena.

"Ma'am, forgive me, but my father insulted Miss Tremayne and I intend to apologize."

"Oh, dear, Keturah." Lena glanced from one to the other.

Ket glared at Blake. But in the glaring she couldn't help noticing that he had shaved. Gone was that unsightly stubble of brown hair. His jaw was now smooth. Her heart fell to her stomach. Clean-shaven, he posed an even greater threat, or so it seemed. His blue eyes conveyed a jolting combination of earnestness and merriment.

"Give me a minute, Ket. Please. Just a minute."

He wanted to apologize. He could never . . .

Horrified, Ket realized that deep inside she was pleased. That insidious heat swept through her, and with it the elusive memory returned. The only difference now was that it chose this of all moments to flash through her mind in full-blown focus.

It was the most prevalent of all her memories. Throughout her adolescence it had returned time and time again. Gradually she had come to know, or to think she knew, the reason she could not shake its grip.

Once wonderful, that memory had soon turned bitter. Every time it reared its head, it had filled her with dread . . . until the day she met Blake.

Mesmerized by the beckoning blue eyes of this man she hated for many reasons, she strangely felt no fear or anguish associated with the memory. Perhaps that was why it had taken so long for it to come into full focus. The tone of it had changed. The memory of that long-ago day no longer filled her with fear and anguish.

That in itself was frightening. The fear and anguish associated with that memory had served her well. It had kept her safe for a long time.

She had been nine when it happened. It was the year before Sabrina stole her father, the year before she fell into the fire. It was summer and raining; the rocks where she played were so hot that rainwater steamed from them. Beyond the rocks ran a creek that today was called Apache Springs. While she sat there on the rocky shelf, shielded from the rain—and from sight—by an overhang, she had heard laughter.

Her mother's brother, Chi Caliente, and his wife Doré, parents to Emily, had emerged from the stream. They were naked and beautiful and happy.

The steamy air had been laden with the sweet scent of sage and juniper, which Ket always smelled recalling the dream. At the innocent age of nine, she had thought they were dancing through the heavy air, and it was the most beautiful dance she had ever seen. No beating drums, no war chants. Only the two of them, their bodies glistening like wet copper, their hair wet and clinging, their urgency compelling even to one so young.

Even at nine she had sensed the tenderness between them and had been overwhelmed by an intense sense of longing.

Doré's hair had come down from its braid and hung in wet lengths about her shoulders and over her face. When Chi kissed her it was through this veil of black hair. It covered her breasts when he took them in his mouth, as though he were a babe, Ket remembered thinking. Enthralled, she had felt the connection, the security that a babe feels and that a motherless child longs for the rest of her days.

Before that time, Ket had witnessed the mating of animals—dogs, horses—so when Chi and Doré lay on the ground and accomplished the deed, she did not recoil from either shock or disgust. Rather, the natural act performed in the falling rain by these two beloved people touched her with its intimacy and left her longing for the intimacy she had known as a child.

Not until much later did she understand the eroticism of what she had so innocently witnessed. By that time, Chi and Doré and many others were dead, and Ket had begun to associate this once-beautiful memory, not with life and love, but with death and hatred. For not a year afterward, while the memory had been still fresh in Ket's young mind, Chi and Doré were murdered by white soldiers. Soon after that, Ket fell into the ceremonial fire, which led to her father bringing Sabrina to Apache Wells to treat her burned leg, which led to her father abandoning her for the fiery-haired soldier's daughter.

The day Ket witnessed her father embracing Sabrina outside the cabin at Apache Wells was the day all the tenderness and love inside her died. After that, as she grew to womanhood and experienced the stirrings of sexual longings, she identified them with death and betrayal and defied herself to be deceived by the false promises of suitors.

Intimacy led to death and betrayal. That was the one fact of life of which Ket was absolutely and unequivocally certain. She had long since hardened her heart against this traitor, intimacy.

But now as she stared through the fall haze at this white eyes' smooth handsome face, she realized an even more certain truth: The worst traitor of all was inside herself. For hearing Blake's voice had made her heart skip a beat; seeing him caused latent longings to pool heavily in the pit of her stomach. Even knowing who he was, she longed to reach for him—to hold him and be held by him.

Angrily she turned aside, only to have him block her path again. She tried to push past him, but he caught her arm and drew her to a halt.

"All I'm trying to do is apologize, Ket."

She'd heard that before. *All it was was a kiss.*

With a mighty jerk, she freed her arm. "You've done it. Turn me loose. I must go to Emily."

Incredibly, Lena interfered. "Ket, dear, perhaps you should hear him out. I'll run on to the hospital. Take your time. I'll tell Emily you'll be along."

"But, Lena, I . . ."

By this time Blake had claimed her arm. Helplessly, or so she felt, she watched Lena step lightly over the yellowed grass, headed for the hospital.

Blake pulled Ket in the opposite direction. He crossed the clearing and didn't stop until he had dragged her behind the steward's house on the opposite side of the hospital.

It was a two-story whitewashed building with no windows in the rear, since that side was close enough to Sleeping Lion Mountain for rifles and arrows to find their mark. With two hands to her shoulders, he forced her against the wall of the building.

Deliberately she squeezed her eyes closed, not trusting herself to look him in the face. "Let me go."

"Not until you listen to my explanation."

"I don't want to hear your explanation. I don't care."

"I think you do, Ket. I think you're mad as an old wet hen that I deceived you."

Startled, she was unable to keep from opening her eyes. She tried to glare at him, to deny his claim. Even though she could never deny it to herself, she wouldn't give him the satisfaction of knowing so.

"I wanted to tell you who I was from the start," he said.

"At first I didn't want to drag my father's good name through the mud—"

"Good name?" When she struggled to free herself, he brought his body closer to hers, effectively imprisoning her. Blown against her face, his breath was hot and steamy, like her memory of Emily's parents. She had the strangest feeling that were he to suddenly step aside, she would fall to the ground. Still, she protested. "Let me go."

"Wait a minute. Let me . . ." His words stopped but his lips remained parted and she thought he intended to kiss her. When he didn't, she recalled the memory, the wet hair, the tenderness. Her body flushed, betraying her yearnings in the most intimate places.

As in respite, Blake's breath blew gently across her face. "After hearing the rumors about my father," he continued, "I was afraid to tell you."

Afraid? She curled her lips inward, pressing them between her teeth, lest they betray her, too.

Blake studied her with an absorption that made her want to squirm, to run—no, to stay right there against him forever. Amusement flickered in his blue eyes.

"I didn't want to be left out there afoot to face Victorio's warriors or the Comancheros or both."

She inhaled a deep breath in an effort to steady her senses, but she only managed to fill her lungs with the scent of him. A new, clean scent, which suddenly reminded her of her father in earlier, happier times.

Desperate now, she renewed her efforts to escape. No white eyes would ever betray her again. Not ever again.

But Blake persisted. "Ket, please listen. I was going to tell you. I wanted to tell you myself. I never intended for you to find out from someone else. Especially not from—"

"You owe me nothing," she spat. "Why should it matter to me?"

"I don't know the answer to that." His response was

quick and his tone honest. "But it does matter to you. The same way it would matter to me if you deceived me."

His statement made no sense. "I would have no reason to deceive you." Although she tried to express her anger, she knew she fell short, for with him so near she could hardly draw a decent breath.

Still, Blake held her in rapt attention, and she had no idea what he was thinking. "I'm sorry about my father," he said after a long moment. "He had no right to talk like that. He shocked me, too."

This she understood, better than he ever would. "I don't apologize for my father, you don't have to apologize for yours."

Blake's reaction was to draw away, even as his grip on her arms tightened painfully. "You think you're the only one who was ever abandoned by a father?"

The question, voiced in such a harsh tone, took her by surprise. She held his obstinate gaze, waiting—for what she wasn't sure.

"I was abandoned by my father, too, Ket. At least he was never around. But I haven't given up on him the way you have given up on your father."

"Given up?" This man had a way of wounding her. It was as if he knew, or thought he knew, the most personal, the most vulnerable and secret places inside her. Places she had successfully hidden from the world for years, he found and plunged his accusations straight to the heart of them. Straight to her most secret desires, straight to the guilt she guarded from her own conscience.

"Coming out here, working with my father, this is the first chance I've ever had to get to know him. That's been the dream of my life—to get to know him. I can't just throw it away. I won't."

What was he saying? What did he mean? That she had thrown away her chance to know Tremayne?

"You think you know so much. You know nothing."

Tremayne had abandoned her, not the other way around. It couldn't have been otherwise. Furious that this white-eyes stranger could open such a painful wound, she lashed out at him.

"What if he fathered Neeta? Would you want to claim him then?"

Blake's expression did not change. "I can't answer that, not right now. Not until I've heard his side of the story."

"Do you expect him to admit the truth about anything? If you asked him about Lon Jasper, he would take up for the man. But I know the truth, and the truth condemns them both."

"Commander Jasper had no right to speak to you the way he did, either."

"You understand nothing," she said again. "How could Jasper hurt me with words? He was responsible for my mother's murder. No words he can ever say will be as bad as that."

"I understand. It is a hideous thing. If it's true, it would be—"

"You doubt me?"

"I don't doubt *you*, Ket, I doubt rumors. Crimes like that and like those you and the boys accused my father of committing are horrible. They deserve nothing but facts."

"Then you should talk to my fath— Ask Tremayne. Or Nick. Ask them for proof that Lon Jasper murdered my mother. Ask them how he got away with that crime and returned to this post as commander."

"If that's true, the facts must not have been presented to the proper authorities."

"You won't give up, will you?" Suddenly she was sad, deeply, deeply sad. At the same time, it made parting with him much easier. "You are just like all the rest of them. Twist and turn the words into your own truth, but that won't make them true for anyone else. You want to believe your father, so you will believe him. Turn me loose. I have worse things to worry about."

Still Blake held her. His gaze penetrated deeply into her, to her very soul or so it seemed. Afraid he might see her sadness, she closed her eyes again.

"Your cousin?" he asked. "Is she in bad shape?"

Desperately she tried to harden her heart against his sympathetic tones. "They say she is dying."

"You've lost a lot, Ket. Endured a lot." With a hand to her chin, he tipped her face. Despite her overwhelming desire not to look at him, her eyes seemed to have a will of their own, for they flew open.

His attention focused solely on her, and she couldn't have looked away if she had wanted to. With a nod of his head he motioned backwards toward Sleeping Lion Mountain, and beyond. "Friends, relatives maybe, were killed out there yesterday."

"I don't need your sympathy." Again she tried to turn aside, but again he used gentle force to move her face back to his. Compelled by his probing gaze, she searched the depths of his blue eyes, unable to quell the fascination that swirled inside her. Even as she hated him, she felt drawn to him.

His hand on her face burned hot spots that trailed down her body. A clamorous hum set up inside her and increased until she was certain he could hear it.

"Since the beginning of time, men have been fighting and killing themselves over land, Ket." He was so close that his breath blew hot and sweet against her face when he spoke. "That's war. It's been going on forever. I'm not saying it's right." As tenderly as though he touched a babe, he cupped her cheeks in his palms. His fingers spread up her temples and into her hair; his voice mesmerized.

"We may not like it," he continued, "but it happens. It doesn't have anything to do with us, not if we don't let it."

"With us?" Her mouth was dry and the words came out like a sigh.

"Us." He repeated the word like a love song and followed it with his lips. They opened over hers, wet and hot and demanding. And she resisted.

And resisted . . .

And resisted . . .

Suddenly she became aware of her body, and this awareness pounded through her veins. The simple white blouse and chemise, covered by the thin woolen *rebozo*, were not nearly thick enough to separate her breasts from his chest. When she inhaled she felt herself swell into him.

He must have felt them, too, for he pulled her closer in a seductive way that made her go limp. The next thing she knew, her arms were around his neck.

He chuckled, lifting his lips enough to look into her eyes. "I forgot to mention that I like your dress."

Defiance swept through her like a zephyr and was gone, burned away by the heat that spread outward from the very core of her. Where before her mind had buzzed like bees in a hive, she now possessed a startling clarity.

This was the way Chi and Doré felt that long ago day in the rain . . . before they died.

But the need he pulled from inside her with his demanding kiss was great, and thoughts of death slipped away on the wings of fantasy. Ket closed the distance between their lips and gave herself willingly.

It was a kiss like nothing she had ever experienced. Deep and sensual, it seemed like the headspring of a river, generating more needs than it eased.

Even before his hands slipped inside the loose blouse and found her breasts, she was on fire for him. Then his palms held her breasts, skin touching skin, and she felt the tremors clear to her toes. By the time he took a nipple in his mouth, she had surrendered to all but the greedy fire that threatened to consume her if he ever stopped.

Then he did stop. Lifting his gaze to hers, he clasped her face in his hands again and kissed her tenderly, almost chastely. "This is what I meant, Ket . . . *us.*"

"No." What was she doing, surrendering to this man? She shook her head to clear it again. This was wrong. The wrong man. He was too white for her. Too . . .

"This is wrong." Her breath was labored and her words sounded weak.

He would have none of it. "It's right. I've never known anything so right."

She felt the calluses on his palms rub against her skin. "You're everything I hate."

His eyes narrowed on her knowingly. "I'm everything you want." As if to demonstrate, one of his hands left her face. Straight as an arrow, he trailed caresses along her neck, across her chest, her breast, her belly.

Although she tried to summon the will to stop him, his touch rendered her helpless to resist. She was breathless; her pulse throbbed rapidly, and inside she was filled with an unnameable yet intense sense of expectancy.

Before she was fully aware of it, he had scrunched up her skirts and cupped his hand around the most intimate part of her. She was wet. She felt it.

And it felt right.

"See?" His lips grazed hers when he spoke, sprinkling her with a shower of tiny sparks. "This doesn't lie."

While he continued to hold the wetness she could not deny, his gaze held hers, too. *Us?*

She wasn't sure whether he had spoken the word or if she had thought it. But it fit. *Us.* Oh yes, the word fit. They fit. But they shouldn't. They couldn't.

Despite his efforts to hold her, she twisted her head away from his remaining hand. Furiously, she tried to wound him. "You're too white for me."

His response was to grip her wetness even tighter. "Fight it if you want, Ket, but it won't go away. There's something here. Something neither of us asked for or want, but by damn, I'm not letting it go until we find out what it means."

It means betrayal, she wanted to say. *It means abandonment. It means death.* Instead she said the only thing she could think of that might save her from this compelling idiocy.

"You know what it meant for Rosa Ramériz."

Blake sobered. For a moment she tensed, thinking she had truly angered him. When he spoke, his tone was firm. "This has nothing to do with Rosa or with my father—or with yours."

She fought against the overwhelming temptation to agree with him, to beg him to never stop holding her, to take her to that magical land of sizzling rain and naked bodies, to lie with her like Chi and Doré had lain . . .

"Like father, like son?" she blurted out angrily.

She watched a painful expression flash through Blake's eyes before he pulled her to his chest and held her tightly against him. She felt his heart throb against her and knew that its erratic pace echoed her own. Moments passed in silence before either of them moved. Then it was only to speak. He held her as if he would never let her go.

His voice was soft, his tone determined. "I saw little of my father while I was growing up. Most of what I know about him was taught me by my mother, and by those in the government in Washington who praised him for his relentless determination to route the Second Transcontinental Railroad through this country.

"I arrived out here unaware that the very people who will benefit most from his lifelong passion hate him."

His breath blew against her hair, and she listened, only half aware of the hope that began to grow inside her.

"I was reared to respect him, Ket. I was expected to emulate him, to grow up to be just like him."

Listening to him, her fear and anger began to dissolve, and she felt only sadness—not only for herself, but also for him. She knew his hopes, his dreams. She understood them better than anyone else ever could.

And understanding him brought a whole new dimension to their relationship. Not only was he wrong for her because he was a civilized white eyes, but he would never stop believing in a man who was the most despicable of all white eyes in this country. She knew, because in her heart of hearts, she had never been able to truly stop believing in her own father.

Us? They didn't have a chance. Instead of anger, she felt only sadness. "Now I know this is wrong," she mumbled against him.

"You don't understand. I was taught to emulate a great man. Not the person who performed the dastardly deeds you and the boys attribute to him." Holding her back, he stared at her solemnly. "I'm not like the Senator J. J. Carmichael you know. I swear I'm not. But I would very much like to be like the father I was taught to respect."

Tears stung her eyes. "There are rumors about me, too," she told him. "They say I try to be like my father. He's skilled at riding, shooting, tracking. They say that's why I wear britches and try to do things girls don't do."

While she spoke, he focused on her face. When she felt the pads of his thumbs on her cheeks, she realized he was wiping away her tears. Shame overwhelmed her. "Tremayne is the last person on earth I want to be like."

"I'm glad you learned some of the same skills," he told her lightly. "I'd hate to have been killed by Comancheros and miss all this." He pecked a kiss on her lips, and she had to concentrate to keep tears from falling again.

"See, we have a lot in common. I don't want to be like the man I heard those stories about, either."

"That's only one thing," she told him, thinking immediately of his whiteness. But could he be right? As different as they were on the surface, could this shared past, as it were, have created a bond?

How could she ever be certain?

"I've gotta get back to the railroad site," he told her. "See what damage Victorio's warriors did. We're supposed to join the rails by spring." Instead of moving away, however, he drew her to him and kissed her again.

And she kissed him, perhaps not as wildly as before, but with desperation more painful than anything she had felt in years. As if he had read her thoughts, he lifted his lips.

"I'm not like the man you think he is, Ket."

"Prove it to me." The demand came unexpectedly, from somewhere deep inside her, and she regretted the words the instant she realized she had spoken them.

"Prove it?"

She had startled him, too, she could tell that in a heartbeat.

"A man is innocent until proven guilty," he said. "Not the other way around."

"Prove it," she repeated. "It's the Apache way."

She watched him walk off, wondering what demon had taken hold of her. Try as she did, she could not dispel the fluttery sensations that remained from his kisses and caresses—nor the intense sense of loneliness she already felt for him. Unspoken promises quivered inside her. He was right.

She wanted him. Wanted him in the most desperate way. Suddenly she was gripped by a new fear, worse even than the fear of death and betrayal that would surely follow any joy she might know in Blake's bed. It was the fear of never being there, of never experiencing the ultimate passion with this man who had already taken her to places she had never dreamed she would go.

How could she have come to this point? Fatalistically, she decided it was meant to be. Realistically, she knew he could never prove himself to her satisfaction. How could he, a white eyes, live up to the standard by which she judged all men?

Tremayne. The thought came of an instant, and she rejected it out of hand. She would never consider Tremayne a standard for any man to live up to. After a while, she decided it had been an errant thought, held over from their earlier conversation. Certainly she did not admire the man who had caused her such pain.

But thinking of her father as a role model was no more a flight of fancy than thinking of Blake Carmichael as a lover. Although she could dream of being with him, it would never come about. By the time Blake returned to the fort, she would be gone.

As soon as Emily could travel, Ket planned to take her back to the Apachería. Emily had left Fort Davis to live with the People. The last act Ket could perform for her cousin now seemed destined to be the fulfillment of her wish to return home.

Her own decision to follow the People, however, seemed foreign now. Most among them considered this journey to Mexico to be a journey to their own death. No longer could she summon the desire or even the willingness to voluntarily travel to a faraway place from which she would certainly never return.

Somewhere deep inside, she wanted to live again. Maybe not forever. Nothing lasted forever. But for long enough to experience the mysteries promised by Blake's caresses.

Somewhere deep inside, she wanted to live.

Chapter Five

Prove himself! Keturah's demand offended Blake to the depths of his civilized soul. *Prove himself?* What the hell had she taken him for? What had she thought he was asking of her?

That, of course, was the question. He wasn't sure of the answer himself. What *did* he want from Keturah Tremayne?

He hadn't left Chihuahua for the rail site until after dark, because, true to his nature, he wanted all the facts set down in black and white before he began the journey. The most important consideration, to his mind, was the safety—or sanity—of riding out so soon after the Apache attack.

For information, he consulted the Officer of the Day at Fort Davis.

"Stay on the road an' you'll be all right," the officer had assured him. "Them red devils've hightailed it back to their stronghold in the Diablos by now. Our detail returned this afternoon with confirmation. Besides, savages don't gener'ly raid at night. Something about their souls being consigned to the devil or some such nonsense. Git there by mornin', you should be safe enough.''

Blake could never know how he would have felt about the racial aspersions expressed by the people he met out here, including his own father, had he not spent time with Ket. Since he had spent time with her, however, he was acutely aware of the bias of these men and women Ket called white eyes. Military and civilian alike, male or female, black, Anglo, or Mexican descent, all despised the Apache. As far as Blake could determine, most of them based their hatred on personal experience.

On the other hand, he knew for fact that death and destruction had been wrought by both sides. From what he had ascertained in the last few weeks, as far as killing went, the burden seemed to weigh heavily on the side of the white eyes. If Ket was representative of the Apache view, they considered all white eyes worse than savages.

He hadn't challenged these sentiments and felt somehow traitorous for not having done so, rationalizing that he couldn't change the attitudes of the whole country. Indeed, he hadn't come out here to pass moral judgments on anyone. He'd come to survey sites his father had sold along the future railway. That was his job.

His mission was to get to know his father. A few weeks earlier that had seemed a simple task. Now, riding into this vast, largely deserted land, he wondered.

Topographical maps Blake had collected of the region west of the Pecos River showed the land to be a huge high plain, dotted by a scattering of more than a hundred different mountain ranges. Ordinarily he enjoyed nothing more than to ride through this wild, untamed land. So much of it showed little sign of having ever been touched by the metamorphosing hand of man.

Tonight, however, as he left Chihuahua headed for the rail site, Blake knew that *he* had been touched by the metamorphosing hand of, not man, but woman. Not just any ordinary woman, either, but the wildest, most intriguing, and most outrageous woman he had ever known.

Roughly halfway to the rail site at Van Horn's Wells he passed through El Muerto Station. A week earlier the place had almost lived up to its name, Dead Man's Station in English, for that was the site where Comancheros had overtaken him and the boys.

Tonight it lay quiet under a clear sky. Although Blake had no cause to doubt Ket's claim that the Comancheros had ridden south, he was relieved to leave El Muerto behind. Which wasn't to say he had passed out of the realm of danger in this wild land.

Due north of the Wells lay the Diablo Mountains, and in the heart of them, the Apachería. Victorio's defeated warriors would have traveled this road or some parallel route. Even with the Officer of the Day's report he rode warily.

Blake loved riding in this high, wide country, especially at night. The great dome of sky stretched across mountain and plain, and the stars seemed close enough to touch. On a clear night such as this they served him well as a star-map, guiding his way. Riding alone, his thoughts drifted. For the most part, he wasn't thinking about Comancheros or Apaches or even his father.

He couldn't keep his mind off Ket. The woman confounded him. After two hours under the stars with her on his mind, he finally figured he knew what he wanted from her, and it was all physical.

Prove himself, hell! For what he wanted—and from every indication Ket wanted the same thing—he could prove himself in a heartbeat. He pulled the collar of his shearling coat around his ears and allowed his erotic images full rein.

That was it. It had to be. He wanted her in his bed. Until that afternoon, he hadn't been able to understand his attraction to this woman who tried her damnedest not to

look or act like a female. How could he be sexually attracted
to her? He certainly couldn't want her for a companion;
she was from a totally different culture; she barely spoke his
language; she hated him and his entire race and culture, to
boot.

At last it was clear. He wanted to bed her.

Time and again his mind returned to the vision of Ket
walking across the clearing. He hadn't immediately recognized her, for he had been ill prepared to see her dressed in
skirts. Not that feminine attire detracted from her wildness.
Indeed, that particular feminine attire had accentuated
her wildness.

His body had instantly responded to the vision of eroticism when she advanced toward him. In the initial few
moments she had been unaware of his presence, and he
had felt like a voyeur for secretly watching her.

His inner thighs twitched against the saddle even now,
recalling the swing of that full black skirt around her sway-
ing hips. When he had realized who she was, his attraction
soared, for he had once hugged those very thighs between
his legs on the bare back of her palomino stallion. Nipped
at the waist, her hips had swelled seductively beneath the
black skirt.

Lady was not the correct word to describe her, for no
lady Blake had ever met would have ventured outside her
own dressing room in such a loose-fitting blouse, sans corset. Beneath it her ample breasts spread and swayed in
sensual invitation. He had stood as though hobbled, unable
to move, for his body had become embarrassingly inflexi-
ble. Want seared through him like a brush fire, and he
knew one thing and one thing only to be true: He must
bed this woman.

At the time he had been distressed by the way his father
had treated her. Now, like cream rises to the surface in a
pail of milk, his want for Ket became clear.

Prove himself? Hell, he would have no trouble, no trou-

ble at all, filling that request. But then, as the four-hour ride
to Van Horn's Wells continued, Blake's thoughts traversed
other paths, and he wondered whom he was kidding.

For even as he rode through the night with the fall air
chilling his clothing, he sensed that there was more to his
attraction to Keturah Tremayne than the mere physical.
Even with the memory of those full, mounded breasts
against his chest, even with the erotic memory of her wetness against his palm, Blake sensed there could be more
to this attraction.

For he couldn't shake his other memories of her: her
sorrow on the battlefield, her fear for her cousin Emily,
her anguish for the fatherless Neeta.

The last image created deep anguish for Blake, too.
Before leaving Chihuahua he had confronted his father
about the vulnerable little girl.

"Believe the rumors if you want," J. J. had retorted.
"Makes you no better than a gossipy old woman."

"Put the rumor to rest," Blake had quietly pled. "Did
you or did you not father Rosa Ramériz's child?"

"What right do you have to question me?" J. J. had
stormed about the sparsely furnished Chihuahua residence. Suddenly he turned on Blake. "There are two ver-
sions to that child's parentage. You heard the Tremayne
version. The rest of the folks out here have a different
opinion. One that makes a hell of a lot more sense than
defiling an esteemed United States Senator." Advancing
on his son, J. J. stood toe to toe. His once-brilliant blue
eyes might be faded with age, but they had lost not one
whit of their ability to convey rage.

"That no-account, savage-loving Tremayne. He fathered
that child. That's what some say." J. J. hurled the words
at Blake as if they were knives. "No wonder his kin seek
to place blame elsewhere. I'm the victim, Blake. I'm disappointed in you. If you can't take your own father's word
against strangers and savages, you aren't the man I had

hoped you would be. Maybe it's time you returned to the capital, where you can hide from reality behind your mother's skirts."

Chastised, Blake left Chihuahua not for Washington, D.C., but for the rail site, determined to finish his job in a manner that would make his father proud.

Then he arrived at Van Horn's Wells and discovered that accomplishing the job in his father's time frame would be a challenge in itself. As he approached the old stage station, the sun, with its promise of a warmer day, had begun to rise behind him. Brilliant rays sparked off the jagged ridges of the Eagle Mountains that slashed the skyline from northwest to southeast ahead of him.

His father had chosen the site for the joining of the rails with commerce in mind. Situated south of the Diablos and east of Quitman Pass, Van Horn's Wells would provide water aplenty in this arid land. West of the station, the tracks would follow the canyon through the *Sierra de la Cola de Aguila,* roughly translated as Peaks of the Tail of the Eagle, shortened Anglo style to the Eagle Mountains.

The old adobe station that was being used as combined office and living quarters for the railroad staff had just come into view when the first shots rang out.

Two bullets spat into a rock ten yards to Blake's right. Of an instant he had dismounted and pulled his horse in the opposite direction behind an outcropping of gray rock that was too small to offer much cover if his assailants turned out to be either bunch that came readily to mind— Apache warriors or Comancheros.

When the rifleman fired again, Blake was stunned. Those shots had come from the station itself. Fortunately, they'd landed wide to either side of the outcropping. One rifle, Blake ascertained. One gunman?

But who?

There should be half a dozen workers inside that station breakfasting on Charley's *Huevos con Jamón* or whatever struck the old cook's fancy that day. Where the hell were they?

Minutes ticked by, while the sun rose relentlessly behind him. Blake held his fire and his position, waiting. Wondering.

Another volley of shots showered him with rock fragments and sand. It was followed by a crackling, old voice.

"Come on outta there. I ain't got all day to play games. Step on out an' show yerself."

"Charley?" Blake's curiosity increased when he recognized the voice of the oldest member of the crew. Too enfeebled to drive spike or lay rail, Charley, as cook, was the most valuable member of the crew.

"Charley, it's me. Blake." Still uncertain of the nature of the disturbance, he kept his head down. "What's going on in there?"

"That you, Mr. Carmichael? For sure?"

"For sure. Where're the others?"

"You alone?" came the old man's still doubtful voice.

"Just me and my horse. How 'bout yourself?" Eyes trained on the side of the adobe, from where he could see both the entrance and the exit, Blake watched the stooped old man come cautiously out of the exit, rifle at the ready.

"Sure you ain't dead?" came the strange question.

"As sure as I am that that ol' sun's climbing." Still wary, Blake rose and began to slowly lead his mount toward the adobe station.

The old man stared gape-mouthed, showing snaggled, yellow teeth. "We thought sure you was dead."

Blake chuckled to himself. "Came close enough. Where're the others?"

"Ever'body else done left me."

"What?"

"Them what didn't leave after we heard the Comancheros was about hightailed it when them warriors went on the rampage."

"The warriors came here?"

"You bet yer city boots they did."

By this time Blake had arrived at the adobe. He glanced to the surrounding hills. "Are they out there now?"

"Not that I've noticed. Thought you might be them returnin'."

"What'd they do, besides run off the crew?"

"Tore up a few hundred yards of rail. They didn't try to murder no one, just held their rifles on us while they pulled up the timbers."

"Guess that means they don't want us building a railroad," Blake replied sardonically. Everyone had known this was a high-risk job. It was like pouring acid on a dying man's wounds to build a railroad through the last territory the Apaches held in Texas. Everyone knew it was a risk. The crew was made up of seasoned men from this area, all but Blake. Blake was the greenhorn—at least, that's what everybody kept telling him.

At the time his father wrote asking if he would like the job, Blake wondered whether the senator saw it as a test for his city-reared son. Well, test or not, Blake was committed to a task that according to most folks would not be easily accomplished. At least, not until the last Apaches were annihilated.

Since meeting Ket, that thought had taken on an entirely different meaning. Gross injustice, he thought now. Human beings annihilating human beings. This was a big country. It should be big enough for everyone.

Inside he accepted a cup of Charley's coffee and demanded to be filled in on the disappearance of the railroad crew before giving any more information about the notorious woman warrior who had saved him.

Notorious woman warrior was Charley's term when he heard a sketch of Ket's rescue mission. An accurate definition, Blake thought. To a point. Where the woman and the warrior parted company was a secret trail for only him to know and explore. He felt warm inside just thinking about it.

After he was certain he had the rundown on where each crew member had gone, he laid out their plans. "Soon's we finish breakfast," he told Charley, "we'll head out for Jorge's place."

"You sure those red devils won't be back?"

"I'm not sure of anything, Charley, except that those rails have to be joined on time, and there's an awful lot of rugged ground to cover between now and then."

It was past noon by the sun when Blake and Charley rode up to a yard fence that was fashioned from the long straight stalks of the sotol plant. The fence guarded an adobe hut where the foreman, Jorge Sanchez, lived with his wife and six children. Blake couldn't immediately determine whether there were more chickens or children in the yard.

"No, hombre," Jorge replied after Charley translated Blake's plea to round up the crew and return to work.

"Tell him if he doesn't work he won't make any money to buy food for his family."

"No trabaja, no dinero," Charley translated in the roughly but generally understood language that passed for Spanish here in the borderlands. *"Comida pare su familia."*

"No," Jorge replied. *"Los Indios muchos malos."*

Blake understood *Indios* and figured *malo* didn't mean anything too good. "Tell him the Apaches are gone," Blake told Charley. "They've returned to the Apachería and are planning to head out for Old Mexico."

"That true?" Charley wanted to know.

Blake nodded. "Tell him."

Jorge still objected. "He's afraid Victorio will return from Mexico to destroy the railroad."

"He won't," Blake insisted. He wasn't certain, of course, but he had to get the workers back on the job before his father learned of the setback.

At first Blake had resented his father's command to report any work stoppage immediately. Then he began to realize that joining the rails on time was a way to prove his own worth to his father.

Now the situation had been reversed. Now he realized that joining the rails on time was the only way he could prove to the Doubting Thomases around Fort Davis that his father was a man of worth and value.

"Tell him we want him to come with us to persuade the others to return to work."

Charley translated, but Jorge remained adamant.

Blake was stymied. The odds were stacked against him. It wasn't like he had a pool of workers from which to choose. Hell, this was probably the least populated part of the country. There was no one else, literally. Without Jorge and the old crew, he couldn't accomplish the task. It took him another hour to come up with a working plan.

"Tell him that soldiers from Fort Davis will protect us."

"¿Ciertamente?" Jorge asked after Charley translated the latest offer.

Blake understood that word. *"Sí,"* he assured Jorge.

Accompanied by Jorge, Blake and Charley spent the next week in the saddle riding from remote village to remote village, gathering the original crew, or as near the original crew as they could find. A few young men, obviously eager for excitement, signed on in place of others who refused to chance conflict with Apaches, even with military protection.

The men, ten in all, met at Jorge's small hut, for to a man they refused to return to the rail site before the soldiers were in place.

"Donde llegar los soldados, vengamos allí." Jorge spoke for all the men.

"They'll come after the soldiers have arrived," Charley translated. Blake decided then and there that if he remained in this country much longer, he'd best set about learning the language.

"Agreed." Charley translated. Blake shook hands, and he and Charley rode off. In spite of the lost time, Blake felt like a winner all around—body, mind, and spirit.

But it was his body that rejoiced most at this chance to return to Fort Davis. He knew it was a long shot, but if he could get Ket into bed, he figured maybe he could get her off his mind. It seemed the only way.

"I'll build a travois," Ket told Emily. They were alone in Emily's half of the room. Reba Applebee had gone home to get some much-needed rest. Reba insisted on spending every possible hour at Emily's bedside. It was obvious that she loved her adopted daughter.

But Emily had chosen to leave the post, Ket reasoned. Days earlier she had promised herself that she would see that her cousin got to return to the Apachería, even if it were only to die there.

In the meantime Ket felt bound here to Emily's side. Emily must have a link to her true people, and Ket was the only person who could provide that link. And even though she truly wanted to be with Emily, the cost was dear.

Yet she felt trapped by these white-eyes' walls. Anxiety continually struggled inside her. She continually fought the overpowering urge to run from this place, from these soldiers who had murdered the People. To run for freedom, for safety.

Still she could not bring herself to leave her cousin. "When you're ready," she told Emily, "I will take you home."

Emily had lost ground steadily since Ket arrived. Now, a week after being shot, she could barely lift a hand off the bed. Ever so slightly she squeezed Ket's hand and managed a slight shake of her head.

Ket was certain she had misunderstood. "You returned to us once, Emily."

"The surgeon . . . wait . . ."

How long? Ket wanted to cry. The surgeon that Doc Henry sent to Fort Bliss for had yet to arrive. "Don't you want to go home?"

The mortally wounded girl beckoned her close. Even with her ear to Emily's mouth, Ket had a hard time hearing the words. There was no way she could not understand the message, however.

"My home is here."

Ket didn't argue. She wanted to, but the facts were undeniable. Emily was loved on this post where she had lived since she was three years old. Her adoptive parents rarely left her side. Every soldier on the base had dropped in to see her at least once. Jonathan Banks, the soldier on whom Emily had had a childhood crush, had come by a day earlier.

He was at least thirty years old, and even though he wore the hated uniform, Ket could see how a child would fall in love with him. He was not very tall; therefore he would not be threatening. He treated Emily with a gentleness Ket had rarely seen in any man.

Later when he asked Ket and Reba to come into the hall with him, Ket struggled to contain her dislike for all soldiers and to listen to him as Emily would have wanted.

"I feel so guilty," he confessed to the women. Ket heard pain in his voice and saw it etched in fine lines around his soft brown eyes. Although she stood apart from him and Reba, he spoke directly to her.

"When Emily was a little girl, we teased about getting married. I was wrong to do that. I wanted to make her feel wanted and accepted and loved, but that was the wrong way to go about it. I feel terribly sad and guilty."

While Ket tried to accept his confession as she knew Emily would want, Reba offered comfort.

"It is normal for a little girl to choose her Prince Charming," she said kindly. "That's the way she identifies traits to look for in a marriage partner when she comes of age. It's a fantasy shared by girls the world over, Jon. You were not at fault. Don't blame yourself."

But it was obvious that he did. "She ran away from the fort when Jenna and I announced our engagement. If she had stayed here . . ."

"Sooner or later, Emily would have returned to the Apachería," Reba insisted. "Every human being has a desperate need to find his or her own place in the world. It was natural for Emily to return to her blood people. I have known that since the day Sabrina first put her in my arms on the veranda of this very hospital. Regardless of what reason she gave, it was a natural quest to find herself."

To find herself. Those words haunted Ket. She had thought she had long since put aside the need to find peace within herself. She had thought she had come to terms with the fact that there was no peace, no place for one such as she.

Now, she knew that that was what she had always longed for—a place of her own, a place where she belonged, a place where she was loved and cherished. But it was not Reba Applebee who had awakened this hopeless, impossible dream inside her.

It was Blake Carmichael, and she hated him for it.

Two days after Blake returned to the rail site, Doc Henry drew Ket and Lena into a spare room to discuss Sabrina's condition.

"She isn't out of the woods," he confided. "I can't allow her to return to the ranch until she delivers. Is there a chance she would agree to rent a place here? A house on Officers' Row is vacant until after Lieutenant Banks' wedding. Perhaps—"

"No." Ket surprised herself. "Not on this post. Not with Jasper in charge."

"Ket's right," Lena said. "The infirmary is one thing. But living on the post under the command of Jasper . . . Sabrina might be able to do it, but Tremayne would never agree."

"I understand," Doc Henry agreed. "Perhaps in Chihuahua. The Limpia Hotel might have a room."

"They'll need more than a room," Lena objected. "I can't see Tremayne leaving Sabrina in town alone for two months."

After a while, Doc Henry came up with another suggestion. "One of those little adobes on George Harman's property may be vacant. I'll check it out."

Neither woman objected, so he continued. "If I come up with a place, do either of you think Tremayne would object to us moving her there before he returns?"

When they looked to Ket for a response, her anxieties clawed their way to the surface. "Don't involve me in this decision."

Lena came to the rescue. "Have you spoken with Sabrina?" she asked the doctor.

"I wanted to get the opinion of you two first. You're the closest to her. Why don't we visit with her together?"

Ket had no intention of becoming involved in the lives of Sabrina and Tremayne. On the other hand, to refuse the doctor's request would require being downright rude to him, and to Lena too, who with an arm around Ket's shoulders signaled that she understood her dilemma.

Thus unwillingly Ket became a participant in the drama that followed. She hated the way that white eyes had of dragging her into their lives, into their turmoil. Yet she always managed to fall into their traps.

Of course, there was her promise to Emily. Even as Emily grew weaker by the day, her most important mission in life continued to be to bring Ket and Sabrina together.

"It won't work," Ket cautioned her early on.

"Give it a try," the girl had pled. "Just be kind to her. She has been so important to me. She found me a wonderful, loving home with the Applebees. She loved me for who I am, and I think she gave me an extra amount of love, Ket, love that she would like to have given you."

Ket was deeply offended, but she strove not to let it show. Emily was dying. Emily, the only person left in the world to whom she felt truly connected.

Emily, who now chose her white family over her blood family. Which, if the girl weren't so ill, would have allowed Ket to get really angry with her. But Emily was growing worse daily, and she had asked for only one thing—that Ket be kind to Sabrina.

If it gave her cousin pleasure, what harm could it do Ket to pretend? It might have been more difficult were her father around, but thankfully Tremayne was absent. With him gone, she vowed to think of Sabrina as a stranger, the stranger she really was, someone who had never entered her life. But seeing Sabrina was the least she could do for Emily.

So she accompanied Lena and Doc Henry when they went to talk to Sabrina about remaining in town. And to Ket's utter amazement, Sabrina turned to her.

"What do you think, Ket? What should I do?"

"If you mean, are the Apaches a threat, no. You could return to the ranch without fear of another raid. They . . . *we* are leaving soon to be with Victorio in Mexico."

Sabrina nodded, lips pursed, as if considering. "I wonder what your father would want."

Ket fidgeted uncomfortably while her anxieties continued to claw their way to the surface. Why did the woman persist? Why couldn't she leave Ket alone? Lena came to her aid.

"I should think Tremayne wants the same thing we all want, don't you, Ket?"

The room became a cage in which Ket found herself trapped. She turned to Lena, whose expression was calm, as always. She, too, waited for Ket to take up the conversation.

What choice did she have? Emily could hear everything, and see everything, since the separating screen had been folded against the wall. Ket stared out the window through the wavy panes of glass that closed her inside this white-eyes building. She tried to imagine herself on the outside, but that turned out to be a mistake, for an edge of the steward's house was visible through the right corner of the glass and she was suddenly overwhelmed by emotion.

The powerful desire she had felt in Blake's arms could be denied no more than could the anxieties that assailed her inside this room, standing beside her hated stepmother's bed, with Emily lying here dying from a white-eyes' bullet.

"He would not want you to endanger yourself or the child," she told Sabrina tersely.

As though Ket had spoken in the most compassionate of tones, Sabrina responded cheerfully. "Then it is decided. Whenever the three of you feel like helping me move, I'm ready."

Doc Henry clapped his hands. "I'm off to make arrangements, my dear. I'll find something furnished, but it will surely need sprucing up before Sabrina can settle in."

Ket wasn't certain what he meant by that, but in the next couple of days, she discovered that in addition to beds for Sabrina, Tremayne, and Luke, the doctor expected room for Lena, Tres Robles, and even Ket herself.

"I'll help her move," Ket told Lena, "but I will not sleep in that house."

Always good-natured, Lena laughed. "No one expects you to, Ket." But on the day of moving in, Lena conveniently disappeared before Ket could escape.

Lena, whom Ket trusted, had left her alone with a stepmother who was under doctor's orders not to get out of bed or wait on herself. Coming to this fort had been like stepping into a bog of quicksand—she couldn't bring herself to leave Emily alone; yet, every moment she remained trapped here, she was sucked deeper and deeper into the lives of people she hated.

"Ket, dear," Sabrina called from the bedroom. "I know you are anxious to return to Emily. Perhaps you could find Luke to help."

Of course she could find Luke, but it might take hours. He and Tres Robles had disappeared the minute Sabrina was settled in bed. It was now nearing noon, and Doc Henry had left instructions that Sabrina was to take her meals regularly—and in bed. Fixing broth and serving it seemed a simple task.

It would have been, she thought later, had she not made the fatal mistake of remaining in the small bedroom a moment too long.

Two bites into the meal, Sabrina broke the code of separation, rendering impossible Ket's plan to pretend that no ties existed between the two of them. "Luke and Tres Robles are really taken by Blake Carmichael."

Stunned that this woman whom she had hated for ten years would dare broach so personal a topic, she replied sharply, "Until they found out who he really was."

"On the contrary," Sabrina objected pleasantly. "Those boys had grown to like him before they learned his identity. From what they say, he helped keep the Comancheros from . . . uh, from hurting them until you arrived."

"You know those boys," she responded, unable to allow herself to voice a single kind word about Blake in front of this woman. "They tell the tallest tales in this country."

Sabrina chuckled. "They do seem destined for the theater. On the other hand, they said you and Blake made a good team."

"A what?"

"A good team. They said you worked together to get them safely out—"

"They were wrong. They made me go back for Bl—uh, for that man. I should have left him. If I'd known who he was, I would have."

"I couldn't blame you, nor would most folks at the fort. His father is despised. Although Reba insists that Blake shows no signs of being cut from the same cloth."

Never far from an exit, Ket turned to the glass-paned door that led into a small courtyard. She prayed Sabrina hadn't noticed the heated flush that rose up her neck and burned her cheeks.

Her anxiety had soared to the level of sheer panic. Why had Sabrina broached this particular topic? Had someone seen her kissing Blake behind the steward's house? Was that what this conversation was about?

And where was Lena? If she didn't come soon, Keturah vowed to leave Sabrina alone, doctor's orders be damned.

"Lena was also impressed with that young man."

"Lena? With Blake? How could she have been?"

"A man who wants to apologize to a woman and admits it in front of strangers is a rarity. It shows a certain amount of backbone, I'll admit." Sabrina paused, toyed with the frayed edge of the quilt that covered her legs, then looked Keturah squarely in the eyes. "I know this isn't my place, Ket, but with his father's horrible reputation .. Well, please be careful."

"Careful?"

"With your heart, dear."

Ket felt her heart skip a beat at that. She couldn't even concentrate on her anger, for the accuracy of Sabrina's words. They thrummed through her head and, yes, in her heart.

"I'm sorry. I know it isn't my place . . . I also know you can't judge a person by what other people think . . . or know. I learned that with your father."

Talking about Blake Carmichael was one thing. Talking about her father and this . . . this flaming-haired white eyes was quite another. Ket seemed to have lost control of her limbs, however, for before she could escape the room, Sabrina continued.

"Your father was the wrong man for me. I couldn't possibly have been in love with him. I told Lena that. He was the wrong man for me. I was the wrong woman for him. We didn't belong together. But . . . well, we couldn't seem to stay apart. It was like we were meant for each other, whether we admitted it or not. The harder we tried to stay apart, the more we couldn't. I didn't believe it was true, and neither did your father until . . ."

By this time when Sabrina paused, Ket was hooked. Here it was. At long last she was about to learn the truth. What had caused her father to abandon her for a white eyes? She had wondered that for such a long, long time.

"After I heard the laughter," Sabrina said softly, "neither of us could deny it anymore."

"The laughter?" Ket fairly screamed the words, but Sabrina just smiled. "You mean the . . . that spirit laughter that's supposed to be in the well?"

"Oh, it is there, Ket. Believe me. I heard it."

"But you couldn't have. Not you!"

"Because I'm a white eyes?"

When Ket didn't answer, Sabrina added, "It is my opinion, only my opinion, that the laughter is your grandmother's spirit. She became the guardian of the well the day your father needed her to confirm himself to the People. And she has remained there ever since, confirming what we Tremaynes need in our times of distress."

Ket felt as though Sabrina had physically attacked her. Too furious to stop herself, she blurted out the first words that came to mind. "You're as crazy as I always thought."

Sabrina ignored or failed to acknowledge the accusation.

"Like myself and your father, Ket, your grandmother was a white eyes."

"I don't have to stand here and listen to this nonsense."

"I know, dear. I apologize for intruding, but I wanted you to hear the truth. If you ever have feelings for . . . for someone you believe is totally wrong for you, there is one way to find out. Take him to Apache Wells. See if you hear the laughter."

"If there is laughter at Apache Wells, it comes from spirits of the Underworld laughing at white-eyes' fantasies." With that, Ket fled the house. She didn't return for two days, and then her visit was so untimely, she was tempted to think the very spirits she professed not to believe in had sent her there.

For that was the day her father returned.

Tremayne was as surprised to see Ket as she was to see him. She had entered the courtyard by the front door, just as he came into it from Sabrina's bedroom. He stopped in one doorway, she stopped in the other, and they stared at each other.

Her first impression was that he had aged in the years since she'd last seen him. How many years? she wondered. She hadn't kept track. Suddenly she wished she had.

Suddenly she wished a lot of things that she fought to suppress. Sadness, joy, and an overwhelming sense of loss. And of pride.

Tremayne was a handsome man. His dark wavy hair now lightly streaked with white brought a lump to her throat. How many years had they lost? He was still a large man. His frame filled the doorway. And he was muscular. He could wrestle a bear to the ground, she thought proudly.

He'd cut his dark wavy hair, though. No longer did it hang to his shoulders, nor was it banded with red flannel in the fashion of Victorio's warriors. He now wore a conservative rancher's cut, swept back from a broad, tanned forehead. In place of the buckskins she recalled from childhood, he wore white-eyes' dress—denims and chambray, and they fit him well.

But it was his eyes she saw first, and his eyes she returned to. Tremayne green was their color. Like Luke's.

Like her own.

Only his were the original, and hers and Luke's sprang from them. First there were his, then there were hers, then Luke's. She thought of the babe in Sabrina's womb and for the first time wondered if this child, too, would possess the Tremayne green eyes.

The hated green eyes.

Tremayne green eyes. Dark wavy hair. Her nemeses, they proclaimed her an outsider in every man's world, a person who belonged nowhere, except right here. Where she was not wanted.

She jerked her gaze away, but her senses remained alert to this man—her father, whom she had once loved with all her child's heart and soul.

She recalled comparing Blake to him, and in a way the comparison held. But there was also a huge difference. The sight of Tremayne made her feel vulnerable, afraid. Standing here before him, she experienced an insatiable longing for what might have been—a child's need for a father to love, for a father who loved her.

Thoughts of Blake also evoked an insatiable longing, but a longing for what could still be, and in a far different and strangely more powerful sense—physical lust, she thought. She prayed to the spirits that that was all she wanted from Blake Carmichael.

Tremayne was the first to speak. "Sabrina told me of your bravery." It was a compliment such as one of the People would have given a man returning from battle.

"It was nothing," she managed. Most of her effort was spent standing her ground. She had just come from Emily's bedside and had brought a message for Sabrina. How adept white eyes were at dragging her into their turmoil.

"She said those boys convinced you to go back in after Carmichael's son."

"I didn't know who he was at the time."

"I hate to think you risked your life for that bastard's son."

"He was skilled, surprisingly so for a . . ."

Tremayne grunted. "For a white eyes?"

Prompted by this exchange, she said, "I've come from Emily with a message for Sabrina."

Tremayne's expression tightened. He shook his head, obviously anguished. "Life out here is so cockeyed."

Did he think that was something new? She didn't know how to respond.

"How is she?" he asked.

"Dying, in my opinion."

He pushed splayed fingers through his hair. His face was a mask of furrows wrought by pain and suffering. It could have been any man's face—white man or Apache—but it wasn't. It was the face of her father. And he voiced a sorrow she had often felt herself. "Such a damned waste. Such a waste."

"I, uh, wanted to take her back to the Apachería, but she wants to stay here."

"Is anybody left there now? What about your grand-mother?"

"I don't know. I haven't been back since the boys ran away. They . . . uh, *we* are going to Mexico."

"Mexico?" He seemed startled.

"Victorio and most of the men are already there. We're going to be with him. I hope they haven't left yet." The thought of going to Mexico never to return filled her with a strange, unfamiliar despair. She had made up her mind. Long ago, she had made up her mind.

Now she didn't want to go.

"Ket, I . . ." Tremayne cleared his throat. Instead of looking her in the eye, he took in her face, all of it. She experienced the sensation of being observed for the first time by someone who had once loved her. Did he still?

Of course he didn't. But his words . . .

"Ket, I wish . . . I wish you wouldn't go. I mean, I wish you would come home."

Chapter Six

Blake's knock on the heavy wooden door was answered by the child, Neeta, and the sight of her immobilized him. Calling at the Tremayne home had been hard enough. Would he finally come face to face with the man his father called a savage? The thought was unnerving. What about Sabrina, the woman Ket called a demon?

Even thoughts of coming face to face with Ket in the presence of others unsettled him. That he was willing to face all these challenges at once, he figured, said something about his determination to see his mission through to its end.

But he hadn't expected to encounter this small girl who might or might not be his half-sister. Sight of her almost convinced Blake to turn tail and run.

Something he hadn't done since he was four years old. Blake was a fighter, always had been. So he stood his ground there on the packed-earth porch feeling more vulnerable than he ever had.

"Hola, Señor Blake."

"Hello, Neeta." He went down on one knee to study the child. He wondered whether he would have made the connection had he not heard the rumor.

Ket had said she was ten, but she looked small for ten. *For all I know,* he ridiculed. What did he know about children? What did he know about life? Certainly not nearly enough about life out here. Neeta had threatened to put a curse on the McCabe boys for roasting her pet goat. He felt instead that somebody had put a curse on him.

Unable to pull his attention away from her, he felt the rumor to be true. Not only were her eyes blue, not green as in Tremayne green, but he felt connected to her. To her shyness and her curiosity, her bone structure, but mostly to her abominable plight. Some man had greatly wronged this precious child. Could it have been his father, the man he had been reared to honor and respect?

He wished he had waited outside until Ket either came out of the house or arrived. Hell, he didn't even know if she was here. At the infirmary Mrs. Applebee told him the Tremaynes had taken this house in Chihuahua to wait out Mrs. Tremayne's confinement.

"Yes," Reba had confided over Emily's fevered brow, "Ket is still in town. She won't leave until Emily"—unable to complete the statement, her words drifted off as tears pooled in her eyes—"is better."

So Blake had come to this adobe house with one thought—to see if he couldn't once and for all get Ket off his mind. But instead of being met by the woman he'd dreamed about too often lately, this child of clouded parentage stood adoring him with her familiar blue eyes.

"Is Keturah here?" he inquired. From inside the house came a call.

"Who is it, Neeta?"

"Señor Blake."

Blake smiled. This child intrigued him. He felt the need to hold her, to protect her, but that was foolish. Neeta didn't need him. She had champions enough in the Tremaynes.

"Who, dear?" came a gentle voice.

"Señor Blake." Neeta's blue eyes twinkled when she gazed up at Blake who had risen at the call from inside. "The man who got Luke and Tres captured by Comancheros."

"Me?" The accusation amused him. "I was captured, too."

Neeta merely cocked her head, not in a sassy way, but in a serious way that revealed her doubtful assessment.

"Ask him in, child."

At the invitation, Neeta grabbed his hand and pulled him inside. "Tía Breena said come in."

"Thanks." Blake stepped inside, only to find himself entering not a room, but an inner courtyard.

The flat-roofed house was built in an open square design with all rooms opening onto an enclosed courtyard. The entire house was small; he doubted it was more than one-room deep all around.

Following Neeta, he came upon two women who sat wrapped in woolen *rebozos* with army blankets draped across their laps.

One woman was Anglo, her red hair pulled into a tight chignon, and very pregnant. He knew before she introduced herself that this must be Sabrina Tremayne, the demon who stole Ket's father. She didn't look at all like a demon, although Blake would be the first to concede that looks could be deceiving.

"Please come in, Mr. Carmichael. I am Sabrina Tremayne." She smiled and became instantly beautiful. "I realize it isn't considered proper for a lady in my condition to receive male visitors, but I think it is much more important that I thank you for saving my son's life."

Blake shifted his weight from one foot to the other,

careful to avert his gaze from the very pregnant Mrs. Tremayne. "Actually, it was Ket who saved all our lives."

"The boys said you handled yourself extremely well. Ket agreed."

"Grudgingly, I'm sure. For a greenhorn white eyes."

Rather than laugh at his attempt at humor, Sabrina responded seriously. "Ket has difficulties with white eyes. She has reason."

"Yes, ma'am, I know. She told me some of it."

"I understand you are related to Senator Carmichael."

"He's my father." Even though her tone had held no censure, Blake resented the need he felt to defend himself. He already felt guilty enough.

Upon arriving in Chihuahua, he had stopped first by his father's house to wash the trail grime off before meeting with Commander Jasper about military protection for the rail workers. His father had been there, and they'd had a pleasant exchange, from which Blake had come away with hope that the camaraderie he wanted with his father might be possible.

His father went so far as to accompany him to the post. "Not bad negotiating, son," J. J. had congratulated after hearing Blake bargain for military protection for the rail workers. "That's the kind of leadership I expected from you when I brought you out here. Don't need to remind you how important that rail-joining date is. I've got senators, hell, even the vice-president is considering showing up for the event. Can't come in late on this one."

"It'll get done," Blake had promised.

"Then get back out there. We don't have a minute to lose."

Commander Jasper had agreed to send a detail to the rail site by nightfall, along with a wagon full of supplies from the commissary. Blake's job was done. But had he returned to the site?

No, he had gone straight to the infirmary, hoping to

find Ket sitting with her cousin. When she wasn't there, Reba Applebee directed him to this house, not half a mile from his father's.

So here he was, standing in the Tremaynes' courtyard, planning to coax their daughter into bed.

Prove yourself, Ket had ordered. Well, that's exactly what he'd come to town to do—prove himself to the wild Keturah Tremayne.

Sabrina interrupted his thoughts. "Excuse my rudeness, Mr. Carmichael. Please meet my dear friend, Señora Raméríz."

If Blake had been uncomfortable before, he now wished he could vanish into the cool mountain air. Awkwardly he acknowledged the woman, who studied him guardedly. Neeta was cuddled up in the oversized rocker beside her mother.

Blake cleared his throat. "You have a charming daughter, Señora." He hadn't known what to say and realized almost immediately that the comment, true though it was, was the wrong thing.

"I met her at the post," he hurried on. "She was certainly glad to see Luke and Tres return safely."

"*Sí,*" the señora replied. "We were all glad to see those boys. They take care of my Neeta."

Blake responded with a distracted nod of his head. Where was Ket? How could he exit gracefully before the situation worsened? Sabrina might have read his mind.

"I want you to know, Mr. Carmichael, that we are a fair people. If I may speak frankly, your father's reputation . . . well, let me just say that Senator Carmichael's reputation is of his own making. It needn't reflect on you."

Her candor further unnerved Blake. With the señora and her daughter close by, he wasn't sure how to reply, or even how to interpret the statement. Should he thank her for keeping an open mind? Or should he be affronted?

Hadn't she, in a sense, slandered his father? Was this the same proposal Ket had made—prove himself worthy?

"I wouldn't have brought it up," Sabrina continued, "but you are sure to get a hard time from a few folks. They're not the general run of Western folk. Most of us afford each man the right to prove or disprove his own worth."

Yep, there it was. *Prove himself.* Did everyone in this country demand that a person prove himself? Mrs. Tremayne was sweet as spun honey, yet she had offered him neither a chair nor a drink, both common courtesies the world over.

"I, uh . . ." Although he was tempted to turn and run, Blake reminded himself again that he was not a quitter. He'd come to see Ket, and by . . . "Is Keturah here, ma'am?"

"I'm afraid not—"

Just then the front door burst open, and in came Luke and Tres Robles. They were delighted to see him standing here in the enemy's den.

"Hey, Blake! You come to see Ket?"

"We'll show you where she's at."

"One minute, boys," Sabrina called. "Luke, you know your father is expected back this afternoon. You and Tres are to return to the ranch with him."

"Aw, Ma—"

"No argument, Luke. Tres, your parents expect you back at the ranch, and Luke, your father needs your help."

"Yes, Mama." But Luke's attention was on Blake. Grabbing his hand, he dragged him toward the door. "Come on, Tres. We have time to show Blake where Ket lives."

"Me, too." Neeta bounded off the rocker and reached for Blake's other hand, only to have her mother call her back.

"Neeta, my sweet, Tía Sabrina needs you to help prepare dinner."

The child's countenance fell, but instead of arguing, she acquiesced.

"We'll be back directly," Tres told Neeta. "Don't go out where those McCabe boys can find you."

"I won't, Tres."

Blake followed the boys along a steep, rocky trail that ran beside Sleeping Lion Mountain, then across it by way of a narrow cleft in the rocks and onto the post grounds. Every step of the way they barraged him with questions and opinions concerning his parentage.

"What'd you think about Neeta?" Luke asked the lead-off question.

"Yeah, Blake, what'd you think of her? She's your sister, like Ket is Luke's sister."

"Maybe," Blake felt obliged to reply. "Maybe not. You boys should learn that a man is considered innocent until proven guilty."

"You mean ol' SOB ain't her father?"

"I mean Senator Carmichael is innocent until proven guilty. He denies being Neeta's father. He should know."

"Oh, he knows all right," Luke said. "Mama knows, too."

"I doubt that. Even if Neeta's mother told her, the senator's denial leaves the situation in doubt."

"It's okay if you want to take up for him," Tres Robles offered. "I'd take up for my father, too. Luke takes up for his. Don't you, Luke?"

"Yeah. No way my father murdered Rosa's husband, like some say."

"That proves an important point," Blake reasoned. "If your father's word is good enough to keep him from being charged with murder, then my father's word should hold some weight, too."

The boys exchanged doubtful glances.

"Don't make no nevermind to us," Luke replied finally. "Don't reckon you had anything to do with it."

Like Sabrina before them, the boys neither condemned nor exonerated him. They, along with everyone else, seemed to agree that who he became out here was up to him. But these boys possessed a healthy amount of the innate curiosity all boys seemed to be born with.

"What's it like, being a Carmichael?" Tres Robles wanted to know.

The question startled Blake. "What do you mean, what's it like?"

"Well, it can't be like being a Tremayne," Luke explained. "I mean everybody says good things about the Tremaynes."

"About the Bourbons, too," Tres said. "So what's it like being a Carmichael?"

Blake started to remind the boys of what they'd just told him—that some folks around here accused Tremayne of murder. But he didn't. Neither did he relate that his own father said some folks suspected Tremayne of being Neeta's father.

Instead, he responded with, "Back East, Carmichael is a respected name." At least his mother had always taught him so. And he hadn't had any cause to think differently. Neither while he attended George Washington University nor later when he worked as a surveyor in Virginia had anyone disparaged his father, not directly or by implication. Blake decided it was time to change the subject.

"Where is this house where Ket lives?" By now they had left the post behind and traveled up Hospital Canyon. The trail was rocky and dim at best. In fact, it didn't look like a trail. It crossed Blake's mind that these boys might well be leading him on a wild goose chase.

"It ain't no house," Luke responded. The two boys looked at each other as if Blake were about the stupidest person this side of the Pecos River. There'd been times lately when he tended to agree with them.

"Ket wouldn't be caught dead sleepin' in a house," Tres Robles advised patiently.

"Ket's a tad on the wild side," Luke felt obliged to add.

"A tad?" Blake's blood had heated to a slow simmer just talking about Ket's sleeping place. He had to clear his throat twice to ask, "So where is this place?"

"We don't rightly know," Tres blurted out.

"Then where—?"

"We're takin' you back in the canyon to where she's working. She won't let anybody near her sleepin' place."

Figures, he thought. *A predator's first line of defense is to protect her lair.*

The canyon up which they walked twisted and curved. On either side red walls rose to somewhere around a thousand feet. The columnar volcanic rock that formed the mountains had broken off in places and littered the canyon with varying sizes of shattered rocks and boulders.

It wasn't long before the post buildings were out of sight. A hundred yards or so further along, he saw Ket. She wore britches again, those cloud-soft deerskins tucked into knee-high moccasins, and although it was cool enough for a jacket, she wore only a loose calico shirt belted warrior style over it. Except no warrior he ever expected to run across would possess the temptingly rounded derriere that his thighs still felt between them or the magnificently mounded bosom which was restricted only by loose-fitting calico and his own imagination.

Suddenly Blake was lost to all except his mission—to seduce this wildly enchanting woman. He saw only one obstacle, make that two.

"Thanks, boys. You'd better run on back now, before Tremayne comes to take you to the ranch."

"We can stick around awhile," Luke objected cheerfully.

"Yeah," Tres added, "we'd like to see how you manage."

Blake was taken aback. "How I manage what?"

"To persuade her to talk to ol' SOB's son."

"I'll manage." In his mind they had already bypassed talking and gone straight to bed, where sans britches and shirt, her supple, inviting body pressed to his, into his . . .

Blake had never considered himself a lady's man, but he figured he had enough experience to know when a woman was as eager as he was. Ket could profess otherwise all day long, but that day behind the steward's house proved her ready to consummate the hunger that by now had gnawed its way into Blake's very soul.

"Get on outta here," he told the boys. "And thanks."

When they drew nearer to her, he could tell that Ket was working on something, stripping the trunk of a small tree. Before he had time to wonder what it was, Luke explained.

"She's making a travois."

"Oh," Blake responded. He consciously avoided engaging the boys in conversation. Once they got interested, they'd never leave.

"She was gonna take Emily back to the Apachería," Tres added, "but Emily wouldn't go."

A few hundred questions presented themselves, but Blake resisted asking them. He could ask Ket. Afterwards. It was always good to talk—afterwards.

About that time, Ket heard them approach. When she turned, Blake caught his breath. Brushed free of tangles, her hair was thick and glowing. It fell loose about her shoulders, held back with a red band around her forehead.

It struck him then, the enigma this woman presented. In her efforts to deny any trace of femininity, she embodied the best of it: rugged strength and womanly beauty. Every movement of her arms as she stripped bark from the small tree trunk was graceful as well as proficient. When she turned toward them, her long-fingered hands went to the small of her back, a gesture he had seen his mother perform a million times.

But there all resemblance to his mother vanished. For the feelings that soared inside him were the furthest from maternal he had ever felt.

"Blake wanted us to bring him here," Luke informed his sister.

Ket merely continued to stare at him. In her expression he read the same questions he had felt gnawing inside himself for the better part of the past week.

He returned her gaze, figuring that silence was a better method of communicating than speaking at this stage. For silence lent itself well to fantasy, and the fantasy in this canyon had become hot and sweet.

Beside him, Luke and Tres Robles continued to pester.

"You know who he is, Ket?" Tres asked.

"He's ol' SOB's son," Luke responded when Ket didn't.

"Neeta's his sister," Tres added.

"Like you're my sister."

Ket dragged her eyes away from Blake to scan the boys. "I know." When she glanced back to Blake, her curiosity seemed more focused.

He figured he knew what was on her mind—had he brought the proof she had demanded?

In the presence of the boys, he remained silent, favoring her only with a slight grin he couldn't wipe off his face. Cocky, that's the way he felt. Cocky and anxious to prove it. Except not before an audience.

Desperate, Blake decided on a course of action. If he couldn't run the boys off, maybe he could bore them into leaving.

"Think you could teach me how to make a travois?"

That startled her. "What for?"

Luke was clearly disappointed. "You came all the way out here to learn how to build a travois?"

"What'd you need to know that for?" Tres echoed Ket's own question.

"In this country, a fellow never knows. Folks get it in their head to run me off for being a Carmichael, I'd have something to carry my belongings on."

Luke and Tres Robles exchanged deflated looks.

"We'd better get started," he told them. "It'll probably take till dark just to find the right trees."

"We don't have till dark," Luke muttered. "Papa's coming to take us to the ranch."

"In that case you'll probably have to miss the lesson." As with most boys, the word *lesson* didn't strike the interest chord. "Maybe Ket will teach you later. Or I can, once I learn."

Luke frowned. "You aren't fooling us. We intend to hang around and watch you soft-soap Ket."

"Soft-soap?" Blake wanted to know. He glanced to Ket. She still hadn't said more than a couple of words. What was she thinking now? More importantly, how was he going to get rid of these boys?

Then she surprised him. "Since you're going back anyway, Luke, you can take a tin of *pozole* to Emily. She needs the nourishment."

Blake was as astonished as Luke. Mesmerized, he watched Ket approach a cook fire, where she ladled a generous serving of some kind of steaming soup from a large iron pot into a lidded tin, after which she wrapped the whole thing in a length of heavy canvas.

The astonished boys hadn't had time to object. Luke took the package.

"Drop this by the hospital," Ket instructed. "Be careful not to burn yourself."

The boys balked, but they had no choice. Blake and Ket watched them go, not turning to each other until neither the boys nor the dust in their wake were visible.

By that time Blake's want for her had risen like yeast

inside him. It pressed at his pores and clamored for release. He felt stiff and awkward, and when they faced each other, he saw his own needs reflected in her eyes. They fell together.

"They'll be back," Blake worried, still benumbed by the ingenious method she had used to get rid of the boys.

"They won't have time." She pulled apart and stared at him with those hard green eyes. "Why did you come?"

He held her gaze, enthralled by her tenacity and—whom was he kidding?—by the very presence of her. *You know why I'm here,* he wanted to say. Instead he asked, "You mean did I bring proof?"

"Did you?"

"I brought you something better."

"What?"

"Myself."

While his meaning sizzled between them, he freed her belt and slipped both hands beneath her shirt. Her breasts fell into his palms, and the mission he had come to town to accomplish became urgent. His lips took hers, and the wetness of the kiss reminded him of the other wetness and his tongue plunged into her mouth. The kiss deepened and became intense and echoed the rhythmic throb that pulsated through his veins and in his groin and he forgot about the boys.

When he remembered, he lifted his lips. "They'll come back," he said.

Without speaking, she took his arm and led him around her cooking fire and up a cleft in the hillside that he had not previously seen. It didn't matter where it led. At this moment in time, he would have followed her anywhere.

And where she led was rocky and high. Was this the plague of mankind, he wondered, to follow a woman down into the bowels of the earth or up a steep and rocky ladder to heaven? Blake had no doubt where this trail would end, and he was as eager as a schoolboy to arrive.

A hundred yards or so from her cooking fire and work site she stopped. At first he didn't see anything different from the trail they had followed up the mountain. Then she pulled him beneath a rocky overhang and into a semi-darkened shelter, dropped his hand, and proceeded to light a fire. He bumped his head on the low ceiling.

"Ouch." When he caught his breath, he glanced around. In the center of the small space was a fire pit. "You built all this?"

"My family did."

"Your family?" Benumbed, he didn't comprehend. When the fire took hold, its light glanced off the walls.

"My ancestors," she corrected, standing. "See their marks?"

As the petroglyphs came into focus, he saw that they were mostly outlines of hands. Small hands, large hands. Black hands and red. Further around he saw stick figures of men and birds and animals, although he could identify none of the animals.

Ket came up behind him. "That's a white shaman." Gesturing, her hand touched his back. "Shamen are the only people who can pass between this world and—"

At her touch, Blake's interest in rock art vanished as if a shaman had cast a spell. In truth, it was Ket who had cast the spell.

He caught her hand and turned her around. Her breath blew hot against his face. The eroticism of it trailed scorching fingers down his body. "So this is your lair."

"White-eyes' buildings terrify me," she confessed. "I feel safer here. It's like a womb."

His lips grazed hers. She didn't have to tell him that she had never brought anyone else into this shelter. He knew she had not. And that fact added to the magic.

He had planned the seduction well. But as with most of the plans he'd made lately, something interfered. This time it was Ket herself who played havoc with his intention to go slowly, to allow passion to build. Passion had already built. For him, for her. Her lips met his, parted and eager.

When he pulled her close, she pressed into him. There was no holding back. While their lips were locked in a hot, lingering kiss, he stripped her shirt over her head, dropped it to the floor, and felt her tug at his.

Then they were on their knees, then on the floor. She had laid a mat over the rocks and it was cushioned with dried grass that crinkled when they rolled over it. The cool air warmed quickly. The scent of it was musty. The scent of her was all musk and want, and her breasts tasted like mountain honey.

Flames leaped in the fire pit, casting the walls with dancing shadows. He felt as if they were inside a kaleidoscope and a kaleidoscope was inside them.

Remembering her wetness, he found it inside the deer-skin britches, which he unlaced before sliding his hand inside. Her belly was taut. He felt her hipbones and the curly hair he knew would be black.

He tasted her belly button, and her skin was salty. Her fingers were supple. They kneaded the muscles on his back, shooting fiery tendrils to the core of his passion. Eagerly, he slid both hands inside her britches and slipped them down—

She stopped him. Suddenly, without the slightest indication that anything was wrong, her hands gripped his. "No." The word was spoken softly, but it could have been shouted, the way it reverberated inside his head.

"No?" He continued to tug at the deerskin.

Finally she knocked his hands away and pulled her britches back in place.

"It's all right," he said. "I'll remove mine, too."

"No." Panic had built in her voice. Tension constricted her body.

"It's all right," he soothed.

But she would have none of it. He had moved too fast.

But hadn't she led him? Encouraged him? Could he have missed an earlier rejection? There hadn't been one.

"Trust me, Ket. It'll be all righ—"

"No." Rolling away, she jumped to her feet. He jumped up, too, bumping his head.

"Damnation!" He rubbed his head and tried to figure out what to do. She didn't help. She stood in the mouth of the shelter, outlined by the flames, looking nude in those skin-tight deerskin britches.

Coming up behind her, he crossed his arms over her belly, drawing her close. "You want me, Ket. I know you do. And I want you. There's nothing wrong—"

"I don't . . ." When she jerked free again, he stood mystified with arms hanging limp and empty. What had gone wrong? How could he have misread her intentions?

"It's my leg." She stood with her back to him, facing the fire.

"What about your leg?" He fairly shouted, or it sounded like a shout in the confines of the small shelter.

"I don't want you to see it." Her voice was steady again, devoid of emotion.

"Hell, it's practically dark in here. How could I—"

"You don't understand."

"You're right about that. Damn, Ket, you're the last person I would have taken as vain."

"Vain?"

"Worried about your beauty—or the perception of your beauty."

"You don't understand," she repeated in a voice replete with something that sounded like hopelessness. Or was that just the way he felt?

He caught her again and held her until she ceased to struggle. "What don't I understand, Ket? Tell me."

"My leg . . . No one has ever seen that scar."

"But a scar isn't . . . I mean, it's almost dark in here," he repeated when no other words came to mind.

"Not dark enough. You would know."

"Know what?"

She pulled away, and he allowed her to. "It would sicken you."

"I doubt it. I happen to have seen scars before." He was offended, by what he wasn't sure. It was probably his physical pain, he decided. For he was in pain. His passion had built quickly and he had not tried to stanch it, believing that they would consummate this . . . this lust.

Then he realized that, although relief seemed far away, lust was also far from his mind. Consoling Ket became urgent.

"Come here," he called softly. When she hesitated, he drew her close and held her tightly against his chest until she ceased her struggles. "Tell me about it."

She didn't want to, he could hear that in her voice, in the hesitant way she began.

"It's deep. And long. And wide. Most of the muscle is gone. My calf is mostly . . . scarred. It's white and ugly."

"It can't be that bad," he argued. "I've never seen you limp."

"I don't." Her pride would have stood the fiercest of Victorio's warriors in good stead. "They said I would never walk again. They brought me crutches. Sabrina had them made. But I threw them away. I wouldn't use them. I hated her so much, I was determined to show her."

"So you walked."

"Yes. I walked."

"And it was painful?"

"Yes."

"Your hatred for Sabrina fueled your determination to walk, and to walk well."

"I suppose. I mean, I did it because I hated her."

"I met her today."

"And you like her."

"I don't have a personal reason not to," he tried to

explain. "But I'm glad you could use your hatred to learn to walk again." He kissed her softly on the lips. "Do you know what I thought about you that first day after you'd rescued the boys and me from the Comancheros?"

"What?"

"I thought you were the most graceful woman I had ever seen. I've thought that several times since, including today when I watched you work on the travois. Now that I know how much effort it took for you to walk, I'm even more impressed."

She remained silent. For a moment he thought she might be holding her breath, for he couldn't feel it against his bare chest. Finally he gathered her in his arms and lowered them to the mat again, even though she resisted.

"It's all right." He traced small, nonthreatening kisses over her neck. "I know something you will like, and we won't have to remove your britches."

It was, in the end, a greater challenge than Blake had thought it would be. For a time he wasn't sure he was up to it, for in the process of pleasuring her, he was left with an acute, wrenching pain. But when he finished she had been pleasured, and the intense joy that that brought him was at once rewarding and troubling.

Afterwards, like he had planned—well, partially like he had planned—they talked. She fixed them bowls of *pozole,* which turned out to be deliciously flavored soup made with rabbit meat and dried corn. They ate around the fire in her shelter and they talked.

He told her about meeting Rosa Ramériz.

She snuggled against him, pressed her shoulder into his chest. "Is this how your father raped Rosa and begat Neeta?"

"Keturah! I don't know whether to be offended or shocked at your ignorance."

"What do you mean, my ignorance?"

"If you don't know that what we just did could not, I

repeat, could not result in a child being conceived . . ."
Words failed him.

"I know that," she said. "What I meant was, do you
think your father and Rosa were ever this . . . close?"

That was a different thing, something Blake readily
understood and wondered himself. A strange sadness enveloped him. The benefit was a lessening of his own physical
pain.

"If the rumor is true," he told Ket, "if he is Neeta's
father, I would like to hope they were close. But if they
were close like this, why aren't they still?"

She shrugged against him, and he kissed the top of her
hair. He couldn't get enough of this woman, he knew that.
On the other hand, he certainly hadn't had enough of
her. He wondered whether he ever would.

Then she surprised him with an invitation that at first
blush was more offensive than her question about his father
and Rosa Raméríz.

"Will you come with me to Apache Wells?"

"Apache Wells?" He was astounded. "You hate Apache
Wells."

"Well, I . . . we could consult the guardian."

"What do you take me for? You don't believe in that
damned guardian."

"Maybe I was wrong."

It took Blake days to try to figure that out, and when he
did, he didn't like the conclusion he'd come to.

Keturah Tremayne did not play games. She wouldn't
even know how to play the titillating games women used
against men.

But if she wasn't playing games with him, why would she
ask him to go someplace she hated to seek guidance from
something she didn't believe in?

It didn't make one damned bit of sense.

Nor did his attraction to this wild woman.

Chapter Seven

Sitting still was not Keturah's style, especially not inside a white-eyes' building on an army post where men wore the hated uniform of the soldiers who killed her mother and Emily's parents and were intent on driving the People from this land.

Still, she could not bring herself to leave Emily's side. So the week after Blake left again for the rail site, she sat with Emily, escaping only when Reba or Harry Applebee were present. Those times she went into the hills, where she worked on the travois. Even though Emily refused to return home, Ket hoped that after the surgeon from Fort Bliss removed the bullet, she would begin to improve and then . . .

Surely when she felt better Emily would want to return to her birth people. Ket felt driven by an urgency to be prepared for that time.

In clearer moments she admitted to herself that she worked on the travois to have something to do. Working with her hands occupied her mind, too.

Not that she had given up all hope that Emily would recover—look at the great odds she had overcome to learn to walk again—but the girl's condition weakened daily.

As Doc Henry continued to explain, the second wound was still a problem. "Dad-blamed bullet's lodged somewhere between her stomach and her heart. Soon's that blasted surgeon from Bliss gets here, he can set about removing it. Wish I could be more help."

He offered his hands for inspection, as if any of them needed to be reminded of the reason he couldn't search for that bullet himself.

"These palsied old hands aren't steady enough for the job, sorry to say." Doc Henry had been gripped by an unidentified palsy years earlier. The young medic in charge of the hospital at Fort Davis, Lieutenant Conroy, whose hands were steady as stagnant water, freely admitted not being experienced enough for the task.

No one wanted to finish what the uninformed sentry had begun. It reminded Ket of stories about how she had fallen into the ceremonial fire and burned her leg.

Unable to heal her, the shaman had sent her away from the Apachería to the only place he could think of where help might be available—Apache Wells. Instead of calling on the guardian of the well to heal his daughter, however, Tremayne had brought Sabrina to treat her.

The result was a scarred leg that had taken Ket years of relentless, gritty determination to learn to use, all of which amounted to nothing, considering Emily's fate.

So Ket sat beside her cousin's bed, and while Emily dozed, she agonized over the myriad conflicts that had arisen in her own life. She tried to stop thinking about Blake and the magic they had shared in her rock shelter high above Fort Davis.

She longed to be with him like that again. Given another chance, she was sure she could overcome the embarrassment that had overwhelmed her. If it were dark enough, perhaps he wouldn't notice her unsightly scar.

At the same time, while her pulse raced and liquid hot heat pooled low in her body, she hated herself for wanting him. He was a white eyes, and they lived for only one thing—to annihilate the People. White eyes abandoned and betrayed. Life had provided Ket with ample evidence of that.

Yet, she was drawn to Blake in so many ways she could not name them all. Foremost, of course, was the intense longing she felt to be with him, the rampant desire that escalated daily and strangely continued to increase even when she was in his arms. At the same time, it was a beautiful feeling, this insidious craving. It ran deep and hot and made her feel as if she could soar with eagles, as if she could live forever.

Sitting at Emily's sickbed, those thoughts seemed blasphemous. Yet she couldn't shake the memory of Emily's parents making love in the rain—it fascinated her.

Stranger still—strange and abhorrent—the feelings evoked by the memory were no longer those of betrayal and death. Even now, as she watched Emily hover at death's door, Ket experienced an intense yearning to return to Blake's arms and fulfill the promises made there.

She decided that this compelling attraction must, in some way, be tied to death, a fatalistic acknowledgment that if indeed every person had been born to die, she should not deny herself the pleasure of experiencing true lovemaking before her time arrived.

If indeed, as she had since childhood suspected, lovemaking preceded death, so be it. Death would come, regardless of whether she and Blake were to make love.

Make love. Even the words sounded fragile. Unlike *make war,* which sounded harsh and strong and courageous, *make love* sounded like seeds blowing on the wind in early spring, like isolated blades of grass peeking tentatively through the snow in winter.

Fragile, yes it was. In her soul were etched images of the results of those fragile words—*making love.* Death and betrayal. Abandonment.

But now she had begun to understand the emotions associated with making love, emotions that stole one's power to resist, indeed one's desire to resist. For in Blake's arms, she had not wanted to resist.

Instinctively she realized that her childhood fears associated with making love would not necessarily have held true had she relented to Blake's—and yes, to her own—will to do so. The world would not have suddenly come to an end. Soldiers from the fort would not have raided them on the spot.

And, oh, what a joy it would have been. But that brought to mind the other quandary: her leg.

The massive scar where Sabrina had almost doctored her to death would repel the most determined lover. Not in many years had anyone looked upon that scar. The idea of Blake seeing it turned her stomach sour.

She had made the right decision not to allow herself to be seduced by Blake Carmichael. On the other hand, she would regret it to her dying day.

On those occasions when she remained with Emily while both Reba and Harry were away, Ket spoke to Emily about her growing turmoil. Not that Emily, at the tender age of thirteen, could understand the situation any better than Ket did, but Emily seemed relieved to have something other than death and pain to think about, and Ket found relief in speaking of it.

Time passed as in a daze. It was the most confusing time Ket could remember. She often thought that if she faced just one or two problems, she might come to some understanding of them, some mode of action. But the situation had splintered into so many facets that the problems seemed irresolvable.

Blake Carmichael had gotten under her skin in too many ways to count. None of which she understood. She knew, had known since she was a small child, that white eyes abandoned, betrayed, and killed at will.

Still, the fascination that sizzled inside her grew daily.

One morning near the end of the first week after Blake returned to the rail site, Doc Henry arrived at the hospital with Sabrina in tow.

The sight of her stepmother frightened Ket. Doc Henry had instructed Sabrina to remain in bed as much as possible. Emily must be dying, Ket decided, for Doc Henry to bring Sabrina off her sickbed.

But Emily stirred at the sight of Sabrina. The two greeted each other warmly. Sabrina held Emily's head to her bosom and squeezed her eyes closed.

Emily had never given up her crusade to bring Ket and Sabrina together. The failing girl had talked of little else.

"Reba Applebee is such a wonderful mother to me," Emily tried to explain. "I don't even remember how my blood parents looked."

Ket remembered how they looked. She remembered all too well. Now she understood what had transpired between them that day in the rain. Now she understood and longed for the experience herself. And she was a fool for thinking so.

But on this day there was Emily to consider. Doc Henry had decided to cauterize Emily's wound and had brought Sabrina, who had once been purported to be skilled at nursing, to keep Reba company during the procedure.

With the women and Ket looking on, he explained the procedure. "With any luck at all, this will keep the infection from spreading."

Sabrina stood between Reba and Ket at the far side of the bed. That was bad enough, for something inside Ket

had begun to change. Since meeting Blake—more precisely, she chose to believe, since the day they returned to
the fort and she had stumbled upon the evidence of the
Apaches' devastating last-ditch attack on Fort Davis and
the wounding of Emily—the icy wall of hatred Ket had
erected around her heart had begun to melt. No longer
could she depend on a stoic defense against emotions such
as sorrow or anguish or fear.

Although she had acknowledged the fact to no one, not
even to herself in so many words, she could no longer
depend on hatred as a defense, since her hatred of all
things white had lessened considerably.

She couldn't even depend on not crying, something she
was determined not to do in front of Sabrina. To show
weakness was the same as showing cowardice. And she
would show neither to this woman who had stolen so much
from her. She would be civil, she decided, for Emily's sake.
But that was all.

Since the day Sabrina told Ket about hearing the laughter at Apache Wells, Sabrina had not crossed the barrier
Ket had erected between them.

Today she offered a simple "Hello, how are you, Ket?"
upon entering Emily's room. Ket edged around to the foot
of the bed.

Doc Henry administered morphine; Emily drifted off;
and Lieutenant Conroy came in to help. All went well.

Sabrina held Reba around the shoulders. Colonel
Applebee arrived and stood on the other side of his wife.
They clutched each other's hands. Ket watched their
knuckles turn white.

"You might want to wait outside," Doc Henry suggested
once, but no one moved from Emily's side. It was as if by
being there, they could in some way suspend the inevitable.

From her post at the foot of the bed, Ket watched the
sedated girl. For the first time she noticed that Emily's
dark skin had paled to an ashen gray. When had that

Take 4 FREE Books!

We have 4 FREE BOOKS for you as your introduction to KENSINGTON CHOICE!

To get your FREE BOOKS, worth up to $24.96, mail the card below. or call TOLL-FREE 1-888-345-BOOK

Take 4 Zebra Historical Romances FREE!

MAIL TO: ZEBRA HOME SUBSCRIPTION SERVICE, INC.
120 BRIGHTON ROAD, P.O. BOX 5214,
CLIFTON, NEW JERSEY 07015-5214

YES! Please send me my 4 FREE ZEBRA HISTORICAL ROMANCES (without obligation to purchase other books). Unless you hear from me after I receive my 4 FREE BOOKS, you may send me 4 new novels - as soon as they are published - to preview each month FREE for 10 days. If I am not satisfied, I may return them and owe nothing. Otherwise, I will pay the money-saving preferred subscriber's price of just $4.20 each... a total of $16.80 plus $1.50 for shipping and handling. That's a savings of over $8.00 each month. I may return any shipment within 10 days and owe nothing, and I may cancel any time I wish. In any case the 4 FREE books will be mine to keep.

Name _____

Address _____ Apt No _____

City _____ State _____ Zip _____

Telephone ( ) _____

Signature _____
(If under 18, parent or guardian must sign)

KN030A

Terms, offer, and price subject to change. Orders subject to acceptance.
Offer valid in the U.S. only.

AFFIX
STAMP
HERE

KENSINGTON CHOICE
Zebra Home Subscription Service, Inc.
120 Brighton Road
P.O.Box 5214
Clifton, NJ 07015-5214

happened? How long . . . ? Anxiety crawled inside her and she felt guilty for it.

But she couldn't change it. She felt trapped inside this white-eyes' building, surrounded by white eyes, suffocated by them.

She looked at Emily but saw visions of others, other friends, other relatives. Too many others to count. The People had been born to die. But Emily hadn't. She was supposed to have escaped the destruction.

Emily had been taken in and loved and cared for by the white eyes. She wasn't supposed to have been killed by them.

The senselessness of it all overwhelmed Ket. The senselessness of life. Against her best efforts to stanch them, tears welled in her eyes. She couldn't hold them back. She tried, but she couldn't, so she fled. Turning, she flung herself out the door.

But Tremayne had come to the door unaware, and Ket ran straight into his large, firm body. The instant she reached him, his arms went around her.

Involuntarily, she embraced him, too. For a moment she stood, face buried in his chest, his strong arms around her, supporting, comforting and being comforted. She was a child again, returning to the time when they had held and consoled each other after her mother was killed. He had needed her then, as much as she needed him.

But the moment passed and reality returned. Tearing herself away, she raced from the hospital and up the canyon behind it. She passed the post magazine and stumbled up the boulder-strewn draw, headed for her rock shelter, where she could hide from the world and all its trouble.

She had just reached the travois when Tremayne caught up. He grabbed her arm and pulled her around.

"Look at me, Ket."

Stoically she refused.

"How is she . . . Emily?"

"You saw her."

"I just got into town. Rosa said Doc Henry had taken Sabrina to be with Emily. I knew if the doc took Sabrina out of her sickbed, it must be bad. What's happening?"

"He's cauterizing her wound. It wouldn't heal. There's an infection." Pulling away, she turned toward the hillside, up which lay her shelter. Anxiously she paused, fidgeted, not wishing to lead him to her place of refuge. That only brought more anguish, not wanting her father to know where she lived.

"I brought you some things." He handed her a bundle. "Clothing . . . and that robe. It's getting colder."

Again a fit of emotion swept over her. She would not cry, she told herself. Not in front of this man. She would rather cry in front of Sabrina than her father. But in her arms was a bundle of her things. They were wrapped in her fox pelt robe. The one she had made herself.

Generally a woman had a man to trap, and she had only to tan the hides and make the clothing. Ket had been proud that she had trapped the foxes and made this robe by herself, that she had needed no one.

Strangely, though, instead of feeling proud right now, she felt lonely. That's what she was. Alone.

"Your grandmother sends greetings."

Startled, Ket lifted her face from the soft fur. At the last minute, she kept herself from meeting his gaze. "Is she well?"

He inclined his head, and she noticed streaks of white in his dark wavy hair. The poignancy of it caught in her throat. She steeled herself against another show of emotion.

"She took the word of Emily's wounding harder than I'd expected," he said. "She's lost so much in her lifetime. A son and a daughter. Now a granddaughter."

"What of those who raided the fort?" Ket asked. "How many were killed?"

"Two. The son of Navarro and a man I didn't know."

"Delgado," Ket said. "We saw his war horse."

"Mangas Che received a wound in the shoulder."

Ket nodded that she understood, for to speak would reveal too much. Her weakness sickened her. Where had her courage gone?

"I see you're making a travois," Tremayne commented, as if to fill the void.

"To take Emily home," she responded tersely.

"Didn't you say she wants to remain here?"

"Not for now." Ket strove for a monotone. "Afterwards . . . she should be returned to her people." The plan had emerged suddenly from her subconscious, and Ket realized it had been there all along.

"You've given up hope?"

"No." But hadn't she?

"Chi and Doré would be pleased with your plan, but what about her family here? What do the Applebees say?"

"I haven't spoken of it." She regretted having blurted out such a desperate plan without thinking it through. Now he would try to stop her, or he would tell someone who would try to stop her.

Instead of the rebuke she expected, however, Tremayne changed the subject. "The Apachería is packing," he said quietly. "Like you said, they are planning to go to Mexico to be with Victorio."

"How soon?"

"They didn't say. The warriors want to attack the fort again."

When she continued to stare into her cooking fire, he called to her. "Look at me, Ket."

Compelled by his tone, she obeyed him.

"Man is born to die," he told her in a stern voice. "You and I both understand that. It's what we were taught, and it is true. But I . . . I don't want you to . . . to die so young. A child shouldn't have to die before her mother, much less before both her parents. This trip to Mexico, I have a bad feeling about it. I studied on it all the way to the Apachería and back, and the way it looks to me . . . It looks like a journey no one will ever return from. It's over for the People. I . . . I don't want you to go with them. What good would your death do?"

She had no answer, so she remained stoically silent.

After a tense moment, Tremayne squatted before the travois and studied its structure. He ran a large hand over the frame she had fashioned from the trunk of a small tree.

She could tell he wasn't thinking about this travois, for he gazed into the distance, as though remembering something. "This reminds me of . . ."

When he glanced up to find her staring at him, his words caught. A sheen of tears covered his eyes. Her father, the great Tremayne, with tears. What was this world coming to? He looked up the canyon again, as if seeing into the past.

"The sun was just beginning to rise that morning," he began, his words no more than a whisper on the wind. "I rode back to Apache Wells preoccupied. I'd been up all night. I had just realized that I had feelings for Sabrina, and that she probably had feelings for me. We both understood how hopeless those feelings were. She was practically promised to Lon Jasper, and I . . . Well, we were certainly wrong for each other.

"I'd reached the well before I saw them. Three young men from the Apachería walked toward me. They pulled a travois . . ." His words drifted off again.

This time she realized it had been on purpose, for when she looked at him, he was staring at her, and she sensed he had paused to gain her attention.

"You were covered in robes of fur," he continued. "I thought you were dead. I rushed over, looked at you, listened to the tale of how you had fallen into the fire. The shaman said he couldn't save your life, so he had sent you to me, to Apache Wells and the guardian.''

Ket watched him closely. Had he forgotten that she knew the story, knew it by heart in all its gory detail, never to forget it? Then she suddenly became aware of something else in him. Intensity lit his green eyes. His brow furrowed. He needed to tell this story . . . to say the words . . . to her.

"I was angry.'' His voice rose with remembrance. "Angrier than I had been since your mother died. So much had happened in such a short time. Chi and Doré had been murdered only a few days before. Little Emily had been orphaned and given to the white eyes. None of it made any sense. All of it was tragic. Now there you lay, reeking of that shaman's witches' brew, so near death that he had sent you from the village. And there I was, alone with no one to turn to for help. I had to save you, Ket. I had to. You couldn't die. You were all I had left. I couldn't let you die. But you see, I couldn't take you to the fort, either.''

Again he looked off into the distance, as if seeing beyond the far hills. This time he shook his head with something vaguely akin to amusement. "Oh, Sabrina fought me for that. Did she ever! She wasn't skilled, she said. She couldn't save you, she said. You must be taken to the post, to the hospital . . . where Emily is now.''

When he looked back, his green gaze pled for her to understand. "I couldn't take you there, Ket. Better that you die first. You had seen your mother murdered by white-eyes soldiers. I couldn't take you to a fort full of the bastards. It would terrify you. I couldn't . . . Sabrina said only the guardian could save you, then. But she did her best. She consulted Doc Henry. He almost got court-martialed for allowing her to help you. Did you know that? It was hard for everyone. I ended up losing you over it, but at least you lived. In the long run, that's all that mattered . . . all that still matters.''

Ket was near tears herself and dared not try to respond. What would she have said, anyway? She had known the story. Part of it.

Now he had told it all. "I wanted you to know," he said at last. "I've wanted to tell you for ten years. I never wanted to lose you, Ket. I never . . . wanted . . . to lose you. I still don't want to lose you."

Standing abruptly, he brushed his hands on his trousers. "That's all."

She couldn't respond. Her emotions were too close to the surface. After ten years, her feelings on this topic were still too raw. Now her fears were greater than ever.

"Sabrina believes the guardian saved you," he continued. "I don't know what I think. I don't know if I believe in the guardian or not. Sabrina believes, and I guess that's all that really matters . . . believing in something . . . and trusting. Sabrina says that to believe in anything, first you have to trust. You haven't been given a fair chance to learn to trust. I don't blame you, Ket. After all that's past, all the future holds, I have a hard time trusting, too."

Finished, he lowered his gaze to hers, held hers a long intense moment, then he turned and left.

Standing straight and stiff, Ket watched him go. She held back her tears until he was out of sight. Then they came so fast and furiously she didn't have time for shame to creep into her mind.

She sat on the travois and cried for Emily and for Delgado and for the son of Navarro.

She cried for Emily's parents and for all her friends and relatives. She cried for her mother. She cried for herself, for the loss of her father and all else that had been taken from her.

Why had the Great Spirit put her on this earth if only to suffer one abandonment after another? Why had he put the People here if only to suffer and die?

Her father spoke of trust. For the first time, Ket realized

that trust was the one thing that she and all the abandoned and betrayed of this earth lacked.

Trust. How did a person learn to trust? How could a person trust those who perpetually abandoned and betrayed? Why should a person try?

Tremayne had obviously found a reason—Sabrina, who had believed in the guardian of the well even when her father could not.

Was there a guardian? Could it teach her to trust?

Not if she died in Mexico, came the sudden and unbidden answer.

Chapter Eight

"Will you come with me to Apache Wells?"

Ket's question caught Blake off guard. After a two-week absence, he had come to town for supplies. Leaving the wagon with Edward Bolton at the mercantile, he had headed straight for the fort. He didn't even try to disguise the fact that he had come to see Ket.

As far as he was concerned, time for playing games had ended. For two weeks his haunting dreams had become more and more erotic. He needed to gain control, and he figured he knew the only way to do it.

In fact, he had even forgotten that Ket mentioned going to Apache Wells. Now he recalled thinking it a ploy of some kind. Although exactly what ploy the forthright Keturah Tremayne would resort to baffled him.

Thus when she asked him a second time to accompany her to the seat of the Tremayne family, it took him off guard, but not entirely by surprise. Regardless of what her reasons might be, the trip seemed an answer to his frustration.

"When?" he asked by way of agreeing.

He had found her on the back veranda of the hospital, waiting for Emily's bandages to be changed.

"Any improvement?" he had asked.

"Not much. They cauterized the wound. It doesn't seem to be getting worse, but the surgeon from Fort Bliss still hasn't arrived. Doc Henry can't remove the bullet and the medic here isn't skilled enough. Time is running out."

"When do you want to go to Apache Wells?" he questioned again.

"Now."

"Okay. Tell whoever you need to tell. I'll wait."

"What?"

"Tell whoever . . ."

"Tell them what?" She seemed genuinely stunned by the suggestion.

"That you're leaving town."

"They'll know I'm gone."

"Yes, but—"

"I never tell anyone where I go, why should I?"

So they left. She didn't even return to her shelter. Her independence infected him. He didn't even stop by the mercantile to tell Bolton he wouldn't be leaving Chihuahua for a day or two. That nagged at his conscience a couple of miles . . . but no further.

Neither did he tell his father. That didn't nag at his conscience. He wouldn't have told his father anyway. The senator would have accused him of shirking his duty.

Indeed, Blake hadn't seen his father this trip. He hadn't stopped by the house in Chihuahua, for the simple reason that he didn't want to lie to the man. And he certainly didn't intend to tell him that he'd come to town to see Ket. No sense lighting any more fires than were already lit.

Their ride was fast and furious, hell-bent-for-leather. Ket

set the pace, and he kept up. The day was chilly. He noticed Ket's luxurious fox cloak and commented on it.

"I made it." Her resplendent smile said she was pleased he had noticed. "I trapped the foxes, too."

What a woman!

Once he questioned why the rush. "Is the valley on fire, or what?"

"It's me," she answered. "I've been cooped up in that white-eyes world way too long. I had to get out."

The further they traveled from the fort, the more she relaxed. Her hair hung mostly free. Some of it clung to her face and neck. Her body could have been fluid beneath that glowing cloak of fox fur, it moved with such a sensuous suppleness. He experienced the opposite effect.

He thought of her struggle to learn to walk and knew she was a woman who could do anything she set her mind to. That, in turn, set his mind wandering down erotic trails.

Not much was said during the trip. Ket didn't talk much by nature, and his anticipation of what lay ahead ran so hot inside him that if he had been able to think of some innocuous topic of conversation, the words would probably have incinerated before they reached his throat.

Lust. That's all it was. Nothing a good toss in the hay, or grass, or wherever she chose, wouldn't cure. But when they sat atop the hill and gazed down into the small ethereal valley, his doubts surfaced—one in particular.

What exactly did he want from Keturah Tremayne?

Finding an answer to that question suddenly became imperative, urgent, for below them lay the stuff of fantasy, a never-never land if ever one existed.

No one returned from never-never land, not unchanged.

The thought was sobering. At the same time, wild horses couldn't have kept him from urging his mount down the cliff behind Ket. And nothing short of blindness could have kept him from focusing on the woman ahead of him, the woman on whom all his dreams centered.

He followed the palomino stallion down the steep incline and watched Ket dismount. She stood as though distracted, glancing around the valley. He had the impression she wasn't sure why they had come here.

It was a question he felt compelled to ask. Dismounting, he approached her. "Why are we here, Ket?"

She turned to him with a faraway look in her deep green eyes. Those feral eyes, that wild hair, that fiery red cloak—they combined to make a stunning sight. Standing there with the winter sun sparkling all around her, she took his breath away. He decided it didn't matter why she brought him here, only that she had.

"I told you," she was saying. "I had to get away from the white-eyes' world."

"That isn't what I asked." His voice was thick. "Why did we come *here*, to Apache Wells?"

Again she glanced around. She might have been searching for an answer in the countryside. Her gaze rested on the well, but she did not speak. She looked genuinely confused. His heart constricted.

He stepped closer. "You hate this place, Ket. You told me so. With a whole wide country to choose from, why did you run here?"

That made her angry. "I did not run."

He dismissed her defensiveness with a shrug. "Why here?" he repeated softly. Then he added, as almost an afterthought, although it was the question primarily in his mind, "Why me?"

He watched her grow more and more agitated. A wild thing, he thought her, reminded him of a circus act he once saw outside Washington, D.C.

He had been drawn to the center ring, where a lion tamer worked with a sleek African lion. Now he realized he hadn't paid close enough attention to the tamer.

His attention had been claimed by the wild animal. Ket reminded him of that lion—caged, trapped, eyes scanning the cliffs that enclosed them. She even seemed to prowl, first with her eyes, then with jerky movements of her head, her arms.

He could practically see her mind crawl inside her head, frightened, trapped, albeit by a threat of her own making, but trapped nonetheless. Her imprisoned energies compelled him like that caged lion had done.

Then he became aware of something else. Drawn by her wildness, fascinated, allured, he suddenly saw past it to something he should have seen long ago, certainly since their debacle in her rock shelter—her raw vulnerability. This, too, held him enthralled. Ket's vulnerability, like that of the lion he'd seen as a child, was palpable. She stood before him afraid and uncertain how to deal with the fear.

He wished now he had paid more attention to the lion tamer. Not that he wanted to tame Ket. He wouldn't do that, not even if he could. He would not rob her of this innate and fascinating wildness. But, oh, to win her trust.

Sensing that the best thing he could do at the moment was to give her space, he turned and headed for the creek.

It had been a terrible idea, the worst she had ever had. Blake was right—she hated Apache Wells.

Hated it . . . but truth be known, she feared it. So why had she returned? What had she hoped to find here? Did she believe Sabrina, that there was a guardian who lived in the well and solved Tremayne problems with laughter?

Did she believe in the guardian, after all? If so, exactly what did she believe? Were the white eyes right?

Was the guardian a ghost instead of a spirit? A ghost who imprisoned instead of liberated; a ghost who locked one onto a straight and narrow path, instead of a spirit who opened one's life to endless possibilities?

For the first time in her life, Ket felt compelled to talk about these things. They troubled her, and she needed to talk about them—and about this place she hated. But she didn't have the words.

She glanced to the creek where Blake sat on a boulder and fished with a pole rigged from a sapling branch and a piece of string he had gotten from who knew where.

Blake had words. He asked why she brought him here. Was that the reason, to talk? He had plenty of words. Could he help her express her hatred, her fear, in words?

Was that why she brought him here? To talk about these feelings? These fears that felt suddenly like they would explode inside her if she couldn't get them out?

Could Blake help her find words to make sense out of the insensible? Blake, the greenhorn white eyes, who, she realized upon observing him now at the creek, seemed no longer to be either of those things.

She watched him pull a small perch from the water, remove it from the hook, and deposit it in a clay jar used to dry seeds. Without so much as a glance her way, he returned to fishing.

He belonged here.

That realization toppled a crucial barrier in Ket's mind. It was as if a wall between them had fallen down, a thought at once unsettling and enormously satisfying. She approached him awkwardly.

"Blake?"

He glanced up, held her gaze, which in turn set her stomach to tumbling. Her head was full of sounds . . . rocks falling. The wall that had separated them . . . falling . . .

"Hmm?" He spoke no words, either to interrupt or to interfere.

"I wanted you to come with me because you are the only person I can trust."

Blake watched Ket's vulnerability surface as timidity. He held his breath. He might be a greenhorn white eyes, like she said; he might not know much about this country, as his father charged, but Blake knew a thing or two about human nature. And the nature of the woman standing before him was as clear as the creek water in which he fished.

One false move and she would bolt. One greenhorn, white-eyes quip and he would lose her. He responded with a simple "Hold on a minute. Let me take care of this fish."

As deliberately as his tight muscles allowed, he pulled the fishing line from the water, unhooked the small perch, placed it in the earthenware jar he'd found in the cabin, and replaced the jar in the shallows, where his catch of four perch could get water through the small holes around the sides of the jar.

While he worked, she came close and gathered the fox pelts around her and knelt beside where he sat on a round red boulder. He struggled for composure. "I have no idea what this jar is used for, but it makes a good fish trap."

"It's used to dry seeds." Then she added, "You're inventive."

He knew he shouldn't touch her. But she was so close. He knew he couldn't rush things. As vulnerable as she was, he could easily scare her off. He had a strong sense that her reasons for bringing him here were not romantic, not solely anyhow.

"Not really," he responded to her claim that he was inventive. He dried his hands on his britches. The need to touch her was great and she was so very close, so he reached over and stroked a strand of hair off her face.

No longer defiant or defensive, her expression seemed open for the first time since he had met her. He sensed that all the differences that separated them had been cast aside. Whether permanently or temporarily, he couldn't decide. The latter would be his guess.

But it was a beginning. The first light at the end of the tunnel. Probably the first tunnel.

She sat still, but seemingly relaxed, and peered deeply into him, making a powerful physical connection with only her gaze. It struck him like a beam of sunlight would strike a tiny piece of quartz embedded eons before in the red volcanic rock, glancing off it, searing deeply, producing a brilliant beam of light and heat.

In that instant he felt right, whole, as if her probing green gaze had found the source of an intense ache inside him and had healed it; found a dislocated part of him and set it straight.

Only one question seemed necessary. She hadn't answered it satisfactorily. "Why me?"

Her response was instantaneous and unequivocal. "You never gave up on me."

In the following hours, they walked the small valley side by side until Blake was certain he knew every nook and cranny, every legend and tale that had ever been concocted about this valley with its legendary well and spiritual guardian.

Only later would he understand that every place, every legend was indelibly linked with Ket.

Keturah Tremayne was Apache Wells and Apache Wells was Keturah Tremayne. In that afternoon, the two became linked in his mind and in his heart forever, one and the same. She might hate this place, or profess to hate it, but it was she and she was it and he could only admit that he had fallen in love with both. The precise moment he realized that was not so easy to pinpoint.

It could have been while they stood together beneath a wild cherry tree at the far end of the little valley from the old stone cottage.

"I've eaten jam made from the fruit of this tree." She had looked up into the winter-barren branches. Her voice held the curiosity of a child, and he saw her here as a child.

When he asked, however, she didn't recall ever having

been here as a small child or who might have made the jam.

"The only time I remember staying here"—she paused and glanced quickly at the old stone cottage, then away—"was after my leg was burned."

Even though he knew that that memory was one of the most unpleasant of her life, she didn't dwell on it, but quickly led him on to another sight.

"Inhale," she ordered, after sticking a juniper branch beneath his nose.

He promptly sneezed.

"Why did you sneeze?" She brought the branch beneath her own nose and inhaled deeply. "I love this scent. It reminds me of winter, but not of being cold." She smiled up at him, and he was certain he would never be cold again.

"I love winter," she added, "don't you?"

A few weeks, days even, earlier, he might have quipped that he was surprised that she loved anything. But he didn't, for the simple reason that he was not surprised. "I love winter, too," he agreed, and somehow kept himself from adding *but I love you more.*

Perhaps that was when he realized that he loved her. If so, it hadn't been the only time he'd thought it. After the juniper came the well, but not just the legend of the well, which the boys had demonstrated in a way he would never forget. He still felt the splash of hot red water over his head.

He still recalled the meaning.

"Papa is legendary with the People," she told him. "When he was young, he came here to prove his manhood by drinking from the well."

"He would either die or become a man?"

"He knew he wouldn't die. I recall . . ." Her words drifted off, and when she lifted her face to his, her eyes seemed afire with the sunlight. "Maybe he told me this story one time. I'm not sure now, but his father had given him a drink of the water once, so he knew it wouldn't kill him."

"Your grandparents were killed here?"

She nodded. "Papa's father put him in the bucket and lowered him into the well when he saw the riders come down the hill."

"Then he knew who they were?"

"I suppose. But nobody was left alive who saw them, so no one will ever know."

"When your father climbed out . . . ?"

"His parents were dead. His father's body had been thrown across the well, so he had to climb around it."

"That's a hard thing for a son to see."

"Life is hard."

"Perhaps more so for those who first came here than for those of us who've come later." He spoke without thinking, and she let him know it.

"My people have always been here. Your people came later."

"Your grandparents were white eyes."

"I never knew them, so that doesn't count."

He started to name her father, too, but didn't. He didn't want to dispel the magic. For magic it was. He persuaded her to retell the story of her father earning his novitiate. He'd heard most of it before, from the boys, but this was different.

This time it wasn't the story that captivated him, but the storyteller. She enchanted him. He found joy in watching her transformation from a frozen, defiant half-breed who belonged to no world, to a winsome, desirable woman who *was* the world.

And, oh my yes, he desired her. Did he ever desire her! He glanced around at the red cliffs. Even in late fall when most of the trees had lost their leaves and the grass had turned a mellow shade of gold, the place was magical.

Piñon, desert willow, and that wild cherry tree. He couldn't begin to imagine it in springtime.

"If there were ever a place where spirits would dwell, this must surely be it."

"Spirits can reside anywhere," she countered. "The People believe the world is full of spirits."

"I never thought much about all that," he admitted. "Spirits are hard to conjure in Washington, D.C., with the streets full of clattering carriages and hawkers. Men rushing about in business suits are concerned with secular powers, not spiritual."

The only dark moment came when he suggested they look inside the cabin. "It's the only place we haven't investigated."

She tensed at his suggestion. He could tell immediately that her defiance had returned. "I've conquered a lot of fears today, but not that one. I will never enter that cabin again."

"Because Sabrina ruined your leg in there?" It was a measure of how comfortable they had become with each other that he chanced mentioning her scarred leg. And it was a measure of how far Ket had come this day that she could answer truthfully.

"Sabrina didn't ruin my leg. Papa explained how it happened. He said she begged him to take me to the fort, because she wasn't qualified to treat me, but he refused. Since my mother had been murdered by soldiers, he knew I would be afraid of the uniforms."

"You spoke with him recently?"

"He came out to the canyon where I was building the travois. He'd been to the Apachería and"—she grabbed the lapels of her fox robe—"he brought me this and some other things."

Blake was astonished, both by her having spoken with Tremayne about the painful subject of her scarred leg and by her calling him Papa.

"I still blame Sabrina. She took my father away from me, but it doesn't matter all that much anymore. Everyone's leaving. Soon no one will be left." She glanced to the west as though she could see beyond the encompassing red hills. "He took Sabrina there once."

"There? You mean to the Apachería?"

Ket nodded. "I was terrible to her. My grandmother was, too. But I was worse. I spit in her face." She looked back at the cabin, as if daring it to attack her. "I stood beside Papa and watched her ride away with Nick. I'd driven her away and I was proud. But Papa was angry. No, he wasn't angry, he was sad. I'll never forget his voice or what he said. 'She only wanted to love you,' he told me. Those were his words. I've always remembered them. 'She only wanted to love you.'"

Ket gazed up at Blake with a solemnity that should be felt only at a gravesite. "But I had already learned to hate."

Amidst the poignancy of that admission, it struck Blake that that was what he wanted, too. At least, that was when he voiced it.

He opened his shearling coat to her, and she stepped into it, and he closed the coat and his arms around her and buried his face in her glorious hair. "I can teach you, Ket. Let me teach you."

He hadn't startled her, not half as much as he had startled himself. She lifted her face and their noses touched. Her eyes probed with questions. He sensed she hadn't understood his meaning.

"I can teach you to love, if you'll let me." For untold moments they stood, scarcely breathing, looking into each other's eyes. Before she could deny him the right to dream, he closed the space between their lips and lost himself in her.

She met his kiss eagerly, as she had in her shelter, her own lips open and receptive. He felt her arms snake up his chest and close around his neck. She pressed her fur-encased body into his and he held her there and she felt so right. She belonged.

This time was different. Not the intensity. Not the unrequited need that flowed into him at a rate that caused him to think he might explode if he couldn't get inside her.

But everything else was different this time. For now he knew he loved her. He had told her so . . . almost.

Ket dislodged herself from Blake's arms. She had begun to tremble, and only partially from the desire that escalated rapidly inside her.

Mostly she trembled from a new fear. The strength of her desire was much greater than she recalled. How could it be? What could she do about it?

"What's wrong, Ket?"

She heard confusion in his voice, along with disappointment.

He tipped her chin. "I thought you trusted me."

The reminder of her earlier claim further frustrated her. "I do, but . . ."

"But what?"

She didn't know. "Not like this," she said finally.

"Not like what?" He sounded confused.

Well, she was confused, too. And she was afraid. If he hadn't used that word—*love*. If only he hadn't used that hateful word.

"What do you expect from me?" she challenged.

"What do you mean?"

The way he stared at her, she could see his temper rising. She began to fear that he might walk away. That made her anxious. She didn't know what to do about it.

Now she was confused and anxious. Her earlier contentment faded, and that angered her. She hadn't felt contentment like they had shared today in a long time. Truth known, she had never felt that kind of contentment with a man.

They had walked the valley. She had talked, and he had listened, and she had never felt as fulfilled.

Of course, there had been that empty, hollow sense of longing that she'd grown accustomed to feeling when she was with Blake. She knew what it was. She wanted to be in his arms. She wanted to kiss him and hold him and, yes, to make love with him. Wasn't that the reason she had brought him here? The true reason?

But *making love* was not the same as *being in love*. Making love was a free, spiritual, wonderful activity.

Being in love was not an activity; it was a way of life. Being in love meant all the things she feared most in this world—betrayal and death, yes. Even before that, though, being in love meant a total loss of freedom.

Being in love with a white eyes was undoubtedly worse than anything she had ever imagined. In the white-eyes' lifestyle, she would be no better than a prisoner. Look at Sabrina. Look at Reba Applebee. Look at Lena. They did nothing without their husbands' consent. Why, they hardly could think for themselves.

Take the case of the boys running off to Apache Wells. With their husbands gone, Lena and Sabrina had not been able to find their own children. They'd had to call her to find their children.

And she had met Blake. Now she wished she never had.

"Don't shut me out, Ket. Tell me what you're thinking."

She searched for words. He wouldn't let her off without a response, and to be truthful, he deserved one. Yet what could she say? How could she tell him she could not, would not, be in love? What were the alternatives?

"What do you expect from me?" she demanded. "You want to make love with me . . . then what?"

"Then what?" he asked in a weak, not at all certain tone of voice. His uncertainty confirmed her fear.

"Am I to be like Rosa and bear your child?" That offended him.

"You know better."

"How do I know better?"

"Because I'm telling you. I would never father a child and not accept the responsibility."

"You expect me to be your responsibility?"

He dropped his arms and moved apart. Anchoring his hands on his hips, he stared up at the clear sky. "You aren't making a tinker's damn worth of sense. I told you I'm not like that."

She watched his eyes become dark and explosive. They faced each other, not touching now. Each waited uncomfortably . . . for what she didn't know.

When Blake broke the silence, he sounded weary more than anything else. "You claim not to be like your father, too. Yet didn't you say people think you emulated him? Why did you follow in his footsteps, Ket? You hate the man, so why did you set out to be just like him?"

She understood only about half his words, but that did not diffuse his meaning. "What you say has nothing to do with . . . with being in love."

"You're damned right it doesn't. Our fathers don't have anything to do with this, either."

"Rosa—"

"And don't bring Rosa into it. If my father raped her, it was despicable. Even the rumor is despicable." His eyes found hers, and she felt him plead for her to understand. "What's happening between us isn't like that. It isn't rape or anything close to it. You know that. You know what it is, too, but you're afraid of it."

"Yes, I'm afraid of it." Even saying the words frightened her. She felt trapped and vulnerable.

"Thanks for admitting it." Then he smiled a bit crookedly. "I think."

When he reached for her, she moved her head aside, so his hand landed on the side of her face. He kept it there, and his fingers felt hot and good against her neck.

"This won't go away, Ket. Not even your fear can stop it now."

"It will." But the blood that coursed through her veins mocked her. He was right. And she was so afraid.

"You asked what I want from you." With gentle force he turned her to face him. "I'll be honest," he continued when they stood eye to eye again. "When we rode into this valley today, I wanted this." Slowly he moved his hand down her face, along her neck, over her chest.

While his gaze held hers, his touch heated her through and through. His hand cupped her breast and she drew an involuntary breath.

He didn't stop until his hand covered the space between her legs where he had first felt wetness that day behind the steward's house. She was wet there today, too, but her clothing hid the truth.

He squeezed her anyway and held his hand there. "I wanted to satisfy the craving I feel for you. It's stronger than anything I've ever felt. I can't deny that." His blue eyes bore into her. His gaze was like a tether, and she entertained the strange fantasy that it was all that held her upright.

"I won't deny it," he rephrased. "One day you won't be able to, either, because it's the same for both of us. You feel it; even if you can't admit it yet, you feel it."

When he dropped his hand, she felt bereft.

"That isn't all there is to it, though," he continued. "Today I learned"—for the first time he looked away from her—"there's much more to this relationship than the physical, Ket. As strange as it sounds, I know we belong together."

"No."

He held her gaze, nodding his head, solemn, determined.

"How can you think that?" She wished he had never said it.

"How can you deny it?"

"Because you're wrong. We're different. Even if you aren't like your father, we're still different in important ways . . . ways that can never be changed."

"Name one."

"You know as well as I do."

"You mean our cultures? Our upbringing?" He grinned. "Or the fact that you can't stand to have a roof over your head?"

"Make light of it, but all that is important."

"You bet it is," he replied good-naturedly. "But we can work it out."

"I should take you to the Apachería; then you would see the impossibility of what you say. The stupidity."

"I'm ready. Let's go."

"You're crazy."

"I'm serious."

She knew he was. "It wouldn't prove anything. Just going there wouldn't. You would have to live there day in and day out—"

"Isn't that what I've been trying to tell you? I can only prove that I'm not the womanizer you think my father is by living day by day without being one. The only way you will ever know is by living with me day by day and letting me show you who I am and"—he stroked her cheek with the back of his fingers—"how much I love you."

His words might have been a rawhide garrote. They cut off her breath. She swirled away. He caught her shoulders. She jerked to free herself.

"Come on, Ket. Look at me."

"You're crazy." She fought for control of her senses. Where had all her hatred gone? Had he stolen her ability to resist temptation?

"No, I'm in love."

Chapter Nine

The woman confounded him. Blake watched her ride away from Apache Wells and wondered how he could have ever imagined that a relationship would work out between them. *Absurd* didn't begin to describe such an idea.

"You're right, Ket," he had told her after her latest fear surfaced. "This will never work. We might as well stop trying. I'm not one to play games with people's hearts. And, frankly, I don't like mine trampled on, either."

He'd turned his back on her then, left her standing there beside that damned well. What had possessed him to think he was in love with a wild woman? Hell, it didn't begin to make sense.

At the creek, he upended the clay pot, emptying his catch of the day back into the fresh, cold water. A moment of melancholy enveloped him, watching the perch flounder a moment, then regain their bearings and swim away. He wished briefly that he could regain his own bearings as quickly. Well, he would.

He'd planned to fry those damned fish for supper. Some

supper that would have been. What the hell had he been thinking?

He hadn't been thinking with his head, he reasoned. He'd been thinking with his body.

Later when he rode off through the cold night headed for the rail site, his piqued feelings settled down and he began to logically piece together the puzzle.

Ket wasn't the sort of woman to play games, not consciously. She was really afraid. But she kept replacing one fear with another. That made a relationship with her impossible. No sooner had he helped her understand one fear than another surfaced. He couldn't live with that, and he'd told her so, albeit more harshly than he should have.

"What'll it be tomorrow, Ket? Yesterday you were afraid I would turn out like my father. Today I'm too civilized. And you know what? I am. You may be half white, but you're too proud to admit it. I'm too white for you, Ket. I'm too damned civilized. And it's time we both admitted it."

She had just stood there and watched and listened to him shout without saying a word. She knew he was right. Hell, they were her words that he'd thrown back at her. And they were true. He was too white for her to ever trust. Too civilized in the worst definition of that word for her to ever begin to understand.

The hell of it was, she was too wild for him to ever forget.

He'd left her there standing by the well and headed for the rail site thinking only to escape. He'd get over her. Sooner or later.

When his thoughts finally settled down, he recalled the wagonload of supplies he'd left at Bolton's store. By the time he returned to Chihuahua, waited for the old man to open the mercantile, and got on his way again, it was mid-morning the following day.

What a waste of time. If his father found out, he'd be justified in his displeasure.

* * *

Ket dealt with Blake's rejection the only way she knew how, by stoically refusing to think about him. It didn't work all the time, but she was nothing if not experienced at denying feelings too painful to acknowledge. She was always able to bring her wandering mind back to the present.

She bided her time at the post, taking care of Emily, not daring to wish to return to the Apachería now that she had a half-formed plan, for she had no wish to return with Emily's body.

Blake was right, though. She would never be able to trust white eyes enough to live in their world. That he was also right about her being too proud to claim her white heritage, she refused to ponder. Then one day while she was preparing a rabbit stew to take to Emily, her father appeared at her camp.

"Howdy."

She glanced up to find him standing on the opposite side of her cook fire, hands resting loosely on hips, his attention riveted on her stew.

"Rabbit stew?"

She nodded.

"Neeta said I'd find you here."

Little Neeta had become an uninvited but welcome companion in the days since Ket returned from Apache Wells. With Luke and Tres away from Fort Davis much of the time, Neeta was lonely. But Ket had begun to think that Neeta sought her company for a more profound reason—one wounded soul seeking solace from another, as it were.

Hadn't they both been wounded by these people in the most intimate way? The white-eyes soldier who ordered her own mother's murder still walked this earth, right beside the white eyes who begot Neeta.

The presence of this child, who was destined to grow up

condemned for her father's evil ways, should have added to Ket's distress; instead the opposite was true. Ket found solace in Neeta's company. They were both outcasts.

"I haven't seen Neeta in a day or so," she told her father now.

"She's with her mother," Tremayne said. "Rosa's health is failing. Consumption, Doc Henry suspects. That's why . . ." He hesitated, then retreated from whatever his true mission might be. "Don't know what will happen to Neeta if Rosa dies."

The statement aroused Ket's defenses. *Neeta would survive,* she wanted to retort. Hadn't she herself survived after her mother died and her father deserted her? But she sensed that Tremayne's statement had been one of fact, not intended to dredge up their own past, so she tried to hide her defensiveness.

But Ket could not deny that Neeta's situation was worse even than her own. Neeta had no grandmother to step in and rear her. The child's closest relatives, two grown brothers, Diego and Felipe Ramériz—half-brothers if Neeta's rumored parentage was true—disowned any claim to her. Not actually estranged, they nonetheless had little to do with their mother, either. The only thing Ket had heard about the men in years concerned their hatred for Tremayne.

To this day the Ramériz brothers held Tremayne responsible for their father's brutal murder, an allegation disavowed by everyone else in the country—everyone who chose to make his feelings known.

Senator Carmichael refused to comment, claiming that his animosity toward the renegade Tremayne made him an unreliable judge in the matter.

But Tremayne had not come to discuss the senator and Rosa Ramériz. "I've come to ask a favor, Ket."

His statement, blurted out in the midst of her reverie, startled Ket. She found his troubled green gaze, wondering what he would say next, what he would ask, he who had asked nothing of her since the day he rode to the Apachería to tell her he intended to marry Sabrina, and to ask that she come and live with them.

"She only wanted to love you, Ket," he had told her once. He repeated that statement when he asked her to live with him and Sabrina at Apache Wells. It had been his last request.

She couldn't blame him. That day she had flown into a rage that brought tears to his eyes. That day, she hadn't cared.

He squatted before her now, hands dragging the red earth between his bent knees. His Stetson was pushed back on his head, and she wondered suddenly if he ever wore his Apache headband. Of course he didn't, she countered. He might have been reared by the People, but he was no longer one of them. A white-eyes orphan when the Apaches rescued him, Tremayne had returned to his white roots. Her father was white eyes through and through. She couldn't decide how she felt about that.

"You may be half white, but you're too proud to admit it," Blake had challenged at Apache Wells.

Was it pride? She had wondered about that ever since. She'd always thought of it as hatred.

Tremayne cleared his throat. "I need to head back to the ranch for a couple of days, but . . . Lena isn't in town, and Mrs. Bolton, well. I'm sure you've heard the stories about Sabrina's mother. She would hover too much."

Yes, Ket had heard stories about Martha Bolton. The woman stood out as a symbol of the weakness of all white-eyes women. Mrs. Bolton had never recovered from the death of Sabrina's twin sister when the girls were three years old.

Apache mothers could teach these weak women valuable lessons about life and loss, but of course white eyes never considered anyone but themselves.

"I don't know how to ask this, Ket," Tremayne was saying. "Sabrina's taken a turn for the worse. Some of it's worrying over Emily, I suppose, but Doc says she could lose the babe if she gets out of bed. I can't leave her alone." He stared steadily into Ket's identical green eyes, his concern for his wife obviously outweighing his own pride. "There's no one else, Ket. No one I could trust to watch over her."

Although his request had not been voiced as a direct question, his appeal was open and honest and desperate. He wanted her to stay with Sabrina while he returned to the ranch.

"A week at the most," he assured her. Then he repeated his earlier claim. "I can't trust anyone else."

Trust. That word again. What did it mean? When Tremayne said he trusted her, what did he mean?

When she told Blake she trusted him, what had she meant? Blake had certainly misinterpreted her meaning, yet Ket was the first to admit she wasn't sure, not even now, what she had meant or why she told Blake he was the only person she could trust.

Trust wasn't something she believed in. Certainly not the sort of trust that would be required if she were to live the rest of her life in his world.

"This isn't a ploy, Ket," Tremayne assured her. "I'm not trying to force you to—"

"I know that." She stirred the stew, thoughtfully considering this request from her father and its implications in her life. He wanted her to stay with Sabrina while he went to the ranch, pure and simple. Nothing more, nothing less. She would be a fool to read meaning where meaning wasn't intended.

"When?" she finally asked.

"Soon as you can." After a while he added, as if further persuasion were necessary, "I know you need to be with Emily. Mrs. Bolton can come once a day to relieve you."

Ket pursed her lips and nodded. She peered into the stew as if she expected the pieces of cooked rabbit meat to take form and jump out of the pot. She was making too much of this request. Far too much. Yet, for the life of her, she couldn't squelch the sense of connectedness this simple request kindled inside her.

She knew better. Angrily she tried to grip her emotions, her expectations. She, who had never entertained expectations in her adult life. She knew better than to trust her heart to one of these people. Even if he was her father.

"I'll wait while you get ready," he offered.

She wanted to tell him to go ahead, that she would follow, but she didn't. And in the end it became easy to be with him, much too easy.

"What'd you want to do with this stew?" he asked when she returned from her shelter. She wore her fox robe and carried a few belongings in the rawhide pannier she had removed from Delgado's dead horse that day outside Fort Davis. She had never shown it to Emily. Emily was burdened with too much pain already. Strangely, Emily had never asked about the raid. What did that mean?

"I made it for Emily," she told her father of the stew.

"I'll dish it up," he offered. "We can drop it by the hospital. What do you carry it in?"

She showed him a covered tin she'd brought from the hospital mess hall. "Do you think Sabrina would like some?" Tremayne didn't glance up, and Ket was grateful. The offer had come unbidden and she had surprised herself.

For the longest time he stood inhaling the aroma from the stew, but was otherwise motionless. After she had given up on his answering, he said, "I'm sure she would love it."

So they left the camp each carrying a tin of rabbit stew. Tremayne stopped by the hospital with her, always a somber task. Today Emily was asleep. Lieutenant Conroy said they could awaken her, but neither had the heart to do so. Ket left the stew for Reba to feed Emily when she returned.

"Send for me if she gets worse." Ket told the medic where to find her.

Tremayne was quieter than usual after they left the hospital. "I'm glad Chi isn't here to watch his daughter die," he said once, beneath his breath.

Ket responded with a nod. Even now, under these stressful circumstances, the mention of Chi Caliente called forth her single image of Emily's parents—the image she had carried in her mind through the years—of the falling rain gently pummeling their entwined bodies. Her earliest memories had been pervaded by an aura of love and peace, both of which she had felt from the beginning in Blake's arms.

But Emily's parents' love had been followed by an epoch of death and destruction, which continued to this day. And Blake had the audacity to ask her to trust him.

How could she trust him? How could she trust any of them?

On the other hand, if death and destruction were inevitable, why not take the chance? Shouldn't she choose a moment of joy over no joy at all?

Even with a white eyes? Even with a Carmichael?

Tremayne carried the remaining tin of stew as they walked the few miles to the house he had taken for his family in Chihuahua. Ket's thoughts turned to Neeta—Neeta, an inevitable warning against trusting the Carmichaels, father or son.

The enigma had weighed on Ket's mind even heavier since she returned from Apache Wells. Looking back, she realized she had thought of little else since she rescued Blake from those Comancheros. Would that she had left him there.

No, she did not wish such a thing. She just wished him

off her mind. He was already out of her life, but that hadn't begun to keep her from thinking about him. She decided it was the curse of her white heritage.

The People never dwelt on the unattainable. Fatalistically, they either dealt with a problem or they left it behind. Yes, Blake Carmichael was definitely a curse wrought by her white heritage.

"Do you think the senator is Neeta's father?" Her question surprised herself. It had come from her subconscious desire to erase from her mind all things pertaining to the Carmichael name.

"More than likely," Tremayne responded tersely, then elaborated. "The bastard had ample opportunity, and he was mean enough. You'd have to have known him in those early days to believe that a *civilized* man, a man with much power in the government, could act so *un*civilized. He was already a drinker and carouser when he arrived here. Even when he was on official duty, he was drunk most of the time. The first time I saw him in action was at the mercantile, Edward Bolton's place. Back then it was called the trading post. Half the building was used as a saloon. Rosa worked for Edward at the saloon while her husband, Manuel, spent most of his time up in the hills tending their flocks."

Tremayne shifted the tin of stew from one hand to the other. "I didn't come to town much back then, didn't get on too well with white eyes, not any of 'em but Nick. I was in the saloon that night to meet with the senator about a peace treaty with the People. Nick had persuaded me to help, but by the time Nick and I arrived, Carmichael was too drunk to parlay. He tried something with Rosa that night, and Edward kicked him out of the house, or tried to. Hell of a fight ensued, followed by the senator threatening to seek a court-martial against Edward. Sabrina knows more about the rest of it than I do. She and Rosa were real close back then. All I know is something happened to Rosa after the senator arrived in town; even before Manuel's death, she was doing poorly."

"Coughing, you mean?"

Tremayne shook his head. "Not that. Had more to do with her spirit, her will to live. Then Manuel turned up murdered, and she was pregnant and she almost lost the babe."

"And they accused you of Manuel's murder."

"Yep."

"And of fathering Neeta."

He turned sad eyes on her. "You heard that one, too?"

She nodded.

"Neither of 'em are true. Both are lies. Carmichael and Jasper were behind those tales. After Nick and I proved that Jasper was the one who gave the orders to raid that village, when you were little and Nalin was . . . Well, after we confronted Jasper with the facts, they let up on the rumors. Everyone figured it was mostly jealousy. Sabrina was expected to marry Jasper, not some renegade white man like me."

"What do you think? Was it jealousy?"

"Lon Jasper doesn't have a heart to get broken. I reckon it could've been his pride, though. As far as Carmichael . . . his kind shouldn't be allowed to walk this good earth."

Ket didn't know what to say. She had considered talking to her father about Blake; she certainly needed advice. Tremayne knew more about those early days around here than just about anybody. And he was fair. Regardless that he had abandoned her, she knew he was a fair man, considered so by both white eyes and the People.

Now that he had expressed his animosity toward the senator, she wasn't sure how to approach the topic of the senator's son. As it turned out, Tremayne did it for her.

"Luke and Tres think you went off somewhere with that . . . what's his name? Carmichael's son."

His remark took her by surprise. "What do you mean?"

"Couple of days last week, nobody could find you," he prompted. As if she needed reminding! "Luke and Tres consider themselves quite the detectives. I was anxious about your absence, thought you might have returned to the Apachería. When you weren't there, Luke and Tres came up with some cockamamie story—"

"You went to the Apachería looking for me?" The idea was astonishing. It struck a chord somewhere in the soul of Ket's lost childhood. *Why now?* she wanted to cry. *Why did you wait so late?*

"Sure I went to find you." He sounded as if he had looked after her all her life.

Her defenses up, she replied sharply. "What exactly did Luke and Tres say?"

"They said you and what's-his-name went off—"

"Blake," she supplied, aggravated by his offhanded treatment. How dare he come into her life at such a late date and start taking control! "His name is Blake."

"Blake? Well, they said Edward told them this, uh, Blake took off for parts unknown and left his supplies at the mercantile for a couple days. Those boys figured the two of you went off somewhere together."

She couldn't deny it. She wouldn't. Why should she? She owed Tremayne absolutely nothing. Was this what it meant to be trusted? She wanted to ask him that but resisted for reasons related entirely to self-preservation. "Luke and Tres spent a few frightening days with Blake. According to them, he kept the Comancheros from killing them. He's their hero." She left out the part about *them* setting *her* cap for Blake Carmichael.

"They're just boys," Tremayne excused. "They'll grow up, shed those foolish notions."

"Foolish?"

"Stupid might better characterize anyone who put their trust in a Carmichael."

"Like father, like son?"

"You bet, Ket. That's why I didn't put any stock in what those boys dreamed up. When you decide to trust us white eyes, you won't pick a loser to start off with."

Start trusting white eyes! For the next two days Ket stewed over Tremayne's fateful statement. When had he set himself up to judge someone for foolish encounters? That took nerve, coming from one who had fallen under the spell of a redheaded demon. But she held her tongue until he left for the ranch.

Not once during the next week did Sabrina intrude on Ket's time or on her privacy. Indeed, she continually expressed gratitude to Ket for coming to her aid.

"This rabbit stew is wonderful, Ket," she complimented.

Ket had waited until Tremayne left for the ranch to heat the stew. Not even after he showed her how to build a fire in the newfangled iron cook stove in the kitchen would she put the stew on. She figured he took time to explain the contraption to her because he wanted a bowl of stew.

It was childish, she knew, but she wasn't about to share her culinary skills with him, not after the way he'd tried to take control of her life.

"Your coffee is perfect," Sabrina complimented the following morning when Ket brought a cup to her stepmother's bed. "Your father likes his to stand by itself without a cup, but I prefer mine just like this."

Ket assured herself she would not be taken in by all this civility. Not that she considered Sabrina insincere. In truth, she tried not to regard Sabrina at all, but for Emily's sake she endured the vivacious woman whose radiance seemed to be returning daily.

Sabrina's vivaciousness was contagious in a way; not that Ket went about with unbridled abandonment, that wasn't her nature. But as the days passed, her intolerance of her stepmother waned.

Feeling less threatened, she recalled her father's claim that Sabrina knew more about the Rosa Raméríz and Senator Carmichael affair than anyone else. Her father had been too hardheaded to keep an open mind, but Sabrina might be more forthcoming.

Even though, as she feared, she was setting herself up for disappointment, she had to talk to someone about Blake. She hadn't been able to forget his distress when she rejected his feelings for her.

Proud, he had called her, saying she was too proud to accept the white half of her heritage. Was it pride that kept her from returning Blake's love?

Or was it fear?

Those questions haunted Ket. By birth she was half white, but by upbringing she was all Apache. How could she abandon her people, especially now in what could prove to be their final hours?

On the other hand, she couldn't deny the depth of her feelings for Blake Carmichael. Guiltily she ran through the list of objections she had to him—his race, his culture, his family.

Blake had admitted it. He was too white, too civilized, too everything Ket had hated most of her life—and hated still, she assured herself.

By contrast, the list in Blake's defense was dreadfully short. Basically it contained but one item—he wasn't a soldier. For most of her life the white-eyes soldier had topped her list of evil persons. And still did, of course.

Still, she couldn't dismiss the feelings she had for Blake, guilty as she felt even thinking about them. He made her feel strong and needy at the same time. He made her feel giddy and serene at the same time. He made her feel valued, she who had never felt valued. He made her feel needed, wanted, good, right. He made her feel loved.

Nothing about it was right, though. Everything was wrong. Even her father said so. Her father, who had never cared enough to give her advice. Now, when his opinion was most needed and when it should be most valued, she resented him for offering it. She had to fight herself not to reject it out of hand.

So with confusion muddling her mind and uncertainty gnawing in her belly, she decided that the only thing left for her was to approach Sabrina.

After dinner one evening, she lit the lamps and sat in the upholstered rocker her father had brought to town from the ranch. To rock a baby in, Ket assumed. Without fanfare she blurted out the question.

"Tremayne said you knew Rosa before Neeta was born."

Sabrina, to give her credit, showed no sign of surprise. Her smile came easily. "Oh, my, yes. Rosa and I were close friends. She's a bit older than me, and she was certainly wiser in the ways of the world. She'd been married ten or more years by the time I met her. My mother was . . . well, Mama wasn't exactly a person one could turn to with questions all girls have about life, so I turned to Rosa quite a bit."

"Was it the senator?" Ket asked. "Did the senator father Neeta?"

Sabrina studied her solemnly before responding. "Your father did not."

"That isn't why I'm asking. I want to know if Senator Carmichael is as bad as everyone says."

Again Sabrina took her time before replying. "He's probably a lot worse than anyone suspects."

Ket drew a sharp breath and held it. When Sabrina patted the covers near her in invitation, Ket moved to the bed without consciously deciding to sit beside her stepmother. The ominous tone Sabrina had used to speak of the senator filled Ket with dread. How could she ask something that might give away her feelings for Blake?

"If this is about Blake Carmichael," Sabrina began sagely, "that's a story with a different twist."

Ket felt her face flush. Was she so easy to read? "What makes you think I want to know anything about him?" Even though she was sure her defensiveness sounded in her voice, Sabrina smiled gently.

"Because I was young once, too. Young and in love with the wrong man."

"You've told me that. This is different."

"I doubt it. Maybe the details aren't the same, but the feelings . . . ah, those feelings are universal." Sabrina smiled broadly. "Your father was definitely the wrong man for me. You should have heard the gossip. No one was on my side. Not even my father, who had always been my rock. Papa didn't dislike Tremayne, but he did not approve of him for my husband."

"Then how . . . I mean . . ." Unaccustomed to sharing confidences, Ket was completely ignorant of what to say next. Strangely, she felt more secure discussing such a personal matter with someone she had disliked for so long. Sabrina's approval had never mattered to her, so if she shocked her, what could it matter?

Although Ket had never confided in anyone in her life, Sabrina seemed able to read her mind. "How did I convince them? I didn't try. The major obstacle, besides the senator's threats to court-martial Doc Henry if I didn't marry Lon Jasper, was your father himself."

"Papa?"

"He didn't think I could survive life out here."

"Blake is accomplished. He probably would have managed to save himself and the boys from the Comancheros if I hadn't come along. It's me. I'm . . ."

"You're afraid you couldn't live in this world." It was a statement of fact, and it startled Ket.

"How did you know?"

"I married your father, dear. He used to climb the walls in that cabin at Apache Wells. That's why our house at the ranch is so . . ." Her words trailed off, as both women thought the same thought.

Ket had never seen her father's house at the ranch. Sabrina recovered quickly, in that easy way she had.

"We have a lot of open spaces," she said lightly. "High ceilings, mostly rock walls. A lot of glass, even though it was dreadfully expensive." She smiled inwardly. "The house looks like part of the hillside," she added. "Like it grew there rather than was built by man."

"How did you persuade Papa?"

This time Sabrina did not hang her head. She held Ket's gaze for a long time before saying simply, "It's true, what I told you. I heard the laughter."

Neither of them moved for the longest time. Ket wanted to deny Sabrina's claim, as she had the first time Sabrina mentioned the guardian of the well. But what if it turned out to be true? What if the guardian of the well was her own grandmother—her *white-eyes* grandmother?

"What if he's like his father?" Ket finally asked.

"That's a much tougher question. No one would want you involved with a man like the senator."

The statement was so true it required no response. Then Sabrina surprised her with a twist that Ket had not heretofore considered.

"What if he isn't?"

Again Ket had no answer, but this time she felt as if a heavy weight had been lifted from her shoulders. "I would have to be sure."

"We would all want to be sure," Sabrina replied.

Ket felt no animosity toward this woman for implying that the Tremaynes had a say in her life.

"Have you spoken with your father about this?"

Sabrina's question brought a return of her defensiveness. "He spoke to me. He said he knew Luke and Tres were wrong, that when I decided to trust a white eyes I was too smart to start with a Carmichael."

"Oh, my." Sabrina sighed. "That sounds like a father."

"Well, it's too late for him to start acting like one," Ket retorted. This was a topic she had no desire to discuss, but Sabrina pressed on.

"Emotions are strange things, Ket. You can fight them, but you usually don't win. Take your father. There hasn't been much communication between the two of you, but that doesn't mean he hasn't always loved you."

Ket kept her seat against all instincts to jump up and run from the room.

"He's kept up with everything you've done through your relatives at the Apachería and through Nick and Lena. He never stopped loving you or caring about you. He has always considered you his daughter, and his business."

Still Ket sat, stiff and unrelenting. The conversation had taken too personal a turn. She wouldn't endure much more . . .

"It's the same way with all relationships," Sabrina suggested. "Your feelings for Blake Carmichael won't go away just because he's a white eyes or even because he's a Carmichael. If they're real, if you've really fallen in love with him, you will always be in love with him."

Ket lifted stricken eyes to Sabrina. *So what do I do about it?* she wanted to cry.

"Sometimes, Ket, you have to trust yourself."

"Trust myself?" The weight that had lifted from her at Apache Wells had been gradually descending upon her since her return. Now with Sabrina's admonition it fell like a mountain over her back.

Trust herself? She didn't even *know* herself.

"You need time to discover how strong your feelings for Blake really are. If your feelings for Blake are strong, and if you give yourself time to get to know what kind of man he is, then you'll have to allow yourself to take a chance. If you don't allow yourself to be wrong, you may miss out on the most important things in life."

Their conversation was interrupted when Reba Applebee arrived with the suggestion that she and Ket change places for a while. Ket grasped at the chance to escape this conversation, even though she had initiated it. She needed to be alone. Time to think.

But on her walk to the fort, she found herself thinking more about Sabrina than about either Blake or her cousin Emily. She had never had anyone to confide in, never had someone to give her advice.

Her people were too busy fighting to save their way of life to fret over matters of the heart, she reasoned, trying to stoke the anger that had burned inside her for so long. But the coals of her anger had banked, and she couldn't help but wonder whether she had been wrong about Sabrina. Her dimly held vision had been formed by a sick child in a dimly lit cabin. Until lately she had never seen Sabrina in the full light of day.

Certainly she had never thought of her as a person, as a woman who could give advice and counsel. As a woman who could love and be worthy of being loved.

Emily had rallied by the time Ket arrived, so she fed her cousin a bowl of leek soup from the hospital mess hall and tried to make light conversation. Ket wasn't good at conversation, but she tried.

"You should have seen him fishing in the pond," she told Emily. "He is very inventive. He found an old clay jar, you know, the kind with holes all around the sides, used for drying herbs. He put the fish he caught in there and sank them in the water. Isn't that resourceful?"

"Did you eat the fish?" Emily asked.

"No, we got into an argument."

"What happened to the fish?"

Ket shrugged. "I'm sure he would have poured them back in the creek."

"That would show compassion," Emily offered. "You must have seen compassion in him."

"Perhaps I saw fear," she retorted. "Perhaps he's like everyone else, afraid of the guardian."

"Who's afraid of the guardian? She's a good spirit."

"Those who hear her laugh think so." Ket related some of her conversation with Sabrina, just enough to reassure her cousin that she was following her wishes.

"I'm glad you two have become friends."

To say that she and Sabrina had become friends was going too far, but Ket did not deny her cousin the pleasure of thinking it true.

By the time Tremayne rode back into town at the end of the week, Ket had to admit that she and Sabrina had made progress, thanks to Sabrina's common-sense approach to her difficulty with Blake.

"Take your time. Don't rush it. Get to know him."

Sabrina was right. Only by getting to know Blake would she be able to judge the situation accurately. That decided, her plans began to settle down. Maybe she shouldn't go to Mexico with the People. She realized that Blake was partially right. She was half white. Perhaps she owed herself the chance to explore her Anglo heritage.

Most importantly, she was not ready to die, and from every indication, that was what would happen to the People in Mexico. As guilty as she felt for thinking it, with so many of her friends and relatives having given their lives to satisfy the white eyes' greed for land, she was not ready to die. She felt even guiltier for something else.

Lately, she had begun to wonder whether she could adjust to the white-eyes' world.

Her father had adjusted. Her father, who had been reared by the People, had not abandoned them, as she had believed, or tried to persuade herself to believe. Neither had he abandoned his Anglo heritage. Curiosity about her father's people had begun to creep into her cynicism and disavowal.

She was at Rosa's house when Neeta arrived with news

that Tremayne and the boys had returned. Sabrina had sent her there with a quart of broth for her old friend.

"Maybe it will cheer Rosa up, dear, knowing we haven't forgotten her. And your broth will surely improve her health. I know it has mine."

Ket doubted that her broth had anything to do with it, but Sabrina was like that. In a week's time she had begun the slow task of erasing the pain of the past ten years. For the first time in her life, Ket began to see a future that included her stepmother—and her father, too, if he wouldn't try to control her life.

Cautious not to expect too much from this fledgling relationship, she nonetheless realized that a frightening sense of hope was taking hold inside her. Could the future be better than the past?

That thought always brought more guilt, for the future was dark and hopeless for the People. How could she abandon them?

"*¡Señorita Ket, Señorita Ket, andale!* Come quick. Señor Tremayne is bringing my new goat!"

"No wonder they call her Goat Girl," Rosa sighed.

"She's a fine girl, Rosa. See how she cares for you?" Eager to be off, Ket nevertheless took time to see that Rosa was settled in. "Do you want me to stay until Neeta returns with her goat?"

"Oh, no, niña. I am fine. Thank Sabrina for me. She is such a comfort. I don't know what I would have done without her through the years."

"She feels the same way about you." Ket was sorely tempted to sit down right there and ask questions, but she would not be so thoughtless. Even if Rosa knew anything that would separate Blake's reputation from his fathers', Ket would have to learn it from another source.

"If you're sure you're all right," she said, "I'll be on my way. I'll see that Neeta returns soon."

By the time she reached the Tremayne yard, Luke and Tres had spotted her. "Ket, we want to ask you something."

"What now?" she challenged.

"Can we have that travois you made?"

"No."

"Please, Ket. Since Emily won't go back to the Apachería, what use do you have for it?"

"A better question is what use do you have for it? It belongs to me."

"Well . . ." Luke glanced at Tres. "You tell her."

"We thought we might strap you on it and carry you out to the rail site."

"What?"

"Figured ol' Blake is probably lonely for you, and since Papa's so against you marryin' him—"

"Marry? Who said anything about me marrying anyone?"

The boys glanced toward the house. For the first time, Ket realized that an argument was in progress. Tremayne's voice would have trumpeted his displeasure to anyone passing on the road. Fortunately, at the moment the road was clear.

"I'll say it again, Sabrina, and for the last time. No daughter of mine will marry a Carmichael."

Chapter Ten

"Halt right there, Miz Ket." The corporal stepped into the roadway, blocking her path. Beyond him Ket saw an old rock stage building. Further along, a jumbled collection of army tents dotted the frosty landscape.

After overhearing her father's ill-timed ultimatum, she had fled to her rock shelter where she spent a restless night trying to come to terms with this new hurt.

Would she never learn? Was she so desperate for a family that she had allowed herself to believe she had one? How dare that man who had abandoned and betrayed her appear suddenly out of nowhere and assume he knew what was best for her?

She didn't even know what was best for her. Come morning, however, she had made up her mind to show her white-eyes father that he could not control her life.

Arising early, she had put out her fire, wrapped herself in her fox pelt robe, and dusted frost off the palomino. Unsure exactly where the rail site was, she had followed the road to El Paso as if headed for the Apachería.

Now, four hours later, it was near noon. Sunlight sparkled from the few remaining patches of frost. Melting ice dripped from tree branches.

"State your purpose, Miz Ket. Cain't have no wild one comin' in an' wreckin' things."

Grittily holding her temper in check, Ket studied the collection of tents. They resembled an Apache village, except that these structures weren't large enough to live in, nor were they made to last.

"My purpose is with Blake Carmichael. Is this where I find him?"

" 'Fore I tell you, which side of you wants to know?"

"Which what?" Ket's patience was nearing its end.

"Which side o' you?" he prodded. "Your white side or your Injun side?"

She glared at him, offended but not surprised by the comment. "I have come to see Blake Carmichael on personal business." When he remained reluctant to let her pass, she added, "From Fort Davis." That did the trick.

"Well, then, I suppose it's all right." He glanced back over his shoulder. "That there's Carmichael's tent, the far one, off by itself. He ain't connected to the railroad building. He's surveying for his old man, and he's already out in the field. I suppose you could wait for him, but you oughta leave your weapons with me."

She ignored the last two suggestions. "I'll go on to the field, if you will direct me."

"Well, now, Miz Ket, I don't rightly see—"

"Don't rile me, Corporal." She shifted about, moving her rifle from beneath her fox robe. "I've ridden four hours in freezing weather, and I'm prepared to ride as far as it takes. Where is this field?"

Backing off, the corporal eyed her rifle, then relented. "Off down that draw. If you reach Bass Canyon, might as well turn around, you've gone too far."

Fifteen minutes later, she found Blake where the corporal had said. The draw cut through the hills to the south of where the tracks would run, then opened onto a plain. Blake didn't see her emerge from the draw, and she took the opportunity to watch him unobserved.

He wore the heavy shearling coat he had worn at Apache Wells, its collar turned up against the weather. The memory of him opening that coat to her did strange things to her stomach. But even as anticipation swelled, she wondered how he would react to her coming here. After the way they'd left things at Apache Wells, he might not want to see her again. Hadn't he said he was through?

She kicked the palomino and proceeded toward him slowly. Intent on his work, he didn't look up immediately, and she thought to tease him about that. No wonder the Comancheros had captured him. She knew, of course, that he wasn't being as careless as it seemed. She approached from the direction of the campsite, which, as she had learned, was well guarded, especially while that corporal remained on duty.

By the time he looked around, she was close enough to see the astonishment on his face.

"Ket? Where'd you come from?" It was in his voice, too—utter astonishment. He looked like he'd seen an apparition. A thrill raced up her spine, pleasure at having taken him by surprise.

"The fort." She tried to make it sound as if she rode out to see him every day of the week.

He didn't step toward her. Rather, he rested crossed arms over his tripod and studied her. "Don't reckon you're lost?"

"Don't reckon." The sun shone through the cold air chilling her skin. Her mouth was dry. Inside she was hot—and nervous.

Blake removed his hat and dried his forehead with a sleeve, more a gesture than anything, for the weather was far too cold for anyone to perspire. Still, he didn't take his eyes off her. His expression was intense, and it made her glad she had come. Then he frowned as if he'd just thought of something bad.

"What's wrong? Did something happen to Emily?"

The question surprised her. She wouldn't have come to him if Emily had died. On the other hand, the idea was entirely reasonable. She knew without doubt that he would be a person she could come to for comfort.

"Emily is no worse," she told him.

"Then what—?"

"Nothing. I came . . . I came to see you."

He grinned, and she could tell he was pleased. But she'd learned nothing if not that this man possessed an inquiring mind. She watched the inevitable questions form.

"Just like that?" he challenged lightly. He still stood with his arms crossed over the tripod. She still sat her horse. "You rode four hours through this cold just to see me?"

She felt out of her depth. Seduction wasn't second nature to her. In fact, she had no idea how to proceed. The last time they were together, she had rejected him. What if he now rejected her?

That would ruin her plan to show her father that she and she alone controlled her life. When Blake stepped around the tripod, she held her breath.

A slow grin spread across his face. "Well, then, you might as well climb down."

His blue gaze held her enthralled and went a long way toward settling her doubts. He held out his arms, and she slid off the back of the palomino and into them.

Thoughts vanished. Emotions raced madly through her, joy, expectancy, desire. Relief was present, too—relief that he had not rejected her, that he had not tried to send her back to the fort.

He held her against his heavy coat, and she held him, although her arms could not span the sheepskin-padded breadth of him. He touched his cold lips to hers, and a fire ignited in her belly. The kiss lingered and was wet and hot—so hot it could melt the frost on the ground. He was the first to pull away. When she opened her eyes, it was to that quizzical expression again.

"What?" she asked, breathing into his lips.

"Why'd you come, Ket?"

"I wanted to." Her response seemed enough, for he kissed her softly, before again setting her aside.

"Let me wrap things up here, and we'll head back to the site. Get out of this miserable cold."

She felt anything but miserable. "Show me how to help you." She saw in an instant she had pleased him.

"Sure thing."

It took an hour or more, during which time she forgot about her plan to seduce him and was herself seduced by him—by this white eyes and his work and his nearness.

Her whole life had been spent outdoors, and she loved having worthwhile work to do, even in the cold. She had never seen a surveyor at work, and she was impressed by Blake's expertise, not to mention by the man himself.

"A livery man from St. Louis bought this site," he explained. After he handed her a bundle of wooden stakes and a measuring rod, he returned to the tripod that held some strange sort of spyglass. He peered through the lens, motioning her this way, motioning her that way, until he was satisfied. Then he instructed her to plant a wooden stake, while he recorded something—numbers, she later learned—with a stubby pencil in a book he carried in his jacket pocket. After each notation he directed her to another place, and they repeated the process.

"That'll be the northeast corner," he explained once. They measured and staked four corners; then he called a stop. "Let's pack up and head for home."

Home. Her heart skipped, and she knew it wouldn't be hard to seduce this man. Doubts swept swiftly through her mind, then vanished. Although she wouldn't want to tell him why she had changed her mind about making love, she was certain he would be pleased.

On the ride back to the rail site, cobwebs cleared from her enraptured brain, and she was struck by the reality of what she had helped him do. "I don't like what we did back there."

"What?"

"Marking off plots for white eyes to claim. The land can't be bought and sold. It doesn't belong to you or to your father, or to your government. It belongs only to the Great Spirit. Land is a part of all life. It is to be used by everyone."

"I understand, Ket. But this is how things work."

She shook her head. "Those stakes mark off land my people have used for longer than the old ones know."

"*Half* your people," he responded quickly. When she glanced to see his expression, he was looking across the distance between their horses, staring at her with a solemn expression. "That makes it hard. Half your people fighting the other half."

She turned away.

"It isn't the first time, Ket, and it won't be the last. Since the beginning of the world, men have been barging in and taking other men's land. Half of mankind is the pursuer, the other half the pursued. It isn't right, but it isn't really wrong, either. There's no right or wrong. It just happens."

"That's easy to say when you're on the taking side."

"I know." They had reached the old stage station, and Blake guided his horse to the hitching rail. "Don't blame me for this. If it weren't me out there marking off plots, it'd be someone else. And if it weren't happening, I wouldn't be here with you."

"I didn't come to talk about these things." She regretted

saying that, but he didn't pursue the topic. Instead he dismounted.

"Let's go inside, see what ol' Charley's cooked up today."

At first Blake had thought her an apparition, a summer nymph conjured by his frozen brain. One minute he was immersed in his work, the next he looked up to find her coming toward him wrapped in that fiery fox pelt robe, riding her proud palomino stallion. He watched, half expecting her to vanish into the icy air.

His first thought was that he loved her. Damn his soul if he didn't love her. The sight of her warmed him like no fire could have done. He loved her, this wild woman who would never be tamed.

Her fox pelt robe shone with a rare brilliance in the chilled air. He recalled its softness. He recalled her softness.

He recalled her rejection. Had she come to recant? To say she had set away her fears and was ready to give them a chance? That would be the answer to his prayers, but experience told him that prayers weren't answered that easily.

It had been little over a week since they left Apache Wells by separate trails. What could have happened in so short a time to change her mind?

What could have happened . . . ? He could tell that something was wrong with her. Even after she assured him that Emily was no worse, he had trouble believing that she had come solely to see him. He couldn't squelch his skepticism.

Something was wrong. He could feel it.

When they drew rein at the stage station, she decided to wait on her horse while he went inside to order a pail of Charley's daily fare, which turned out to be *carne guisado*, in plain English a thick beef stew, and a dozen tortillas.

"Who's that you left out there in the cold?" Charley wanted to know, peering through a smudged spot in the windowpane.

"Friend," Blake replied tersely. "We'll eat at my tent."

His tent was not equipped for entertaining visitors. No table, no chairs. One single cot, a canvas floor, and thankfully a pot-bellied stove vented through a flue in the roof. First thing Blake did, coming in, was to light the stove. He motioned her to sit on the cot.

"Make yourself at home. It'll get warm in no time."

Ket wandered about, which required no more than a few steps in any direction. "I thought you said you lived at that stage station."

"I did until the soldiers came out to protect us. They had a tent left over and I claimed it. It's actually warmer than that old station with all the chinks out of the walls."

They sat on the cot to eat, side by side, warming their innards with Charley's stew. This close to Ket, Blake didn't figure he needed stew or even a pot-bellied stove to keep him warm. His heart pumped pure heat through his veins, the result of all those pent-up, unrequited expectations.

"It isn't very large," she commented once.

She appeared more captivated by his living quarters than by him, he thought, finding that more strange than offensive.

Why had she come?

"These tents are for enlisted men. They're designed to hold two, three men at most."

"What is this cloth?"

"Canvas," he told her. "Treated with oil to make it water resistant." She hadn't come all the way out here in the cold to check out his living conditions. He started to tell her that, but he didn't.

She was here. That was the important thing. She had come all the way out here in the cold to see him. The reason didn't matter.

Why couldn't he believe that?

By the time they finished eating, the tent had heated up considerably. Blake stashed their plates in a pan under the stove. He took off his coat and hung it on a peg, and turned to her, a hand outstretched.

She understood, and he watched her shuck her fox pelt robe. But when he reached to take it, it fell to the floor and she came into his arms. His body heat climbed by double digits.

His lips took hers and hers were open and wet and eager, like always. And like always this reminder of her wetness surged through him. He had never wanted a woman as badly for as long.

What did it matter why she had come? She was here, in his arms—in *his* lair this time, and this time they would carry this project through to the fulfillment he craved. Without breaking lip contact, he scooped her in his arms and carried her to the cot.

"I've been dreaming about you holed up in your shelter," he mumbled, depositing her on the cot, "wrapped in that fur. I'd rather have you right here"—he unbuckled her belt and slipped her deerskin shirt over her head— "in my arms."

Quickly settling alongside her, he pulled her close and absorbed the insidious jolt of her breasts settling against him.

She snuggled into him. "You've been dreaming about some other woman," she said lightly. "Except for last night, I haven't been in the shelter."

Her banter pleased him. Yet it baffled him, too. It wasn't her style. "No? Where've you been?" His lips found her breast, and he knew this encounter would of necessity be all too brief.

"I've been staying with Sabrina."

"Sabrina?"

"Tremayne asked me to stay with her while he took care of things at the ranch."

Tremayne? Last time they were together, she'd called the man Papa. "How'd it go?"

"Better than I expected. She was ... I've never had a woman to talk to."

This was better, he thought. Now they were getting somewhere. "Ah, girl talk," he mumbled against her other breast.

She sighed, and he felt her swell seductively into his mouth. His passion built quickly to excruciating levels. He lifted his face to hers, partially an attempt to prolong his response time, partially from a startling curiosity. "Tell me, what did those girls talk about?"

"You," she told him without the slightest bit of self-consciousness.

It was one of the many reasons he loved this wild woman. She was fresh, devoid of the games so many women played. He shed his shirt, then his pants. Clad only in longjohns, he drew her closer.

But his brain worried with the problem. He wouldn't have expected Sabrina Tremayne to help his cause. Then again, Ket was here in his arms.

But why? There it was again, that persistent nagging thought—why had she come all the way out here in the cold? With his hand against her skin, the word *cold* sounded like something spoken in a foreign language.

"The way we left things at Apache Wells," he told her honestly, "I'm surprised you wanted to speak my name, especially to Sabrina."

"I didn't start out to talk about you," she admitted. "I asked about Rosa and Neeta."

He wasn't anxious to bring that up again. "I can guess where I fit into that conversation."

"Sabrina mentioned you. At first I was furious that she would pry into my life, but she didn't try to give me advice, not really. She understands. She said that when she was young she had fallen in love with the wrong man, too.''

Blake wasn't sure he had heard her right. His hand stilled on the soft curve of her buttocks. His heart leaped to his throat. "In love with the wrong man?" he finally managed.

Ket snuggled closer. "No one in Sabrina's family accepted Tremayne. But ... Sabrina said they, she and Tremayne, couldn't help it. They tried to stay apart, but they couldn't.''

Blake wasn't interested in Sabrina and Tremayne. His heart skipped a beat at Ket's words. *Young and in love. Ket loved him!*

"She didn't give you any advice?''

"Well, some. She said no one would want me involved with a man like the senator, but that I should give myself time to learn the truth. That I should trust my feelings.''

There it was, her reason for coming all the way out here in this freezing weather. "You aren't afraid anymore?''

"I'm still afraid,'' she admitted. "Sabrina said Tremayne had a hard time adjusting to the white-eyes' world. She said living in a house was hard for him.''

"Hmm, it would be. Do you want to try?''

She answered honestly, as he was certain she always would. "I don't know yet.''

"Sabrina is wise,'' he whispered into her hair. "We'll give it time.'' But even as he spoke of time, his body warned him he was running out—at least for this encounter. Conscious of Ket's fear when he tried to remove her britches in the rock shelter, he was a bit surprised, although greatly relieved, when she assisted him this time. Working together, their hands scrunched the soft deerskin down around her knees. Then he was lost.

For a moment caught in time he stared at her. Light filtered through the canvas and seemed to glow from the smooth dark skin on her mounded breasts. Bending low, he took one darker nipple in his mouth and felt her contract in rhythm with his own throbbing heart, his own desire.

He trailed hot lips across her taut midsection, where he kissed her belly button, then her belly . . .

Lifting his face, he absorbed the beauty of her. Her lithe but muscular thighs, a dark patch of . . .

His fingers sifted through the curls. He watched light glimmer from the wet strands . . .

She was so beautiful it took his breath, so inviting, nothing like the frightened woman in the dark rock shelter.

The compassion he had felt for her swelled with his own rising passion. Conscious of not causing her undue embarrassment, he reached for a blanket before removing her britches the rest of the way.

"Need some cover?' he asked lightly.

"No." He watched her eyes dart toward her leg. He felt her tremors, saw terror flash across her face. She tried to smile, to erase the fear, but it didn't work. "Yes . . . please."

Compassion won out. "We don't have to do this, Ket. We can wait."

"No."

"At least for dark?" he suggested.

"No. Now. I have to . . ."

"You have to what?"

"Get back to town." Her eyes were filled with genuine fear.

"Emily?" he asked softly.

"No."

Now it was he who knew fear. Something was wrong with this perfect setting.

"Then what?"

She turned her head away, closing her eyes.

"What, Ket?" No longer was this the perfect setting. Fear did something to a man's libido, especially when that fear was somehow wrapped up in his whole future.

"What the hell's going on?" he asked when she refused to either answer or look at him. "Last time you wouldn't remove your clothing in that dark rock shelter. Today you're willing to let me see your leg in full daylight, even if you die from the fright of it."

When she flinched at his accusation, he knew he was right. "What's going on?"

"Nothing. I . . . I thought you wanted—"

"Damn right I want you. I've wanted you for weeks. I wanted you in the shelter, but I didn't take you."

She pursed her lips and looked like he might have struck her.

"I wanted you at Apache Wells. Hell, I thought you took me out there to make love."

"You did?"

"Damned right I did. So don't go asking me if I want you. That's a fact." Taking her hand suddenly, he closed it around his swollen evidence. "Feel how much I want you?"

As quickly as he had taken her hand, he released it and jumped to his feet. In the far corner of the small tent he stood facing the canvas, letting the cold air that seeped through it cool his body. His breath came hard and painful.

When he felt her touch his back, he flinched. "What's going on, Ket? What suddenly made you pretend to have all that courage?"

"Tremayne."

The word was spoken so softly he had to strain to hear. He didn't understand.

"What about Tremayne?"

"Sabrina said he's acting like a father. But it's too late."

Turning, Blake took her by the shoulders. Strangely he didn't even notice her bare breasts or that her britches were pulled up but remained unlaced. "Too late for what?"

"For him to control my life."

It took a few more questions for Blake to get the complete story, and afterwards he realized that today's tryst had ended like those before it, before it had ever really begun. He kissed her tenderly on the lips.

"Put your clothes on, Ket."

"My clothes?"

"If we make love today, Tremayne will be convinced that I'm just like those rumors about my father. It's called seduction."

"You said this wasn't wrong."

He remembered telling her that. "This is different," he said now. "When you do it for the wrong reasons, it's wrong. It's no better than what happened to Rosa."

"This is nothing like that."

Hearing the pain in her voice, he couldn't help but take her in his arms. "You'll have to find some other way to get back at Tremayne for abandoning you when you were ten years old, Ket. You can't do it in my bed."

She didn't understand. He should have known she wouldn't.

"I thought it would be all right because you would want it—"

"I told you this has nothing to do with want. I take that back, it has everything to do with what I want. I want us to have a future together, or at least the chance to see if we want a future together. I don't intend to ruin that by playing games."

When she lifted her face, tears glistened in her eyes. "I wanted it for more."

"I know. So did I. So *do* I. But right now there are a lot more desperate matters. We'll find a way to handle this, Ket. Go on back to town. Take care of Emily. I'll be in in a few days. Maybe I can meet Tremayne."

"You don't have to do that."

"Sooner or later I do."

When she demurred, he added, "I'm not giving up on

you, Ket. I'm not giving up on us. I told you before, I love you. You're the first woman I've ever said that to. I've never been in love before, and I'm not about to let you get away from me.''

Chapter Eleven

Even bundled in her fox robe, Ket thought she might freeze on the ride back to Fort Davis. Snuggled into her robe, most of the cold came from inside her, where confusion reigned.

She would never understand white eyes, Blake Carmichael least of all.

"I love you, Ket," he had said. And she believed him. She was terrified of love. She always had been. Then he had compounded the issue by adding, "I'm not about to let you get away from me."

What did that mean? Never let her get away? It sounded like another trap. At best an ultimatum.

Like Tremayne's. *No daughter of mine will ever marry a Carmichael.*

That was the trouble with white eyes. They wanted to own things—land, people. With people they called it love, but it amounted to the same thing—control.

Tremayne had loved her, yet he abandoned her. Now he had come back, wanting to control her life.

Blake loved her so much he vowed to never let her get away from him. Already she felt trapped.

Riding swiftly, she inhaled deep drafts of the cold air. Ahead of her rose the majestic Davis Mountains. They were beautiful, yet inside them was the fort where Emily lay wounded; where Ket must bide her time inside the confines of the white-eyes' buildings. The thought suffocated her.

Behind her lay the wide-open spaces of the land she loved. She was tempted to turn around and run from these white eyes who seemed bent on capturing her.

Never let you get away . . . She felt like a prisoner already, caught in a vicious fight with white eyes trying to own her, control her, take away her freedom. Maybe she should go to Mexico with the People, after all.

At the fort she went directly to the hospital, and as so often happened, the distress in her own life became unimportant. Although the hour was late, she found Reba keeping vigil at Emily's bedside.

"The surgeon finally arrived today," Reba whispered when Ket entered the darkened room.

"Did he operate?" By this time she had reached the bed. Lowering her face, she listened and was relieved to detect breathing—shallow, raspy, but breathing.

"He didn't leave us with much hope, Ket."

The room was cold; the only light came from a kerosene lamp on a table across the room. A circle of light clung around the lamp, but most of the room was in darkness. The odor of kerosene hung in the cold air and was both unfamiliar and unpleasant.

"Did he remove the bullet?"

"Yes, but it had been in there so long, he said the infection . . . is bad."

"He took too long to get here." A slow, hot rage had begun to build inside Ket and accentuated the distress she had already felt coming into this room.

This was what allowing white eyes to love you always

meant—death. Destruction of a person, of a way of life, of a People. While she struggled with these inner fears, Reba rounded the bed and took her in her arms.

"It has meant so much to Emily to have you here," she whispered. "And to me, too. Sabrina was right, you girls needed each other. I'm so glad Emily had you at the . . . end."

"It isn't the end," Ket objected. "You've been here all day and you're exhausted. Go home and get some rest. I'll stay the night."

Reba glanced down at Emily, who had yet to rouse from the chloroform the doctor had given her during the surgery and the laudanum he'd given her afterward. "I hate to leave her for even a moment."

"I know. But you need rest, too. I'll send for you at the slightest change."

For the next forty-eight hours Emily held on, with either Ket or her adopted mother or father, often all three of them, by her side. Although she regained consciousness, it wasn't the lucid sort of awareness that would allow conversation, so when Ket spoke, it was as much to herself as to her cousin. She tried to keep anger from her voice, mindful that angry feelings would not be conducive to recovery. She mopped Emily's brow with wet cloths and sponged her body to keep the fever down.

Nothing worked.

Although Emily was often fretful, crying out in delirium, not once did she call for her birth parents. Not once did she utter an Apache word. Hour after hour, Emily called to the white eyes who reared her. Only her world here lived in her consciousness, only these people, they who had murdered her mother and father, and ultimately Emily herself.

The night she died, Ket was alone with her. It was late, well past midnight. Reba hadn't been gone over an hour.

Ket had dozed. Of a sudden, she awoke, shivering. A chill wind had blown in from somewhere and awakened her.

She hurried to draw the covers up to Emily's chin. Then she knew. Her hands froze over her cousin's still chest. It had not been a chill wind that awakened her, but Emily's last spasmodic gasp for breath.

Time passed. How much, Ket didn't know when she thought back on it the following day, for along with Emily, time seemed to have died that night. Ket stood transfixed over the bed with tears falling onto the slate-gray army blanket.

Even after she realized she was crying, she couldn't stop. She had thought she'd cried all her tears the day her father had come to her camp and told her why he had brought Sabrina to treat her.

The day he told her that he had never wanted to lose her.

Now she found she had more tears to cry, and they were for the same people. It was as if she hadn't cried for them enough the first time. As if she had to cry enough for all of them before she could stop.

She cried for Emily, of course, but more . . . She cried again for Delgado and for the son of Navarro, for Chi Caliente and Doré, she cried for her mother, Nalin.

She cried for all the People, those who had gone on to the other world and those who remained, for even those who still walked Mother Earth would not do so for long. The time of the People had passed, cut short by white eyes who coveted this land.

Finally she cried for Blake Carmichael. Not for his death, but for the death of his dreams . . . and of hers. For she did love him. She couldn't deny that she loved him, any more than she could deny the past that would keep them from having a future together.

As suddenly as they had begun, her tears dried, and Ket knew what she must do. She must carry out the plan she had told no one of except her father. She would take Emily home.

The logistics were tedious, but the venture would not be difficult, because it was right. She had never felt so right about anything she'd ever done.

The hour was late. The hospital steward had retired to his adjacent home, leaving an orderly on duty. Ket dispatched him to the mess hall with a request for hot tea for Emily. It would take time to stoke the coals enough to boil water and make tea.

As soon as he was gone, she wrapped Emily in the gray woolen blanket that covered her bed and hefted her over her shoulder. Two steps and she reached the back veranda. Another twenty yards and she was out of sight behind the cistern. Stumbling through the dark night with her cargo tight in hand, she made her way steadily up the canyon toward her camp.

A crescent moon shone through a shroud of clouds, more ghostly than ever. Tonight the steep red cliffs that rose above Hospital Canyon stood like a cadaverous honor guard, while Ket stole along the rocky path beneath them with her secret plunder.

Once she arrived at camp, it took no time to strap Emily's body onto the travois. At the last minute she retrieved Delgado's fancy rawhide pannier, the one Emily had made and she had taken from his dead horse. She bound it as a badge of honor around the corpse of her cousin.

With the travois harnessed to her stallion, she was ready to go. Before setting out, she glanced around in the darkness, wondering whether there was anything of hers she should take along.

She would not return. If Emily belonged with her birth people, so, too, did Ket.

Half your birth people, she heard Blake object. The memory of his voice was a feeble reminder of the robust baritone she would love to hear one more time. But riding up the canyon on this journey of death, she knew she would never hear that voice again.

For a moment she allowed herself to experience sadness for all the things she would never experience again—she would never feel his touch again, never taste his mouth again, never look upon his attractive, no, more, his fascinating, alluring, desirable body again.

She mourned all this, and the reverse, as well. She would never experience the heady wellspring of being admired by him, of watching him see her, hear her, touch her, taste her. Even the thought of him viewing her withered, scarred leg seemed inconsequential now. She wouldn't mind him looking on it. She knew in her heart of hearts that his reaction would be neither horror nor sympathy, but acceptance.

For in Blake Carmichael, she had been accepted, wholly and completely accepted for the first time in her life. He saw her as a whole. Not as half Anglo, half Apache, but as a whole woman.

He had told her so. And she believed him. And she loved him for allowing her to be whole.

But he possessed all the hated white-eyes traits. *Never let you get away . . .* He sounded like all the others, those who had destroyed her mother and her people. She had hated white eyes too long and too hard to ever forgive them for all they had taken from her and from the People. If she couldn't forgive all of them, how could she expect to live with one?

And if she couldn't live with Blake, she would have to do the next best thing, leave this land with the People. If her father proved right, she would die with the People.

The night was cold and the stars were few. She found her way by instinct, following the dark outline of mountains through this pass, across that plain. By the time she arrived at the Diablo Mountains, snow was falling. She had no idea how long it had been snowing, but now she realized that she had been bucking a strong north wind for miles.

At the western edge of the Diablos, she located the promontory that marked the canyon entrance. Atop it stood the guard.

Her first thought was one of relief—the People had not left the Apachería. It had started snowing the night she left the fort and had snowed on her the entire way, slowing her progress considerably. She had worried she would arrive too late. Had the People left for Mexico?

In which case, she had decided to perform the funeral fire herself. Emily deserved no less. But Ket was now relieved to discover she would not have to.

With a motion of his rifle, the guard waved her into the steep-walled canyon, at the winding end of which lay the stronghold of the People.

She was home. She wished she were happier about it. Emily's death prevented happiness, of course.

The palomino took the path wearily, and Ket knew the feeling. Once inside the canyon, she had experienced the full weight of the melancholy that had been creeping up on her during the long, depressingly cold journey.

When the walls opened up and she entered the path that led through the middle of the assemblage of brush and hide wickiups, she wished for a moment that she hadn't returned at all.

She wished she hadn't left Fort Davis. No, she wished she were with Blake.

Lost in this moment, as black as any she had known, Ket suddenly remembered why she had come, and she chastised herself sharply.

Emily was dead. At least Ket had her own life.

"Tremayne's already left to fetch her, son." Edward Bolton, stooped from years of carrying everything from cases of rifles to sacks of flour, stood behind the mercantile counter.

Blake stood before him. He still reeled from the shock of hearing that Ket had disappeared. He had come to town hoping to sit down and settle things with Tremayne, only to learn that Ket was nowhere to be found. Not only had she disappeared, but she had done so with her cousin Emily in tow.

Some claimed Emily had died and Ket had taken her back to the Apachería for an Indian burial.

Others insisted that Ket had taken Emily to a shaman for help, since white man's medicine hadn't worked. Either way, that put Ket at the Apachería.

"Give me a week's supply of . . . hell, whatever you figure I'll need for a week or so out there in that wilderness." He hadn't come to town outfitted for an expedition into the frozen unknown. "Add a couple of water bags, too, Edward, in case I miss the water holes."

"Coffee pot? I just ground some Arbuckles."

"No time. I won't stop to make camp."

Edward folded his arms across his chest and peered over the stack of goods he and Blake had piled on the counter. "This isn't a good idea, son." The older man's serious tone could not be ignored.

"I realize that, sir. Thank you."

"It isn't a good idea," Edward Bolton repeated.

"Got a better one?"

"Sure do. Like I said, Tremayne's already gone after her. He's a good man, Blake. They don't make 'em any better'n Tremayne, even if I do say so, him being my son-in-law. Most folks out here feel the same way about him. You can trust him, son."

While Edward talked, Blake began stuffing goods in a tow sack. Edward helped him, even though he continued to try to dissuade him from the dangerous mission.

"Besides all that," Edward added, "Tremayne's considered one of 'em. He's the only man I know ... I'll go further ... Tremayne's the only white man in this country who could get into that stronghold alive and get out the same way, hide, scalp, and all.''

"You may well be right," Blake acknowledged. The decision had not been easy. But it had come quickly. And it was right. "I still have to go. If I don't, she'll run off to Mexico with them and get herself killed.''

"Let Tremayne bring her out.''

Blake hefted the tow sack full of supplies to his shoulder, then extended a hand to Edward. "She won't come out for Tremayne.''

Edward grasped his offered hand in both of his. "Likely you know her better'n I do. But take care, son. We need men like you out here.''

"Thank you, sir. That means a lot. More than you know.''

"We're all aware of the reputation you've had to overcome. For what it's worth, in my books you've done a good job of it.''

Blake's next stop was at the post Headquarters. To his relief, Commander Jasper was nowhere around. Colonel Tom Sandhurst was on duty, along with Captain Jake Lewis, who was considered an expert on the terrain west of the Pecos. Blake figured he was about to test the captain's reputation.

"Reckon you know that what you're suggesting is something even the Army hasn't done yet," Sandhurst observed after Blake outlined his rough plan to penetrate the Apache stronghold in the Diablo Mountains.

Blake attempted to make light of the situation. "Someone's gotta be first, Colonel. I wanted to get the lay of the land from the experts before I head out.''

Captain Lewis spread a map of the area west of the Pecos River on a large oaken table in the center of the room. "My first advice is not to do the obvious.''

"Such as?''

"Don't attempt this," Sandhurst quipped. "It's suicidal, nothing short of suicidal."

"Could be you're right." Blake motioned for Captain Lewis to continue.

"Don't take the obvious way into the Diablos," the captain began. "As you're well aware from the trouble the railroad's had with those red devils, the southern rim of the Diablo Mountains fronts the new tracks. Those savages are sittin' out there primed and ready to take out anyone who attempts to enter their stronghold from the south."

"I should head north from Van Horn's Wells?"

"Don't even get that close to the southern ridges of the Diablos." Using a wooden pointer, the captain sketched a line north through the Davis Mountains, roughly parallel to the Diablos, where Victorio's Apachería was rumored to be. "This route will take you a day or so longer, but if you use it, you might—I say might—stand one chance in hell of making it through."

Blake grinned. "I came here to improve my chances."

"Chances?" The colonel was serious. "If there'd been any chance of penetrating that nest of savages, we'd of done it long ago. I'll say it again, Carmichael, what you're attempting is suicide."

Blake didn't doubt the colonel. Thing was, he had to try. If he stayed here where he was safe and sound and let Ket ride off to Mexico and get herself killed, he'd have to live with that the rest of his life.

A week earlier he might have given Tremayne half a chance of persuading her to come out. After she overheard his plans to lord his authority over her, she wouldn't listen to any plea the man made.

"Doubt if anyone can give you better than one percent odds," the captain was saying. "Take the southern route, you don't stand even that."

"You've convinced me," Blake told him. "Show me."

Captain Lewis turned back to the map. "Head due

north. Ride all the way up to the foothills of the Apache
Mountains, then skirt them headed west, like so.'' The
captain drew an imaginary line around the lower edge of
the mountain range. ''From there head north again for
ten, maybe fifteen miles.'' The captain laid aside his
pointer and looked Blake squarely in the eye. ''Hug those
foothills. Don't get out in plain sight.''

''That's the long way around.''

''You asked my advice.''

''Go ahead. I won't do anyone any good by not getting
there alive.''

''As you see here, there's a pretty good stretch of open
ground between the Apaches and the Diablos. Cross it in
the dead of night. Enter the Diablos here.''

Blake studied the map. ''As the crow flies, that's the
long way around,'' he commented again.

''Yep. There's a draw coming out of this overlap right
here. That's where you need to be. It leads into a narrow,
winding canyon that will eventually take you back south
and into the valley where reports place the remnants of
Victorio's band. Travel that by day. You'll think you're in an
English maze as it is. At night it will be most inhospitable.''

Blake gave the map one last concentrated perusal. ''How
heavy do they guard this north entrance?''

Captain Lewis shrugged. ''We don't know for sure, of
course, but I doubt they'll be guarding it at all, what with
rumors of them heading out for Old Mexico.''

''If there are lookouts,'' Blake persisted, ''what'll they
do? Come out in the open after me or hole up and wait?''

''Ambush?'' Colonel Sandhurst didn't hesitate to
respond. ''They don't generally resort to ambush, but
that's why we say you should cross that open area during
the night. No use giving them a target.''

Blake took it all in, gave the map another last sweep.
He felt as if he might be procrastinating. Time was wasting.
Still . . . ''What about landmarks?''

"You mean mountain ranges?"

"Anything I can use for markers if the stars don't come out."

Both the colonel and the captain looked as if he'd just given them a new and unexpected piece of the puzzle.

"You're waiting for this storm to pass."

"You wouldn't be that—"

"I don't have time for the storm to pass."

Both the colonel and the captain held him in their gazes, like in the cross hairs of a rifle, he thought, feeling himself a target even before he set out. He offered his hand to Colonel Sandhurst first.

"I appreciate your time, Colonel."

"I'm not sure we should have given you the time of day. For your own good, of course."

"I won't hold you responsible." He shook Captain Lewis's hand next.

"Applebee must have promised you the moon and the stars for you to go this far to bring Injun Emily's body back to the fort for burial."

"I haven't spoken with Colonel Applebee."

Again the men reacted in unison, raising their brows.

"This is a personal matter," Blake told them without elaboration. "I'd best get on with it. Thanks again."

Before he reached it, however, the door banged open with a force that slammed the doorknob against the wall, dislodging a chunk of plaster. Senator J. J. Carmichael ignored the mess he had made. He stopped in front of Blake, barring his exit. "Not so fast!"

The colonel and the captain each took a step and straightened their spines, as if coming to attention. Blake felt like he'd received a swift kick in the gut. The senator fairly exploded into the room. His bewhiskered jowls shook with his fury.

"I won't have any son of mine chasing off after a half-breed and leaving my work unfinished."

"The survey stakes are in place." Somehow Blake kept his voice low. "Jorge Sanchez helped me every step of the way. He can show your investors everything they need to know, in case I don't return by the time they arrive."

"Don't be impertinent with me. I order you to get back out—"

Blake stepped around his father. "Don't worry, Senator. I won't sully your fine reputation." He only half-heard the sputtered response. Outside, he drew a deep breath, pulled his collar up against the flying snow, and summoned his courage. The officers had given him little hope, and contrary to what he told them, their assessment weighed ominously—

"Hey, Blake, we're comin' with you." Luke and Tres Robles sat their mounts at the hitching rail, to either side of his own snorting, stamping horse.

"Like hell you are." He meant every word.

"We know this country a lot better than you do."

"So you said just before the Comancheros came down on us."

"Aw, those ol' Comancheros are already long-gone to Mexico."

"Those Apache warriors are probably not." Hopefully not, Blake thought. Not that he relished meeting up with renegade warriors who hankered for revenge, but he relished even less the thought of losing Ket.

"Mangas Che won't hurt us," Tres Robles insisted. "Don't you remember? We proved that we're chiefs—"

"That legend only applies at Apache Wells," he interrupted. "You're not coming with me."

"Aw, Blake. We've never been to the Apachería."

"We've always wanted to go."

"This might be our last chance."

"We can be a big help to you."

Blake listened with half an ear. He unhitched his mount

and drew the reins over the saddle. "I recall how much help you were the last time."

"That's not fair. Ket came after us, didn't she?"

This time he was going after Ket, and time was wasting. "I said no and that's final."

"But we're packed and—"

"One more word and I'll march you both into Headquarters and have Colonel Sandhurst lock you in the guardhouse."

"You wouldn't do that."

"Don't try me. Get back home before Sabrina takes sick worrying about you two. And don't follow me."

The boys exchanged looks that asked where Blake could have gotten such an outlandish idea.

"I mean it, boys. This is serious business. If you want to see Ket again in this life, get yourselves back home and wait for us."

He rode off without a backward glance, but his show of nonchalance was just that. He wouldn't have given a dime on a bet that they would obey him, but as the minutes turned to hours and the day waned, he saw no sign of them.

Of course, he had ridden around town a couple of times to throw them off his trail, an act he later regretted. If they tried to catch him by riding up to the southern side of the Diablos, they could find themselves in a peck of trouble, according to Captain Lewis.

The next couple of days passed in a blur of blowing snow and dismally gray skies. Blake had never been so cold in his life. He finally pulled the two blankets out of his pack and wrapped them around his coat, and that helped.

The only thing that would truly help, of course, would be to find Ket and bring her safely out of that stronghold.

He rigidly followed the officers' instructions and was glad for his penchant for doing so. From an early age he had believed that planning a task beforehand generally kept a person from making rash decisions on the spot.

Although, when he thought about it, he wasn't certain how anyone could classify this trip as anything but rash.

Time in the saddle gave him opportunity to think, and think he did. He relived every moment spent with Ket, from that first rash decision to kiss her right there in the middle of the Comanchero camp.

He hoped and prayed he would have another such chance. For several weeks he had known he was in love with her. Now he realized how much he loved her. Before, he had wanted to spend the rest of his life with her; now he didn't want to consider facing life without her.

It would take all his persuasive skills and then some to convince her to take the chance, but if he lived long enough to make it to that Apachería, he knew he could do it. He wouldn't just try to do it, he would do it. He would bring Ket back, marry her, and live happily . . .

Well, perhaps not too happily. Such a request might test fate too much. But he did intend to win Ket's mind. He already had her heart. If he hadn't believed that, he couldn't have undertaken this journey. If he hadn't known she loved him, he would have been a fool to attempt it.

And Blake had never considered himself a fool. Except perhaps, he decided on reflection, in his rigid devotion to a father who had daily proved himself more and more unworthy of anyone's devotion.

The country Blake traveled changed dramatically once he left the quiet serenity of the Davis Mountains. Miles upon miles of desolate plains stretched ahead of him, bounded on either side by various and changing mountain ranges. With skies overcast and snow blinding much of the route, he was glad he had asked for landmarks to guide his way. Late the first afternoon he arrived at St. Martin's Springs. He watered his mount, stretched his legs, and headed out with an icy wind blowing down his collar and the rugged foothills of the Delaware Mountains looming ahead. And west of the Delawares lay the Diablos.

More than once he considered turning due west and riding straight for the Diablos and the Apachería and Ket. Always he talked himself out of his rashness. Impatience would only get him killed. Then who would save Ket?

From the way she had talked at the rail site, he knew she wouldn't give Tremayne half a chance. Day faded to night and night to day, and his greatest battle became, not the weather or even time, but himself. Anxiety knotted inside of him. Had she already gone? Was she packing to leave? Would she be gone when he got there?

If he got there?

Twelve hours after leaving St. Martin's Springs, Blake arrived at the second watering hole, Rattlesnake Springs. He had entered the foothills of the Delawares and was closer than ever to the northeastern edge of the Diablos. Taking out his spyglass, he studied the distant terrain. No sign of life.

Temptation nudged again. Why not cross here and be done with it?

Again discipline prevailed. Captain Lewis had cautioned that the canyons inside the Diablos were a maze, waiting to befuddle a foolish traveler. He must stick to his plan.

His inner fears had become his constant companions: Had Ket left for Mexico? Would he ever see her again?

Still he held to his sanity and to the route Captain Lewis had outlined. He turned north, hugging the foothills of the Delawares. Four hours later, with the foggy light of the gray day fading into night, he arrived at Apache Springs. Due west, across that wide-open plain the officers had termed an open area, loomed the Diablos.

He watered his horse and himself and filled his water bags, out of habit, for sometime the next day he would find the Apachería, or be found by its warriors.

He huddled against a protruding boulder and ate some

hardtack and jerked meat. He tried to doze, but for the most part kept his spyglass trained on the distant hills. He thought he located the overlap Captain Lewis had described.

With this weather, he couldn't be certain. One way or another, come morning he would know.

Crossing the valley floor that night, his fears began to change. He still worried that Ket might have left, but fear for his own safety surfaced now.

Although snow had fallen continuously since he left the post, it wasn't deep. Even so, he knew his tracks would be there in the morning to give him away. What if he were ambushed before he reached the camp? Ket might never know he had set out. She would go to Mexico . . .

She had called him many things since he met this wild woman of the mountains and none of them complimentary. Now he was beginning to see the validity in them—one in particular. *Greenhorn*.

She'd called that one right. No one but a greenhorn would attempt what he was now attempting. Hell, the Tenth Cavalry hadn't even tried it.

Blake had always prided himself on being practical, on taking his time, deciding a matter on facts, not emotion. From the outset this journey had been undertaken on emotion and only emotion—pure and simple.

He successfully crossed the plain and arrived in the foothills of the Diablos a couple of hours before daybreak, as best he could judge. No sun would rise today, but he did see a glimmer of light in the east.

He wondered whether this would be the last morning he would live to see. Dramatic or not, he realized that he could well have just cause to wonder.

Proceeding ahead, he soon found the opening Captain Lewis had described. With a glance to the world outside, as if he perused his life for the last time, Blake entered the labyrinth. He guided his horse onto the rocky trail.

Steep cliffs rose to either side, but they were nothing like the lush vegetation and beautiful red rocks of the Davis Mountains. This land was gray and brown, streaked here and there with yellow, for the most part barren. Instead of mountain willow, piñon, and mesquite grasses, he saw mostly dirt and several species of cacti, including two he could identify—prickly pear and cholla.

Victorio's stronghold inside these desert mountains could be nothing like— Then they were upon him.

He rounded a bend and they sat their horses, three abreast, at least two deep, although in the foggy winter air his vision had blurred and he could have been looking at a thousand warriors or at three.

Their horses were not painted for war, like those outside Fort Davis. Nor were the men painted. But that did not diminish this, the most menacing sight Blake had seen since the Comancheros came upon him and the boys.

His encounter with the Comancheros had been different. For one thing, he had the boys to worry about when the Comancheros came upon them, so all his fear hadn't been concentrated on one life—his own.

He recalled asking Ket if there was a difference between Comancheros and Comanches.

Pray you never find out, she had replied.

Well, he was finding out, for these men were warriors, like Comanches would be. He would never have to ask that question again. Saying he lived long enough for the topic to ever come up again.

The Comancheros had been a noisy, lusty lot. They shouted, cursed, fired their weapons. Even with rifles leveled on him, these Apaches made no sound. He might have said they were dignified.

He might have said they looked defeated. But he never doubted that they intended to kill him.

He, on the other hand, hadn't come all this way to give

up. He was a fighter, even though it was a little hard to believe, given the circumstances.

"Keturah." He searched their faces for recognition. He knew no words in Apache and felt the fool for never attempting to learn a few. He didn't even know how Ket was identified to the People.

"Keturah," he repeated.

The warriors exchanged looks. One, the obvious leader, shifted his rifle. Blake felt his heart skitter.

He tried another name. "Tremayne."

The warrior frowned, but this time Blake knew he had seen recognition. So he tried again.

"I have come to see Keturah Tremayne. Will you take me to her?"

Chapter Twelve

Dismally, Keturah decided that she had never made a right decision in her life. Lately everything she had done had turned out wrong. Whether she had acted for the wrong reason—retaliation against her father—or with the noblest of intentions—returning Emily's body to the Apachería for a proper Apache funeral—she had failed in her mission.

Her attempt to use Blake to get back at her father had been wrong. She understood that now. She knew she had offended him. She regretted that, for Blake had been the one person in her life who had accepted her for what she was—or what she would like to be—a person of worth.

And what had she done? Instead of thanking him or appreciating him, she had wounded him.

"You didn't come to make love with me, Ket," he had observed angrily. "You came here to make war on Tremayne, and I won't help you."

Intrinsically she realized that by what she had attempted, she could well have lost more than what she'd tried to take away from Tremayne. It wasn't Tremayne she would have hurt, but Blake. While he struggled to prove himself unlike his lecherous father, she had thrown herself at him and tried to undo any progress he had made.

"Tremayne already believes I'm like my father," Blake had stormed at her. "Or like my father is rumored to be. If I take you to bed under these circumstances, he will *know* I am."

But she hadn't stopped there. She had gone straight from that debacle to another one. She had stolen Emily's body and returned it to the Apachería with the noblest of intentions.

But this act, too, had been wrong. The ragged remnants of Victorio's brave band refused Emily the final rites of passage into the Afterworld.

The journey from the fort had been arduous. Snow had begun to fall by the time she left Fort Davis, and Ket had never been as cold in her life.

Even wrapped in her fox pelts, she had thought she might freeze. Pulling the travois along icy trails made the going slow; it took her an extra day to get there.

She hadn't stopped to sleep or to eat, so she arrived weary and famished. Her scarred leg was so cramped she doubted she would be able to stand on it.

But her cause had been honorable. She knew this in her heart, so she nudged the palomino up the steep trail that divided the camp in two parts. To either side stood brush-and-hide wickiups that she would have thought deserted, except for smoke rising through their vents into the icy air. She saw no sign of movement, not at first. Even the dogs had gone inside to escape the snow and bitter cold.

What happened after that stunned her. Someone must have heard her horse, for soon people began to emerge from the warmth of their shelters. Then boys were running, carrying word of her arrival from wickiup to wickiup. Soon the trail to either side of her was lined with people—old men and women. Children.

They watched in silence as she nudged the palomino up the slippery hill to the furthest shelter, that of Mangas Che, who had assumed leadership in the absence of the elders.

Well before she arrived there, however, she became aware of the keening. It began softly and rose in crescendo as more women joined the dirge.

Ket heard it as a tribute to a fallen daughter. Even after one of the women rushed into the road, she didn't understand. When the woman spat on Emily's corpse, Ket recognized her. *Delgado's mother.*

Her mind dulled by weariness and hunger, Ket gradually began to comprehend that something had gone gravely wrong with Emily's final homecoming.

Delgado's mother was joined by others who followed her up the hillside. Their keening became deafening. Then they started to tear off pieces of the pannier Ket had so carefully bound around Emily's body—a sash of honor, she had thought it. Now it was being torn to shreds by the women of the village. They threw pieces of rawhide and red flannel to the icy winds.

She kicked the palomino to a trot. Her heart pounded blood through her chilled veins, heating her. She had to get to Mangas before the women tore Emily apart.

Suddenly she felt like the victim. She had seen how the women mourned. And for the first time in her life, she was afraid of her own people.

In a moment of startling clarity, a memory came to her—the memory of Sabrina riding straight and tall away from his very village with jeers of the women ringing in her ears and Ket's own spittle on her face.

Mangas Che had come out of his wickiup by the time she drew rein. He stood tall and straight and was wrapped in a bearskin robe that came to his feet and dragged on the ground behind him. His relentless expression was as unwelcoming as the women's cries.

"You should not have brought her here," he said after a long moment.

Ket summoned the stoic courage she had hidden behind for so long. "We are her blood people. She belongs here."

"No longer is she one of us," Mangas Che returned. "She alerted the white-eyes soldiers to our raid. She is responsible for the deaths of the son of Navarro and of Delgado to whom she was promised."

Ket did not beg, although she fully expected to be turned out into the cold with her unwanted cargo.

It was a measure of her father's standing with the People that she was not, for before her confrontation with Mangas Che concluded, Tremayne arrived at the Apachería.

The compromise he worked out would have stripped a warrior of his pride. Ket, not being a warrior, was left to her own anguish.

She was to remain inside her grandmother's wickiup until the storm abated enough for her to safely leave the Diablos.

"And what of Emily's body?" she demanded of her father when he returned to her grandmother's wickiup to tell her of the agreement.

Nourished by her grandmother's *guisado* and warmed at the fire, she had successfully loosened her cramped leg by pacing the ground cloth.

"Mangas covered her with a robe belonging to your grandmother," Tremayne explained. "He will post a guard to keep the women from desecrating the body."

He left her then, and she slept. When she awakened sometime later, she expected to find him gone, but he was still in camp.

He, too, waited for the storm to pass. He did not, however, return to her grandmother's wickiup, and she was not allowed to leave it for two more days.

When he returned, it was to her chagrin.

"Feeling better?" he inquired.

"I'm not so cold, if that's what you mean."

Tremayne did not respond to her caustic tone. "We have to decide what to do about Emily," he said.

"You decide." Ket didn't want to talk about it. "I brought her home, but nobody wants her. If you've come to take her back, take her."

"That isn't the reason I came."

The wickiup was dimly lit, and she studied him skeptically. He squatted on his heels beside the fire pit, but something about him didn't look right. In his white-eyes clothing and hairstyle, he looked out of place. She wondered how he had been able to form an agreement with Mangas Che, looking like a white eyes.

"I came to persuade you not to go to Mexico."

His voice was low and sad, not strong like she remembered, and it fired her anger. "Why have you suddenly started acting like a father?"

She watched his jaws twitch. She had hurt him and she was glad. He deserved to hear the truth. "You have no say over me. I can do anything I like."

"You're right, Ket," he agreed solemnly. "You can do anything you like." He didn't look at her but into the fire. He held his hands, palms out, toward it, as if warming himself. When he spoke, it was to the fire. "You can do anything you like. As long as you're alive. You won't be able to do much of anything when you're dead."

He had turned then and left the wickiup. That had happened the day before. This morning she heard him again outside the wickiup arguing with her grandmother.

"The child must leave here," Ket heard her grandmother say. "She no longer is one of us. She cannot go with us on our final journey."

Ket listened in disbelief. Coming from Mangas Che she would have believed it, or from Delgado's mother. But this was her grandmother, the woman who had raised her after her mother died. The woman who had stood beside her when she drove Sabrina away from this very Apachería.

Never had Ket felt as lonely or as lost. If she didn't belong here, she belonged nowhere. If she couldn't follow the People—her people—to Mexico, where would she go?

She felt wounded, herself, and frightened. Inside her that caged animal began to clamor for escape. She wanted out. She wanted to escape.

But where would she go? The People had always been her refuge. If she must leave them, where would she go? Where did she belong?

Nowhere. She belonged no—

"Ke-tur-ah!"

Later she realized it hadn't been the shouting of her name that drew her attention, but the voice that shouted it. Disoriented, she listened and it came again.

"Ke-tur-ah!"

Blake? It couldn't be. Not here. She was mad, losing her wits . . .

"Ke-tur-ah!"

Hearing it again, she jumped to her feet and rushed outside. She stopped dead in her tracks. It was Blake. She hadn't conjured him. He stood in the roadway surrounded by six mounted warriors who prodded him with the muzzles of their rifles.

His clothes were torn. Blood ran down one side of his face. He looked as weary as an old man, but there was a fight in him that caused her heart to contract.

"Ket . . ." he called, seeing her. One of the warriors rammed a rifle into his back. He stumbled, caught his balance, and called again, "Ket, I love you! I love you!"

Then she was running. And shouting. As though she had never been banished from their lives, she ordered the warriors about in a stream of bitter words. Mangas Che appeared, and she turned on him. In the language of the People, she told him to order his men aside.

Stumbling between the warriors, she fell to her knees beside Blake. She stared at him through the cold and falling snowflakes, and he stared back. As weak and frightened and cold as he must be, all she saw in his expression was his love for her. Then he reached an arm for her, and she realized he was close to collapse.

"Come." She helped him rise and supported him with her weight.

Mangas Che had spoken to the warriors and they had moved aside. When she moved between them, she saw Tremayne. He stood beside Mangas Che, as stony-faced as any warrior. Although she was afraid he might, he did not follow them inside her grandmother's wickiup.

"What on earth . . . ?" She stroked the side of Blake's face where blood had dried.

"I was afraid I'd be too late," he said weakly, as if with his last breath.

She sat him on a stack of robes, fetched a gourd filled with water, and held it while he drank.

"How did you get here?"

"Through the north pass," he said. "At least that's how I started."

"You walked through that storm?"

He grinned. "Just the last day."

"They took your horse. It's a wonder they didn't take your life."

"I told them I had come to find you and they brought me. Not my preferred escort, I'll admit, but here I am."

"It's a wonder they didn't kill you," she repeated. "Those warriors are primed to kill someone. That's why they haven't left for Mexico. Some of them argue to return to the fort to kill more soldiers."

"Lucky I'm not a soldier."

But Ket's mind had rushed ahead to other worries. "I don't know how we'll get you out."

"With you."

"I'm not going your way." Now that the People refused to allow her to go with them to Mexico, she certainly wasn't returning to the post. But Blake would not accept that.

"Oh, yes, you are. I just spent the best part of my life getting here, and I don't intend to waste it, Ket. I told you. I'm not giving up—"

"It would never work," she argued.

"If you can't return to the fort or to Chihuahua, I'll come with you. You decide where."

"That's ridiculous." He didn't know how ridiculous. Would he follow a woman who belonged nowhere into no-man's-land? Then neither of them would belong anywhere.

She watched him study the brush-and-hide walls of the wickiup. A wry grin spread across his weary features. "You're afraid of four walls." He scanned the contours again. "Can't see the difference. A person's shut up in here, too."

She glanced around, surprised. "There is a difference."

"Not in theory. You're afraid, Ket. To be honest, I am, too, a little. But what I came all this way to tell you is that you don't have to try to adapt to my world. I'll try to adapt to yours."

He was serious. Before she could respond, he took the wrong meaning.

"Maybe you're right," he said. "Maybe I couldn't adapt to living in the wilds, but I'm not afraid to take the chance. I don't see why you are."

She jumped to her feet. "You're too cold and tired to talk about this." She grabbed him another fur robe and busied herself at the fire pit, dishing up a bowl of *guisado*. "We can talk about this later. Right now—"

"Later won't change things. I told you once, and I'll say it again. I will never walk away from what we have together."

Before she realized he had risen, he was behind her. "Put down that bowl. I'm not hungry . . . not for that."

She felt faint at his words, but still she gripped the wooden bowl. How could she tell him the truth? Only days earlier she had despaired of losing her freedom. Now her freedom was all she had.

His arms felt strong and warm around her waist. "I love you, Ket."

"Don't say that. Please."

With force that belied his recent treatment at the hands of the warriors, he turned her to face him. He took the bowl of *guisado* and set it aside. He then took her by the shoulders.

"Tell me that again," he said, staring into her. "Tell me not to love you. Make me believe I have to stop loving you."

She couldn't, of course. It wouldn't be possible to lie to him. She couldn't even speak the words while she looked into his eyes.

"I don't know what's wrong with you, Ket. In some ways you're the bravest, most intelligent person I know. In other ways you're afraid to take a chance on life. You're afraid I might be like my father or that I couldn't adapt to your way of life. Well, maybe you're right. Maybe I am like my father. Maybe I couldn't adapt to living in the wilds, but if I'm not afraid to take a chance, I don't see why you are."

"Please, Blake." She ducked her head. "There's no sense in this."

"Love often doesn't make sense, or so I'm told."

"You can't love me," she cried, desperate now for him

to listen, to hear. "You can't love me, because I'm nobody. Nobody can love—nothing."

His only response was a tightening of his hands at her shoulders. She had rendered him speechless. After a while, she felt obligated to explain. "I'm not going to Mexico, so you and Tremayne can stop worrying about that."

"He persuaded you—"

"Nobody persuaded me," she cried. "The People won't let me. I don't belong here anymore."

Before she finished her outcry, he drew her into his arms. He held her tightly against his chest, one hand cupping her head. His fingers splayed through her hair.

She felt supported, as though he had snatched her back from a precipice over which she had stumbled, as though he had saved her from some horrible death. But he didn't know what he had saved, and when he did, he wouldn't want her. She stirred.

"You can't go with me. I don't know where I'm going. I belong nowhere."

"When will you stop fighting it, Ket? You belong right here—with me."

His lips opened over hers, and she couldn't have resisted kissing him if it had meant a death sentence.

"This is what I was hungry for," he mumbled against her skin.

She had been, too, but she didn't say it. "You were crazy to come here."

"So I was told."

When she questioned, he described his talk with Edward Bolton and the officers at Headquarters. "I knew you wouldn't listen to Tremayne, not as angry as you were with him the last time I saw you."

"It's a good thing he came," she told him. "When he arrived, they were about to throw me out into the storm."

He was genuinely distressed. "And that's not the worst, is it?"

"What do you mean?"

"Emily." He glanced around the wickiup. "How is she? Where is—?"

"You don't know?"

"Know what? I just got here, remember?"

"I mean ..."

"No one knows, Ket. Some folks think you brought her here for the shaman to treat. Others think she died and—"

"Oh, no. I didn't realize ... She died. I brought her here for a proper funeral, but ... How could I have been so thoughtless ... so ignorant?"

"Ket, come on now. You're not ignorant. You believed—"

"They won't allow her a funeral. She alerted the fort to their raid and some of them were killed and—"

"It's over." He drew her back into his embrace and held her close. "You've had an ordeal, but it's over."

"No, it isn't over. I have to do something about ..."

"When?" he asked, as if he were ready to tackle another trek into enemy territory in the height of winter.

He would, too. She knew that. Whatever she needed, he would be there to help her. Was that what he'd meant when he vowed to never let her get away? Was that what it meant to love someone?

"First we have to figure out how to get you away from here with your scalp."

His eyes widened in mock terror. "It's that bad, huh?"

"I don't know. I—"

"You expect me to worry? With you here beside me? You who stormed a Comanchero camp to rescue me?"

She laughed. How could she not? He sounded genuinely convinced.

"I'll have to admit it sooner or later, so I might as well tell you now," she said against his throat.

"What?"

"You probably could have rescued yourself from those Comancheros."

He held her back and gazed at her with a fondness that brought a catch to her throat. "You mean I'm not the greenhorn white eyes you took me for?"

"You amaze me," she confessed. "Stealing into this stronghold. It frightens me to think about you out there in that storm and being captured by those warriors."

When he stroked her cheek with the back of his fingers, she felt his hand tremble. "It frightened me, too," he admitted. "But it frightened me worse to think about getting here and finding you gone to Mexico."

She couldn't look away or she would have, for she knew he could read her thoughts. She would have gone to Mexico, she might still if they would let her, but she wouldn't want to. She never wanted to go anyplace without Blake.

Before he could understand, she slipped her arms back around him and laid her face on his chest. Yes, she loved this man. She drew strength from him in a way she would never have imagined.

Was this the dilemma her father had faced? He had loved Sabrina every bit as much as she loved Blake, and she had expected him to give Sabrina up.

Neither was aware of Tremayne's presence in the wickiup until he cleared his throat.

"Papa."

Blake released her with all but an arm around her shoulders, extending his free hand to Tremayne.

"Blake Carmichael, sir."

Tremayne just glared at them. "I know who you are." Ignoring Blake's offered hand, he turned to Ket. "Your grandmother and I have agreed that I'll take Emily's body back to town. Your grandmother is right. Emily ceased being one of the People long ago, when I left her at the fort, thinking it was best."

He glanced to Blake, then back to Ket. "You know what your grandmother would say about this."

It wasn't a question, so Ket didn't bother to respond.

"You don't belong with the People anymore either."

"Papa!" Even though she had overheard their earlier conversation, she hadn't expected her father to be the one to tell her.

Tremayne's voice lowered and became more gentle. "You know it in your heart, Ket."

She ducked her head to keep her pain to herself.

"I don't mean you'll ever give up this part of yourself. It's in you, through and through, and with luck you will pass it along to your children."

He took both Ket and Blake by surprise when he offered a hand to Blake. "You came here for the same reason I did, to save my daughter's life. Reckon I'm beholden to you for that."

Blake caught Ket's eye and winked. "Life is looking up already." Then he turned to Tremayne. "Why don't we sit and talk? There are a few things we need to get clear before we leave this place."

Tremayne was obviously taken aback. When Ket found her senses, Blake was talking to her again.

"Can we talk here without being interrupted?"

"Yes," she said, wary now, but curious, too. They sat on the stack of skins, Blake close beside her, an arm around her, protecting her, loving her.

"All my life," Blake told Tremayne, who squatted on his heels opposite them, "I've wanted my father's approval. Ket has wanted the same from you. Well, we don't need that anymore. We have each other. If you think I'm a womanizer like my father is reported to be, I'm sorry. I'm not, but the only way I can prove it is by living a moral life."

"Fair enough," Tremayne mumbled stiffly.

"And if you believe my father stole your land, take him to court, but don't saddle Ket or me with the blame."

Tremayne remained stoic, obviously caught off guard by Blake's forthright attack. For a long, tense moment no one spoke. Tremayne broke the silence.

"Just so you'll know what sort of rattler's den you've crawled into"—he lifted his face and gave Blake a full view of his feelings on the topic of a Carmichael—"your father murdered my parents."

"What?" Ket came to her feet. She had never heard such a charge in her life.

Tremayne shrugged, almost amicable now. "Don't reckon I can hold that against you," he told Blake, "seein's how you weren't born back then. Sabrina says folks out here who've met you say your mama did a right fine job raisin' you, and I'll take her word. Until you prove them wrong."

Now it was Blake who sat stunned. Defensively, Ket wanted to deny the charge out of hand. But she didn't have any grounds to do so. Her father was known far and wide as an honest man.

She wanted to say something to ease the tension, but she didn't have Blake's gift for words. So she moved her shoulder into his side and felt his heart beat against her and knew she was sitting where she was always meant to sit. When he finally responded, his gift for words astounded even Ket.

"I don't suppose this is the time to ask for Keturah's hand in marriage?" he asked Tremayne.

Tremayne actually grinned at Blake's audacity, and Ket was so proud of him she actually felt her heart swell. Not that she was about to marry him, but . . .

"Not that I'm the man to ask," Tremayne offered, not quite humbly. "Regardless what she's always thought, I am and always have been proud to be her father." He studied his hands awhile, and when he looked up at them again, he was serious.

"It's not the senator's womanizing, bad as it is, that I'm afraid of. Don't rightly think a boy who grew to manhood without his father around could pick up on such a habit. It's the ruthless way the man conducts his business."

"I don't know anything about that," Blake admitted. "I feel as if I should be affronted that you would say such things, including accusing my father of murdering your parents. I guess I'm inured to hearing him disparaged. Since I've been out here, I've yet to hear a good word spoken about him. The only thing I know to do is to confront him myself." He turned back to Ket. "I promise to get to the bottom of this. The thing that worries me most is little Neeta." He glanced to Tremayne. "Not that murdering your parents isn't worse, but—"

"I know what you mean. We all hate what's happened to Rosa and Neeta. Sabrina and Rosa have been friends for many years. It's been hard to see her go downhill and to be able to do little or nothing to help her. As for Neeta, the poor child will be an orphan if anything happens to Rosa."

"She'll never be an orphan," Blake vowed. "I intend to get to the bottom of that rumor."

After a few moments passed with no conversation, Tremayne clapped his hands. "Reckon we'd best be getting Emily back to the fort."

Both men looked at Ket. She felt their question, the same question.

"I'll come with you, but . . ." She was feeling trapped again, strangely now, for the last few moments had been peaceful—almost serene, sitting in conversation with the two people she knew now she loved most in all the world.

Later, she thought her father must have read her thoughts, for before she could leave the wickiup, he stopped her.

"Do you remember the day Nick brought Sabrina here?"

Although he had asked the question in a quiet tone, Ket felt herself go stiff. "Of course."

He placed a large palm on her shoulder. "I sent Sabrina away that day, knowing she was the only woman since your mother that I could ever love."

Ket caught a breath just before it became a sob.

"I loved your mother with all my heart," he continued. "After she died I became cynical about all white eyes." He shook his head, remembering. "Sabrina had the devil of a time ridding me of that. Reckon ol' Blake here knows something of what I'm talking about."

Blake squeezed Ket's other hand, but neither of them spoke. The moment was too poignant.

"I know how hard it'll be for you. I know you feel lost and guilty, too, riding away from your grandmother and the others for probably the last time."

Ket stared at the ground cloth and tried not to cry.

"I know your fears about trying to live in the white man's world."

She looked up at that, surprised that he would consider such a thing. Sabrina had, of course. But Sabrina was a woman.

"I had an advantage on you, because I started out in the white world; after that I spent a lot of time with Nick and Lena. They taught me to read and write, to dress the part of a white man, even how to behave at what few social functions I attended. You haven't had much of that advantage. And I know you're probably dreading things you don't even know you ought to dread yet."

"I do," she said softly, for not to acknowledge his kindness would have been to deny it.

"Well, as a wedding present—if that's what you choose to do—or just as a gift for yourself, I want you to have Apache Wells for your own."

For a long moment she didn't understand his words.

Then she did. She looked at him, held his gaze, and it was with the greatest effort that she retained her sanity and remained beside Blake. At that instant all she wanted was to be in her father's arms.

"If you want it, that is," he added.

"I want it." She strove to regain her voice. "Thank you."

Chapter Thirteen

The storm had passed on, leaving behind a sharp north wind. Somehow that made the sad good-byes all the more bitter. What would have been difficult under any circumstances was made worse by the knowledge that this would more likely than not be their final good-bye.

Not only were Ket and Tremayne riding away from the Apachería for the last time, but the People were leaving it, as well. The wickiups would be burned in their wake.

Ket felt wrenched to the bottom of her soul. Watching her father walk solemnly from wickiup to wickiup, from warrior to old man to her own grandmother, she realized that this leave-taking was equally wrenching for him.

The image remained with her on the long, chilling ride back to Fort Davis, the image of her father bidding farewell to the people who had taken him in as an orphaned child and raised him to be one of their own. The image of her father hugging her grandmother, the mother of his first wife Nalin, the woman who had reared Ket after Nalin had been murdered and Tremayne left the People to take up his life as a white eyes.

Now Ket was leaving the People, too. That final day they had come to her one by one, all except the mother of Delgado, to assure her that she would always be considered one of them.

Ket wondered whether her father had had anything to do with that. Whether, indeed, he had promised the People that she would not test their claims of kinship by asking to remain with them.

She hadn't, for she realized that the time had come for her to move on. She must make a life for herself, somewhere. Whether with her white-eyes relatives, she didn't know.

Whether with Blake Carmichael, she was even less certain.

They took the shorter southern route back to the fort and spoke little along the way. The weather was partially responsible. Collars raised against the cold north wind at their backs, each rider was buffered by clothing against the howling wind, each with thoughts of what the future held for him or her.

Since their meeting with Tremayne, Blake had acknowledged Ket's need for privacy, for time to think things through.

"We don't have to talk about all this right now, Ket. I need to see what my father has to say about these accusations. You have things to do of your own. After Emily's funeral, we'll talk about our future. I promise two things— I won't rush you and I won't give up on you."

She knew he spoke the truth, and she knew in her heart of hearts that he was right: they belonged together. Yet it both saddened and frightened her to think about the difficulties ahead for them both. She had never lived in a house; he had never lived without one.

And that was only the first of a vast number of differences they would face.

At the fort, Tremayne offered to deliver Emily's body to the Applebees. But that was Ket's job. Not even a father could shoulder all one's responsibilities.

"I took her," Ket said. "I should explain why."

"Want me to come with you?"

It was an offer she hadn't expected, and one she could not refuse. She dreaded meeting with the Applebees, not because she considered what she had done—or tried to do—wrong, but because of the heedless manner in which she had gone about it.

"I shouldn't have taken her without telling you," she told a tearful Reba Applebee.

"No need to think about that now. We're grateful you returned her." Colonel Applebee comforted his sobbing wife with an arm around her shoulders.

"Yes," sniffled Reba Applebee, "we are grateful. We should have discussed our plans with you, my dear. We want to bury our little Emily beside our first daughter." She blew her nose and smiled ruefully. "In our hearts they have always been sisters."

Ket didn't explain that she had returned Emily's body only after the People refused her the traditional Apache funeral.

"It's the right thing to do," she said. Never had the white-eyes method of dealing with their dead seemed so offensive. No wonder their grieving periods took forever. Placing a body in a tightly secured box and burying it underground would be a difficult thing to forget.

"Let us know when you set the services," Tremayne requested. "Anything we can do before then—"

"You have our eternal thanks." Reba hugged Ket and Ket tried to return the embrace. She had come to care for this woman. During Emily's last days they had become close.

With her own future looming ominously before her, Ket could but wonder how she would ever adjust to a world where she would be expected to bury her dead. So disconcerting was the idea that she was glad Blake had left them at the edge of town.

"I'll come with you to the Applebees," he had offered. But he faced a difficult encounter of his own.

"Go ahead. You have things to do, too."

While Tremayne sat his horse and stared down the road, Blake had leaned across the space between their horses and kissed her on the lips. "I'll meet you at Tremayne's."

Leaving the Applebees later, Ket wondered aloud how she could ever marry Blake.

"How could I even think about making such a big decision?" she questioned, half to herself, half to the wind. "Everything I've done lately has been wrong."

Tremayne responded, startling her. "If this is about that marriage proposal, Ket, my advice is to take your time. There's no rush."

"That's what Sabrina said." For the first time in a long time, actually for the first time ever, when she spoke her stepmother's name, she felt a sense of peace.

She needed time. Sabrina and her father understood.

"Damn your hide, get out of here. Run back to that half-breed. I want nothing to do with the likes of you."

Blake stood just inside the front doorway of his father's two-room adobe in Chihuahua. Outside, snow had begun to fall again, but at the moment he figured it would be warmer out in the elements than in here with his father. The only thing warm in this place was the odor of stale liquor.

Across the room the esteemed senator sat sprawled in an old leather armchair, his neck collar undone and a bottle of whiskey—it looked like the homemade variety—

on a mahogany table by his side. He held a dirty glass of the liquor in one hand.

Resisting the urge to turn around and leave, Blake closed the door behind him and crossed the room to stoke up a fire in the corner fireplace. His father wore a heavy coat.

Blake felt a heavy burden on his shoulders, too, but it had nothing to do with his clothing.

He might have fallen in love with the wrong woman, but if everything he'd heard about his father was true— hell, if any of it was true—he had loved and revered the wrong man all his life.

The burden of learning the truth weighed heavily. He gazed around the cluttered room. His attention came to rest on his unkempt father.

With a shock he realized that he hadn't noticed his father's slovenly nature before. He'd been too busy denying the truth, perhaps.

"Least you could do is light a fire," he told the man. "You'll freeze yourself to death."

"You wish."

"I wish you no ill will."

" 'I wish you no ill will,' " the older Carmichael mocked.

Blake drew a chair closer to the sputtering fire. "We have to talk."

"Talk? You march in here straight from the arms of the enemy and expect me to listen to whatever lies they filled you with?"

"I didn't come to fight with you." Blake drew a deep breath and knew he was stalling for time. How could he proceed with this miserable task? He was grateful his mother wasn't around.

It occurred to him then that he was grateful his mother had never seen the man she admired in such a repulsive state, had never heard the tales told about him. "All my life I've wanted only one thing," he told his father. "The opportunity to get to know you. I came out here filled with such grand expectations, with so much enthusiasm. Mother reared me to revere you. 'Your father is a great man, Blake,' she always said. 'Never forget, your father is a great man.' Then I arrive in this place where you've spent most of your life and learn that out here you're . . . Well, here you are not revered."

"No need to tell me that. These people are the most ungrateful specimens of humanity on earth. But they'll come around, once I make them rich."

"Rich?"

"The railroad. Don't play the simpleton with me. I paid for your college education. I know your capabilities, which makes it all the more detestable that you're bent on throwing your life away."

Blake ignored his father's choleric outburst. He'd like to put it down to alcohol consumption but decided that might be too kind an explanation.

"This conversation has nothing to do with the railroad," he said, exasperated. "Or about getting rich. If you can't manage a serious discussion right now, I'll come back later."

The senator straightened as if Blake had struck him. "Don't go getting high and mighty with me, boy."

"All right. I'll come right out and ask. Did you murder Tremayne's parents?"

J. J. Carmichael glared at his son a long, intense moment, before returning to his liquor. He downed what was left in his glass and reached for the bottle.

"Did you?"

Using his teeth, J. J. pulled the cork out of the whiskey bottle, spat it to the floor, and filled his glass. After he took a gulp and wiped his mouth with the back of his hand, he shook his head as though incredulous. "That damned Injun-loving bastard."

"Just answer the question."

J. J.'s eyes might have been bloodshot, but there was

nothing wrong with their ability to focus. He glared at Blake. "Hell, no. Now are you satisfied?"

Blake swiped a hand over his face and stared into the fire. God, he hated this. His trip to the Apachería, warriors and all, had been easier.

"I don't know," he answered honestly. Turning, he studied his father with no attempt to hide his distress. "I haven't heard one decent thing about you since I've arrived out here. You and I both know politicians are fair game, but with no one on your side—"

"You listen to the wrong people. Ask Commander Jasper what he thinks—"

"Commander Jasper? He's accused of the murder of Tremayne's first wife. Isn't that right? I'm told there's proof to that effect, and that you used your power as a United States Senator to erase the black mark from Jasper's name."

"Black mark?" the senator fairly exploded. "Lon Jasper was well within his rights for what he did. General Sherman had a good way of putting it—'Only good Injun's a dead Injun.' "

"So Commander Jasper murdered Tremayne's first wife?"

"No. Commander Jasper, Captain Jasper back then, gave an order to his troops to raid a village of red devils who had wreaked their own brand of devastation around Fort Bliss. On review, the Army sided with the officer, who in a tough situation had the guts to rise to the occasion. That's why I earmarked him for my team."

"Your team?"

"The railroad."

Blake didn't begin to understand this last, but it hardly seemed worth pursuing given his father's earlier prejudices. There was no arguing with him on that, because at least half the nation felt the same way. Annihilate the inferior red man and the country would be theirs.

"It's our destiny, son." The senator voiced the often quoted phrase as if privy to Blake's thoughts. "Our manifest destiny."

"Tremayne's parents were Anglo. What happened to them?"

If Blake hadn't been the senator's son and his only son to boot, Blake had the distinct impression that the senator would have struck him. He watched his father struggle to remain seated.

"Lies, lies, lies. Damned lies, all of it. How would I know what happened to that . . . that renegade's parents? How old was he when they were killed . . . four, five?"

"Six."

"You know so much about them, you tell me what happened."

"I don't know," Blake admitted. "That's why I came here tonight. He told me you murdered them."

"Me? What age would that have made me? What was I doing back then, running around murdering folks in a land I'd never even heard of, much less seen? Tell me, since you have all the answers, what would have brought me out here all those years ago? Ha! You didn't stop to think about that, did you? You storm in here, accusing me, your own father, your own flesh and blood . . . Some gratitude, all I can say. Some damned gratitude. Just because you want to get into that red devil's pants, you don't have to go around slandering the man who brought you into this damned world."

Blake's will to continue this interrogation was severely threatened by his father's allegations. Crass as the language was, could J. J. be right? In an effort to win Ket, had he jumped to conclusions about his own father?

"Since you put it that way," he continued, "I have only one last question. What about Rosa Ramériz? Did you rape her and father her child?"

"It wasn't rape," J. J. blustered. "Far from it."

Blake recoiled at the insinuation, even though on seeing Neeta, looking into her small blue eyes, he had known without having to be told that she was related to him. "You fathered Neeta?"

"The relationship was by mutual consent," the senator insisted. "Ask anybody who was there. That slut was all over me. Why should I have denied myself the pleasures of the flesh when they were offered on an open platter?"

That wasn't the way Blake heard it, but he ignored the fact. "You are Neeta's father?"

"Don't put words in my mouth," J. J. raged. "No man I know would claim paternity under those conditions. If you haven't learned that by now, you're not the man a son of mine should be."

Thank God for that, Blake thought. "Rosa is ill. She needs help with the child."

"She's got family."

"You don't intend to see that Neeta is taken care of?"

J. J. guzzled the remaining liquor in his glass. "Lordy, lordy, son. You sound like you were raised in a convent. If I'm at fault, I see now that it was leaving your education in the hands of that sissy mama of yours."

"Leave my mother out of this."

"Calm down, son, calm down. I didn't mean to offend your sensibilities. Good God Almighty, she sure made a mess of you."

Blake left the house without another word. He didn't fear he might strike this slovenly, degenerate man his mother had reared him to emulate, but he did think he might regurgitate if he heard one more slur uttered against people he had come to love and admire.

In a matter of minutes, he stood outside Rosa Raméríz's ramshackle adobe home. Blowing snow and wind rushed inside when his knock was answered by the child he now knew to be his half-sister.

Blake stood transfixed. He'd suspected Neeta was his

sister, but until now he hadn't known for sure. Seeing her for the first time as a relative took his breath. She was adorable.

"Who is it, Neeta?" came a call from inside.

"Señor Blake," the child replied.

"Invite him in, *hijita.*"

During the exchange, Blake had stepped inside and closed the door against the storm. He went down on one knee and took Neeta by the shoulders. "Hi," he finally said, finding himself in the unusual situation of being tongue-tied. Finally, he scooped her in his arms and crossed to the far doorway.

In the bedroom beyond, Rosa lay in bed, covered to the chin in a pile of quilts. The house, he realized, was as cold as his father's had been. The difference was that no one here was able to build a fire. He set about doing so without asking permission.

Finished, he turned to find an embarrassed expression on Rosa's face. He ignored it.

"Mrs. Ramériz? May I talk with you?"

She indicated the room's only chair. *"Sí, señor."*

"Call me Blake," he said, taking the indicated seat opposite the bed.

"It'll get warm in no time," he told her. Now that he was here, what should he say? Rather, how should he say it? The visit had been spontaneous, not planned. Although he couldn't call it rash any more than he could have termed his mad race for the Apachería rash.

While he pondered the situation, Rosa went into a fit of coughing, which further discomfited him.

He jumped to his feet. "How may I help? Water? What—?"

She silenced him with a raised hand, then again indicated that he should sit.

"Has Doc Henry been by?"

"*Sí.* He stops by almost every day. Even in this weather. Sabrina encourages him."

"What does he say?"

"Tuberculosis."

"What—?"

"*Hijita,*" Rosa interrupted him. "See if there is coffee for Señor Blake." When the child left the room, she addressed Blake. "The child is too young to understand."

"I'm sorry. I . . ." He took a deep breath and plunged in. "I've come from my father's house." Blake glanced toward the other room, then back. "Neeta is a beautiful, wonderful child."

When Rosa tried to speak, it resulted in more coughing.

"I want you to know . . . I mean, I'm deeply sorry for any . . . for your . . . trouble."

"As you say, señor, Neeta is a wonderful child. A joy to her mother. Of course, I worry . . ."

"That's what I want you to know. Don't worry about her. She will never be alone. She will be taken care of . . . good care."

Neeta returned carrying a pottery cup of cold coffee, which she placed on the hearth. When she faced him, it was with a glowing smile.

"*Gracias.*" A thought occurred to him, another spur-of-the-moment idea that sounded right. "That's about the only word of Spanish I know. How would you like the job of teaching me?"

The child scrunched up her face. "Me?"

"You. Teach me."

She laughed, and Blake felt a pang of joy. "I would pay you, of course."

Neeta tilted her petite head coquettishly. "With a goat?"

"Afraid not. The Tremaynes give you goats. I'll pay you in dollars."

"Pesos?"

"If you like."

"*Sí*, Señor Blake. I would like that. Then I can buy food for my goat."

By the time he rose to leave, Neeta was sitting on his lap and Rosa was crying; tears of joy, at least he hoped they were. Blake felt better than he had in days.

But there was still work to be done. Next stop, the Tremayne house.

"I don't doubt the man denied it," Tremayne observed after Blake related his father's denial that he had murdered Tremayne's parents. "If you're serious about wanting to know the truth, I can show you proof."

"You have proof that my father murdered your parents?"

"Hold on a minute." Tremayne left the room, only to return with a plan. "Spoke with Sabrina. Ket will stay with her while we ride out to the ranch."

"In this blizzard?" Blake blurted out the question, only to be reminded of something he already knew—he was new to this country.

"It's just a little snowstorm," Tremayne objected, and Blake recalled the stories of the man's hardihood.

"I don't need to tell you, sir, I'm not the outdoorsman you and Ket are."

Tremayne sized him up and down with a grin growing across his broad face. "Don't expect to convince me of that—not you, the man who sneaked into the Apachería single-handed—"

"And got himself caught," Blake reminded him.

"Doesn't matter. Any man who would attempt what you did can ride a few more hours in a snowstorm." He clapped Blake on the shoulder. "But I'm not sure I'm up to it. I had in mind waiting until tomorrow morning. If it's all right with you, we'll start out bright and early."

"Fine. I'll be here. By the way, I also asked my father about Neeta."

Tremayne cocked a head.

"He admitted to fathering her but claims the relationship was by mutual consent."

"Mutual, hell!"

"He said anyone who was around during that time would agree."

"No one who was around during that time would agree. But with Rosa sick and all, I don't see how it would do any good to dig into it."

"That's what I figured, too. I don't want you to take this wrong, sir, I mean . . . I'm not trying to toot my own horn or anything like that, but I stopped by Rosa's before coming here."

"Did you?"

Blake nodded. "I told her not to worry about Neeta, that . . . well, that Neeta will be well taken care of and loved. Maybe I should have talked this over with Ket first, but I do have an obligation and—"

"I wouldn't worry about Ket's reaction if I were you."

Blake intended to tell Ket that night, but he looked all over town without finding her. The next morning when he arrived for what promised to be a cold ride on a snowy day, Luke and Tres Robles came tumbling out the door. They dogged his every step, giving him no chance to say a private good-bye to her, even if he'd found her.

"Don't know where Ket ran off to," Tremayne confessed. "She said she'd be back in time to see after Sabrina for a few days."

"She'll keep her word," Blake told him. He was just sorry he hadn't been able to tell her good-bye.

They hadn't gotten far out of town before Luke and Tres Robles set about pestering him.

"We've been thinking about how to help you, Blake," Luke informed him, and thus began what Blake thought would be a long and torturous ride through the cold, but which instead turned out to be an indoctrination of a far different sort.

"What kind of help do you think I need?"

"With Ket. Now that you saved her from going off and getting herself killed by Mexicans, you've got to figure out how to get her to marry you."

"Is that so?" Blake glanced to Tremayne for explanation, but Tremayne just shrugged.

"Don't look to me for help. These boys have been way ahead of me for years."

The Tremayne ranch house was both unpretentious and unique. Built of native stone, it stood on the side of a sloping hill and overlooked a meandering creek.

"It's a dry wash," Tremayne explained. "Comes off Delaware Creek, further north. Only time we see water in it is after a big rain. We call 'em gully washers, and if you're ever here when we get one, you'll understand why."

Blake studied the terrain north and south, then up the hillside. It was another cold winter's day. The air was heavy with chill. A light dusting of snow covered the ground with deeper drifts in the numerous crevices. He should have been cold, but he wasn't.

From time to time during the ride he had wondered where Ket was, but he'd caught himself just short of worrying about her.

Keturah Tremayne had been taking care of herself for a long time, and he would have to learn to respect her need for freedom.

Already he felt like a new man. When the sun glanced off an expanse of glass, he realized they were approaching a dwelling.

"Riding up, you wouldn't know there was a dwelling anywhere around, except for the glass," he commented.

"Sabrina's idea," Tremayne acknowledged. "She figured the more places I had to see out, the less likely I'd feel trapped inside a regular house."

"Not a bad idea," Blake replied thoughtfully.

"You'll come up with your own way," Tremayne assured him. "She's a wild one, Ket is. Wilder than I ever was."

Inside the sprawling house, Tremayne went straight to the kitchen, calling, "Sophia, we're home. Sophia."

A stout, middle-aged woman of Mexican descent hurried into the wide hallway. "Señor Tremayne. ¿La señora? Do we have a niño?"

"Not yet, Sophia. And who's to say it will be a niño. We might come home with a niña."

The woman grinned and bobbed her head. "Buena, buena. A girl would be good."

"This is Blake Carmichael," Tremayne introduced. "The boys are around somewhere. We'll need supper as soon as you can manage. It's right cold out there."

"Sí, señor. I will pour coffee first."

"Bring it to my study, por favor." Leading the way, Tremayne strode through the winding hall and down a flight of stone stairs that led to a separate wing of the house, where for the next several hours he and Blake went over records collected ten years earlier.

The study was large, stone-floored, with wide windows that looked out over the dry wash and a rise of red stone cliffs. Tremayne removed a sheaf of papers from a metal box and spread them across the huge oak desk. He invited Blake to draw up a chair.

"When I decided to marry Sabrina, I looked around for some way to support a family. I knew that the land my father had owned before he and my mother were murdered had been bought up by your father, all except Apache Wells. Looking into it, I discovered that your father had purchased the warranty deeds to that land a short time after my parents were murdered. By my calculations, that would put Carmichael in the area in his early twenties."

Tremayne pushed the papers toward Blake. "Move closer to that lamp yonder," he suggested. "Check the names and dates."

"Roger Carmichael," Blake read. "George Carmichael. Those are my uncles. Although both are dead now. I never knew much about them. You mean they lived out here?"

"That's what it says."

Tremayne showed him other papers.

The first was a marriage license showing that George married one Gwenda Hoffmiester back in 1848. "Where's Marathon?"

"South of Fort Davis."

"West of the Pecos?" Blake wanted to know.

Tremayne nodded. That put his Uncle George in this country before Blake was born.

Next Tremayne handed him a birth certificate, listing Roger Carmichael as father to a baby girl, Beatrice, born in 1842. Attached to it was the child's death certificate and the mother's, one Beatrice Caulderon.

Blake set the certificates aside and picked up the warranty deeds again. His father had signed them and listed his place of residence as Fort Davis, Department of Texas. Well before the Civil War.

Well before Blake had been born.

Well before J. J. Carmichael claimed to have ever known about this land.

The warmth Blake had felt earlier turned as cold as the weather.

Ket faced a huge adjustment, moving from one world to another. But Blake faced an adjustment, too.

"I feel like I just lost my past," he told Tremayne, "my identity. The man I grew up believing to be my father, the man my mother taught me to emulate, never really existed. It's like my past was a lie, or at best, a nightmare."

"I wouldn't dwell on it too much, son. A man who strikes out on his own and makes his way by the sweat of his brow is genr'ly stronger for it." Tremayne returned the documents to the metal box where he had kept them safe from storm and fire for the last ten years.

"At best this is circumstantial evidence," he told Blake. "Your father and his brothers had motive—the land—and opportunity—they lived in this area."

"Which contradicts what he told me yesterday. He said he hadn't known this area existed back then."

"None of this is proof positive. It wouldn't convict in court," Tremayne went on. "I'm not sure I would have pursued the issue if the evidence had been stronger." He studied Blake with those Tremayne green eyes. Blake would never forget the first time he realized Ket's eyes were that deep, feral green. At the *tinaja* the morning after she rescued him and the boys from those Comancheros. Hell, if he ever ran into those fellows again, he'd be tempted to shake their hands and thank them.

"Likely we'll never know the whole of it," Tremayne continued. "Can't say it's important to me anymore. Except for the trait?"

Blake dragged his attention back from the *tinaja*. "The trait?"

"Personality trait. If all this speculation is true, if your father and his two brothers were ruthless killers and thieves, did you inherit the trait?"

Blake sat stunned, both by the documents before him and by Tremayne's audacity. The question, however, in the light of things, was a fair one, so he attempted to address it.

"I'd like to say not," he replied. "If my father was involved in this scheme before he was twenty, I've waited a bit later. I'm already thirty. But I don't guess that's much in the way of proof. On the other hand, I haven't done any of those things up to now, haven't even felt the urge. I can't recall ever coveting another man's property." Thinking of Rosa, he added, "Or his wife."

Tremayne rose and clapped Blake on the shoulder. "Frankly, any time Ket's ready to take a chance on you, I am, too. You have my blessing to marry her, son, if you can catch her. She's a wild one."

"Wild and lovely," Blake mused. "She's the best thing that's ever happened to me."

"I figure you'll have your work cut out." Tremayne laughed. "Especially keeping those two boys off your back trail. They're bound and determined to catch her for you."

Blake laughed. The road ahead might be rough, but he was champing at the bit to get started on it. "Can't say I don't need their help, but this is one task I'd best tackle by myself."

Chapter Fourteen

True to her word, Ket stayed with Sabrina while Tremayne took Blake and the boys to the ranch. She was finding it easier to be around her stepmother, although with her mind in its present state of turmoil, she realized this was not conclusive proof that their relationship had taken a turn for the better.

Sabrina, however, acted as if they had always been close; as if they had always been friends, on an equal basis rather than the way a stepmother would treat an unwanted stepdaughter.

Ket played along. Even when Sabrina spoke of plans for Emily's funeral, she listened.

"I wonder," Sabrina said once, "do you think you could find something for her grave, berries or juniper or something? And maybe some for Manuel's grave, too. Rosa always tended his grave, but with her illness, she isn't able to." That was before they heard that Emily would be buried in the post cemetery, not the one in town.

"I'll see what I can find," Ket had agreed easily, for in

truth her mind was on the turmoil inside her. She began to look for an opportunity to discuss this turmoil with Sabrina and found it when, at the end of the first day, Sabrina inquired about the Apachería.

Ket had cooked *pozole* on the iron cook stove. It seemed an awful lot of bother. Then again, it lent needed heat to the small house.

When she served Sabrina a bowl of the soup, she brought one for herself also and closed the bedroom door against the bitter cold wind that swirled inside the courtyard. She closed the heavy wooden shutters over the windows and stoked the fire in the corner fireplace, and the room became comfortable. "Cozy," Sabrina termed it.

Recalling Blake's observation about the wickiup, Ket gazed around the four adobe walls and willed the animal inside her not to panic.

"Can't see the difference," Blake had observed. "You're shut up inside here, too."

Ket glanced to Sabrina, the woman she had hated for so long. Now she was closed up in a small square white-eyes room with her.

"I don't mean to pry, Ket," Sabrina said after a few bites of *pozole*. "Your father said things didn't go well at the Apachería. Do you want to talk about it?"

No, she thought, recalling her grandmother's final good-bye.

"Go, my child," the old woman had said. "Go to your other world. You belong there now, as surely as your cousin did."

"Why do you say that?" Ket had objected.

"Your young man. You belong with him. Take your place and do not concern yourselves with us."

"How can I not . . . ?"

The sadness of that leave-taking overwhelmed her still. She was sure it always would. The abruptness with which she had been cut off from all that was her past, from the only people she had ever claimed, was a tragedy she knew she would never get over.

Talk about it? No, she couldn't.

But a new and threatening life loomed ahead of her, and locked away with her in this small room was a woman who offered guidance. How could she refuse?

Yet, how to begin? "Did he tell you about Blake?" she asked after a while.

Sabrina took her time answering. "He appears to be a persistent man."

"He could have gotten himself killed!"

"It was a dangerous thing to attempt, sneaking into a camp of armed men who consider him an enemy," Sabrina agreed.

"I couldn't believe it was him. Then I saw him . . . I've never been that frightened. Not even inside that Comanchero camp."

Sabrina laughed softly. "You two make a pair."

Ket recalled Blake's proposal. She still wasn't certain what she could do about that.

"Your father said he asked to marry you."

Ket ducked her head, studying her soup. "Yes . . . well, that wasn't why he came. He and Papa came out there for the same reason."

"Oh?"

Rising, Ket set her soup bowl on a chest. "To keep me from going to Mexico." When she turned to take Sabrina's bowl, Sabrina reached a hand and drew her down on the bed beside her.

"It's a terrible thing, Ket. I know you see us all as being of a single mind, but we aren't. A lot of us would like to live in peace with . . . with your people."

"I know that," Ket snapped. She wasn't angry with Sabrina. "I'm sorry. It's just . . . everything."

"I understand, dear."

"Did Papa tell you the rest of it? The *worst* of it?"

Sabrina shook her head slowly.

"Their trips were useless. Blake risked his life for nothing." Despair weighed heavily upon her. Tears stung her eyes. "I couldn't have gone to Mexico anyway. They . . . my people . . . they're not my people anymore. They . . . sent me away . . ."

Before Ket realized what had happened, Sabrina had set her bowl to the side of the bed and drew her down to cradle her head on her shoulder. Several lengthy, tense moments passed in silence before Sabrina released her.

She pushed Ket's hair off her forehead, as a mother would have done a child's, and smiled wanly.

"Your father told me something else." When she had Ket's attention, she continued. "He said he gave you Apache Wells."

Ket didn't trust her voice, so she nodded without meeting Sabrina's gaze.

"Then why don't you go there? Not this minute, but when the storm passes. Go there for comfort."

Ket turned her head aside.

"I know it sounds foolish, dear, a grown woman counseling a skittish young bride-to-be to listen for spirits. That isn't exactly what I mean. To me the guardian's laughter is an affirmation of the deepest desires inside a person. It's like saying listen to your own heart, but I always found that to be too simple. We are very good at denying what is inside our own hearts. Our past muddles our view of the road ahead of us."

Her view of the road ahead was more than muddled, Ket thought. "I'm not sure there is a road."

"There is a road for everyone," Sabrina assured her. "Sometimes we can't find our way until we go back to the beginning."

"The beginning of what?"

"According to your father, he and your mother took

you to Apache Wells when you were only a few days old. You began your life there; that is your beginning.''

Ket considered this. She wasn't sure she understood, and if she did, she wasn't sure she believed.

"Your life has been a series of disasters, Ket. The worst of all, after your mother's death, was when your father and I married. I can tell you the truth—the decision was wrenching for him, but he always believed you would eventually accept me . . . us. He never stopped loving you with his whole heart. He never stopped hoping you would come back to him.''

"Then why didn't he come for me?" The question was out before she thought, and once spoken, the words could not be taken back.

"We thought about it. We talked endlessly about it. We might've been able to force you to live with us, although I'm afraid you would have just run away, but we could never have forced you to accept us. Maybe your father should have tried harder; it's easy to look back and ask 'what if?' Maybe he should have gone to see you when you visited Nick and Lena. He didn't, because he was afraid you would stop seeing them, too. They were his only link to you. He never gave up, Ket. He's been waiting for you all this time. He's still waiting for you.''

Ket didn't know whether to believe what Sabrina said. She wasn't even sure it mattered anymore. "It was easy to hate him,'' she admitted. "Much easier than to try to figure out what to do.''

"Don't be hard on yourself,'' Sabrina cautioned. "You were a child, a child who had lost too much already. But the only way your father could have pleased you would have been to give up his right to live his own life. Parents must rear their children to live independent lives, but children must also allow their parents to live their own lives. It's a difficult situation, whichever way you look at it. There are very few right or wrong answers in this world.''

* * *

Two days later Tremayne and the boys returned from the ranch in time for Emily's funeral. Before Ket could ask about Blake, her father told her, "Blake's gone to palaver with his father. He said he'll catch up with us at the funeral."

It was a military funeral, complete with bugles, cannons, and flags. The only people missing were the Commander of Fort Davis, Lon Jasper, and the senator in residence, J. J. Carmichael.

"Smart move on their parts," Tremayne whispered to Nick. "Folks would have had a hard time deciding which one to push into that open grave first."

The storm had ended the day before. Sunlight shone through the crisp mountain air and glistened from the icy red cliffs. Nick and Lena arrived that morning, and all except Sabrina attended together. Ket had donned a woolen shirtwaist and skirt, covered with a heavy woolen cloak from among Emily's belongings, which made things even sadder, or so she imagined, for every time Reba Applebee looked her way, the woman's sobs increased.

Or so Ket felt. Then Blake arrived, out of breath and grim-faced until he spied her standing uncomfortably beside her father. When he came quietly to stand at her other side, she felt a surge of relief. Standing here between her father and Blake, she received a renewed sense of warmth, and the situation became bearable.

Bearable, that is, as long as she didn't look at that gaping hole in the ground.

In her hands she held two sprays—blue-berried juniper mixed with red-berried youpon. Scents from the juniper rose to fill her with a strangely sweet sense of tranquility. Strange, indeed, that she would feel tranquil here in this white-eyes graveyard.

After the service she and Blake waited until the others

dispersed so she could place Sabrina's spray on the casket, following white-eyes custom, according to Blake. She was glad to walk away, but one task remained.

"Would you like to come with me to the other cemetery?" she asked him.

"Making the rounds, huh?"

"Sabrina wants me to take a spray to Manuel's grave."

It was a strange time for their love to grow, but that's how she felt as they walked along the snow-laden road bundled inside heavy coats. The wind had died down the evening before and had yet to pick up again.

"Tremayne said it's a sign of more snow," Blake mentioned.

"I'm glad it let up for the service," she replied.

Neither of them was thinking about snow or funerals. At the Fort Davis Pioneer Cemetery, she placed the wintry wreath on Manuel's grave. When she straightened, Blake took her in his arms. The juniper scent lingered, leaving her feeling mellow—until he broached the topic she had hoped to avoid.

"How will you feel about marrying the son of the man who murdered your grandparents?"

"Papa had proof?"

"Not the kind that would hold up in a court of law, but the circumstantial evidence is powerful. Especially taken against my father's denials of ever having heard about this country in those days."

"I'm sorry," she told him. "You had such hopes of establishing a relationship with him."

"I meant what I said at the Apachería, Ket. We don't need our fathers anymore. Now that we have each other, we can take them or leave them." He brought his lips close to hers. His breath blew moist and warm against her face, lathing her with old familiar longings.

Longings she was sure she would always feel for this

man. No longer did she see him as a white eyes. He was just a man—no, a particular man, a special man.

She opened her lips and received his kiss and felt completely and wholly loved for the first time in her life. When he opened the edges of his shearling coat and she slipped inside, she knew she was standing exactly where she belonged.

Yet, her past tormented her. She had belonged to her mother, but her mother had been taken from her.

She had belonged to her father, but he had abandoned her for another.

She had belonged to the People, but they no longer accepted her.

How could she think this would last, when nothing else in her life had lasted? How could she make mistake after mistake and never learn?

Finally, she knew what she had to do. Even if it hurt them both now, it could save them much more pain later. Drawing away, she folded the edges of his coat across his chest. "I can't marry you, Blake."

He didn't understand, of course. "I've already said I'll give you time, Ket, and I will. I'll give you time to get used to things."

"That isn't it."

"Then what the hell is?"

How could she make him understand? "It's me," she said finally. "It's inside me."

"What?"

"Ghosts," she said, using a white-eyes term. "Not spirits, ghosts. They haunt me. I'll never be free . . ."

While she spoke he took her head in his gloved hands, as though he were bestowing a blessing of some sort. To ward off ghosts? Of course it didn't work that way.

"We'll fight them together," he told her.

"No." That animal inside her began to panic again. "I'll never be free."

"I don't care, Ket. We'll live with them, together, one day at a time. I told you, we don't have to rush into anything."

She couldn't answer, so she just shook her head.

"Don't be afraid," he whispered.

"I'm not. It just won't work."

"Damnit, Ket, it will work. You'll see—"

"It won't work." She said it firmly now in an effort to convince him. "I'm sorry. I hoped you would understand." But he didn't. He looked so hopeless. So . . . Suddenly she moved further away from him. "I never made you any promises, I never said I would—"

He stared her straight in the eye, and she flinched at the determination she saw there. No wonder he had sneaked into the Apachería. The man before her could do anything he set his mind to. Anything except reach inside her and snatch out her past.

Her past was a part of her and always would be, and she felt so cold and lonely she thought she might cry.

"Yes, you did, Ket," he told her. "You made a lot of promises. Maybe not in words, but in deeds—in your reaction to me, in your reception of my love. You gave love to me, Ket. That's a promise if ever there was one. And I don't intend to stand by and let you renege on it. You're not deserting me the way you did your father."

He left her standing there in that white-eyes cemetery, saying he had unfinished business with his father and that he would see her at the house.

Well, she wouldn't be at her father's house when he returned. She had tried to explain, but now she saw that he was beyond understanding.

The way she had deserted her father? How could he accuse her of being the perpetrator? She was the victim. She had always been the victim. Sabrina had even admitted it. A victim of the hated white eyes.

Except some of them were not so hated anymore.

* * *

"Just so you'll know where we stand," Blake said by way of greeting when he burst into his father's house. "I spoke with Rosa Ramériz, apologized for your behavior, and promised to take care of her daughter."

"What the hell do you mean . . . ?"

"I mean that I intend to live in this country, too, and I don't want every Carmichael out here tarnished by your disgusting behavior. I plan to marry Keturah Tremayne as soon as she agrees. I will continue surveying your sites, and I would like to remain on good terms with you—"

"Remain? Hell, we haven't been on good terms your whole life. Didn't you know that? I hated that bitch of a mother of yours. Why do you think I stayed away? Living out here where everyone hated me was preferable to living in the house of that whining, prissy—"

Blake turned on his heel and left while he could still control his behavior. If they both remained in this country, he and his father would probably come to blows someday, but today wasn't the day for it. Today, he had more important things to do, such as persuade Ket to take the biggest chance of her lifetime.

Ket did not tarry at the cemetery. She made haste for her father's house, where she slipped in the back without seeing Sabrina or the others, changed into her deerskin clothing and fox robe, and left again. Hours of cold riding later, she sat on the ridge looking down into Apache Wells.

The thought that it now belonged to her fluttered inside her, but that, too, created turmoil, for she had been raised by the People and they taught that man could not *own* Mother Earth. Man, along with all creation, was a part of Mother Earth.

Yet, she felt a kinship, a bond, looking down into this valley she had hated for so long.

Why here? Blake had asked. *You hate this place.*

Hate it? She wondered now. Did she really hate it? If so, why had she returned?

Listen to your heart. Sabrina's suggestion made hardly more sense than her earlier admonition to listen for the guardian.

Yet Ket had to admit that she had never needed to hear someone or something more in her life. Nudging the palomino down the steep incline with its columns of red boulders to either side, she wondered why she was drawn to this place.

Why here? Blake had asked.

It's your beginning, Sabrina later claimed. *To find your way in life, you must return to where you began.*

For the last ten years Ket had allowed herself to recall only recent memories of Apache Wells—memories of her father and Sabrina and her own scarred leg.

But, as Sabrina had reminded her, Apache Wells had played a much earlier role in Ket's life. Her father had lived here as a child. He had seen his own parents murdered here. And she had lived here from time to time as a child, also.

For ten years she had denied that she could have experienced any joy in this place. If she had, those happy memories were buried beneath the anger and hatred of the more recent past.

Now she felt an urgency—and yes, more than a little fear—to recall those earlier times, whether they turned out to have been good or bad.

When she reached the valley floor, it was as if she had descended with the night, for the early evenings that came with the winter season always reached the valley first. She felt small here, insignificant, and for the first time she wondered whether that feeling came from more than her painful memories.

Physically it did, for the land itself rose from the valley floor to a height of a thousand or more feet. Columns of red boulders towered above her like giants ringing a miniature figure. Even though she stood taller than most women, Ket had always felt small here. Now she realized that this feeling could have come from the physical nature of the high mountain valley.

Hitching the palomino at the ancient rail outside the cabin, she stood before it lost in thought.

Her father had lived in this cabin as a child. Later, he and Sabrina began their married life here. Ket had hated it since then. Her memories were painful, and not only because her father had lived here with Sabrina. As a ten-year-old she had lain inside that cabin, delirious from the pain of her burned leg.

Could that pain have etched hatred for this place and for Sabrina so deeply in her soul? Thoughts of this cabin always brought a return of the pain, a pain she associated with Sabrina. Every time she looked at the massive scar on her leg, she felt that pain and she hated Sabrina more. As time passed, the reason became clear—in this cabin Sabrina had tried to kill her so she could marry Tremayne without the burden of a half-breed stepdaughter.

But Ket's history had included this cabin before she burned her leg. According to Sabrina, Ket had lived here with her parents. Would she ever be able to remember those days, or had she been too young?

Had the disasters that came afterward erased those earlier memories from her frightened child's mind forever?

Some of her early days must have been joyous, she reasoned. Else why would she have spent so much of her life grieving over the loss of her parents? The three of them, she and her parents, must have known joy in this valley, perhaps even inside this cabin.

With an enormous sense of trepidation, she pushed open the heavy, weathered door. A musty odor rushed out of the darkened interior, but she held her ground, determined to face this ghost, if no other.

Peering into the dark, she tried to imagine it as it would have been when she lived here with her parents.

The mustiness could be explained by the passage of years, but the taste of gall in her mouth could only be the result of her latest memories. The bed of furs her father had placed her upon; the breathtakingly sharp odor of the ointment.

Witches' brew! Sabrina had covered Keg's leg with it and made bitter tea for her to drink. *Witches' brew!* The words had haunted her for ten years. And every time she thought them, she had envisioned Sabrina.

Witches' brew! It had poisoned her leg and her soul. Now listening to the voice in her mind, she was confused. Standing here in the darkened doorway, it wasn't Sabrina's voice she heard, but her father's.

No! Her father wouldn't have spoken those words. He had trusted Sabrina and her knowledge of medicine, meager though that knowledge had been. Her father had brought Sabrina here to cure her. He thought she was an angel, not a witch. He wouldn't have called her treatment *witches' brew.*

Then what was this memory all about? Prodded by new questions, Ket stepped into the cabin. Again she stopped, mere inches inside the one-room cabin. And again she fought her mind, striving to recall the interior from her earlier, happier days. The struggle was intense, but she was aided by the deep and penetrating darkness—and by an overwhelming desire to conquer her fear of this one dwelling, if of nothing else.

Step by step, she forced herself into the room. She wanted to light a fire but resisted, for to do so would extinguish any hope she had of recalling this place in its former state.

Light would reveal the cabin as it looked now. Or perhaps as it had looked ten years earlier. Light might fall on the bed of furs where she had learned to hate Sabrina . . . and her father.

When she reached what she judged to be the center of the room, she swept one toe around the floor, but felt nothing in the way of furniture, so she sat cross-legged where she had stood.

The cold was stark, even wrapped inside her fox pelts. The darkness was so intense, it seemed tangible; it penetrated her senses and gave her the feeling of being inside a dream, even though she was wide awake.

Snuggling into her robe, she forced all thoughts from her mind and concentrated on the blackness. Time passed . . . drifted . . . She lost track . . .

The darkness became light . . .

A fire leaped in the fireplace at the far end of the cabin. As from a distance, she watched a young woman dressed in a soft deerskin dress kneel before it. She stirred a pot of something . . . *pozole*, Ket decided from the aroma.

The door burst open and a child rushed in carrying an armload of juniper branches. The scent filled the small room.

Turning, the woman jumped up and closed the door. "Brrr, Ket, we must keep the door closed. It is the time of Ghost Face."

The child giggled and dropped her bundle of branches on the floor. Instead of chiding her for making a mess, the mother sat beside the child and taught her to weave a garland of juniper branches, which she then placed on her daughter's brow.

"Make one for you," the child begged.

So the mother complied. When she finished, she took

her daughter's hands and the two of them skipped around in a circle, laughing and singing a song with strange words.

During this the door burst open again and a man entered. A very tall man. When he dropped his bearskin robe to the floor, the child noticed his dark wavy hair; it was so long it fell to his shoulders. Instead of a garland of juniper branches, her father's hair was held back by a band of red flannel.

"What are my girls up to?" The man went down on his knees and opened his arms, and the child and her mother rushed to greet him.

The child sat on one knee, the mother on the other. The father kissed the child on the forehead, but he kissed the mother on her lips.

The child watched while her parents' kiss lengthened. The sight filled her with so much joy, she thought she might burst with it. Before that could happen, she shrieked with sheer delight.

The parents stopped kissing and started laughing. Then they both put their arms around the child. And the three of them held each other so tight, the child was sure they would never let her go. . . .

Daylight came through the open cabin door and cast a stream of light across Ket's face. She opened her eyes but lay there a moment, freezing, yet strangely at peace.

The dream was fresh and she recalled it in detail, realizing that she had seen her mother's face for the first time since that horrible day when the soldiers raided the village.

Rising, she built a fire in the cold fireplace and inspected the cabin in daylight. No ghosts here. It was mostly barren of furniture—a couple of old pieces she had never seen before. No pallet of furs to call forth memories of that painful experience with her leg.

Prompted to recall that time, though, she glanced to the fireplace again and saw an old rocker.

An old woman had sat there, sewing. The memory became clearer. She saw a pair of scissors, heard screams.

Her own screams. The memory rushed back. She had grabbed those scissors and cut her braids. But that wasn't the reason she was crying. The pain in her leg was intense. Sabrina was there. Sabrina had caused . . .

Her memory was of a dimly lit cabin, but she recognized Sabrina by the color of her hair. It glowed in the firelight like the fires of the Underworld.

Suddenly she saw Sabrina run from the cabin. Then her father was there. He held her in his arms . . .

"Sabrina didn't hurt you," he was saying.

She touched his face, in her mind's eye, and felt his tears.

Tremayne, her father, weeping? Holding her and weeping? That was the last time she had allowed him to hold her.

Suddenly her memories became suffocating. She couldn't breathe. Drawing her fox pelt robe tightly around her, she ran from the cabin. By the time she caught her breath, she had reached the well. Her tears fell now. She couldn't stop them.

Could Sabrina have been right? Had her father not given up on her? Had it been as Sabrina said—that he realized one person alone could not form a relationship?

He's been waiting for you, Ket. He is still waiting.

Lifting her head, she stared up at the red hills that surrounded this valley—her valley.

Why here? Blake had asked. *You hate this place.*

She didn't hate this place. She hated what had happened here—or what she believed had happened here. Could she have been so wrong? Certainly at ten she hadn't seen life accurately enough to judge such a complex situation. As a child it had been easy to hate, yes, and it had also been easy to feel abandoned. By that time she had lost a lot in her short life.

But now she was no longer a child.

Inhaling deeply, she drew the chilled morning air into her lungs. She exhaled and drew in some more. Fresh, cold air.

"I love winter here! It's like living in a cocoon. Isn't this a marvelous place, Ket? Apache Wells is a wonderful place to call home!"

In her mind her mother's laughter sounded so alive she could have just whispered the words in Ket's ear.

Suddenly Ket was laughing, too. She couldn't stop laughing. Inside her heart a child's giggles joined a mother's laughter, and she threw back her head . . .

Then she saw him. He sat atop the ridge staring down at her.

Chapter Fifteen

Even though Blake left his father's house with a huge void inside him, an unexpected sense of relief soon began to seep steadily into it. At least now he knew the truth about the man.

Nothing really surprised him. He was shocked, yes. Disappointed, of course. From the first time he saw his father in this strange, wild country, Senator J. J. Carmichael had seemed more foreign than the environment. Blake realized that now. He also realized that with ties to the senator severed, he had work to do.

After stopping by Rosa's to check on her condition and find out what she needed in the way of supplies, he headed for the mercantile with Neeta in tow. The child was her usual quiet self, but Blake needed silence, too, right now. So many things were happening at once, he needed time to organize them in his brain.

"So you're moving out?" Edward Bolton quizzed. Never one to mince words, he came around the counter and shook Blake's hand. "Sorry things turned out the way they did for you, son, but you're gonna be better off. Mark my word on that.''

"Do you happen to know of any houses for rent?"

Edward scratched his head a minute, then his eyes brightened. "Sure enough." He turned toward an open door that led to a back room. "Martha, could you mind the store while I find our new citizen a place to live?"

Thirty minutes later, Edward had tracked down one Mr. George Bently, who showed Blake an unfurnished one-room rock house next to his own larger adobe. "Five dollars a month."

"Now, George," Edward bargained, "that's a mite steep for a young fellow just out of the East. Settle for two and a half and he'll take it."

George wouldn't go any lower than three, but Blake would have given the five to have a place of his own.

"Come on back to the store and Martha and I'll fix you up with a bed and things."

"I wouldn't want to bother—"

"It's no bother. I told you we need good men out here. Besides, it's a loan, not a gift."

Back at the mercantile Blake accepted the loan of a bed and mattress, sheets, towels, and a couple of cooking pots. From Edward he bought supplies for himself and additional sacks of masa, pinto beans, and coffee for Rosa. Edward promised to have the lot of it delivered by nightfall.

Leaving Neeta with her mother, Blake returned to his father's house and removed his belongings without the two men exchanging so much as a word.

Once he finished organizing his living quarters, Blake cleaned up using water from George Bently's water well and a bowl and pitcher Martha Bolton had insisted no home should be without. He changed his shirt, combed back his hair, and for the first time since arriving in this place felt like his life had taken a turn toward normalcy.

He was going courting. His step was light. He decided

to ask Tremayne for Ket's hand again, more formally this time.

But Ket wasn't there.

"She might be at her camp," Tremayne suggested.

Blake wondered why he hadn't thought of that. Perhaps things *were* back to normal. With the two boys dogging his footsteps, he decided that normal in this part of the world needed a whole new definition.

"Ket's a wild one," Tres informed him.

"I know."

"She's not likely to take kindly to a man telling her what to do."

"I don't intend to."

"Where're yawl gonna live?"

"None of your business."

"Are you gonna ask her the question tonight?"

"Not with you two around."

"Aw, Blake, we've never heard a man propose marriage. How're we gonna learn if no one shows us how?"

"Don't worry about it. When the time comes, you'll figure out what to do. No woman wants a proposal of marriage her lover learned from somebody else."

"That sounds awful hard," Luke complained. "If we learned from you—"

"Nothing worthwhile is easy." When Ket's camp came into view, he stopped. "You boys head on back home."

They didn't turn around, not to his surprise, but in the long run it didn't matter. Ket wasn't at the camp. From the look of things, she hadn't been there in quite a while. The absence of the travois reminded Blake of the tragedies she had endured and of all the *ghosts* still left for her to overcome.

"I bet she headed for Apache Wells," Luke suggested.

"Now, why would . . . ?" Blake reconsidered. Why hadn't he thought of that?

"We can be there before midnight."

"Yeah, we can—"

"*We* can't do anything. You boys stay out of this."

"Aw, Blake, you better let us come."

"You're gonna need some help, taming that wild one," Tres observed wisely.

"You're probably right. But this is my business. Mine and Ket's."

"You'd better let us help or you might lose her."

"Listen to me, both of you. I said no, and I meant no. This is something every man has to do himself, and he doesn't want an audience."

"But—"

"No buts. Besides, I'm not riding out there tonight. That would be foolhardy. Comancheros might happen along."

"They've gone to Mexico."

"What's to say they won't come back?"

"They just won't. You haven't been out here long enough—"

"I've been out here long enough to know when I want to be alone. Now you two scram. If I catch you on my back trail, you won't be invited to the wedding."

"Wedding?"

"What'd you think's the result of a proposal?"

The boys broke out laughing in unison. "You think Ket's gonna hitch herself in a double harness?"

"You've got another think comin', greener."

"Scram!"

Instead of heading out right away, he decided to stop by the Tremayne place and find some way to dodge the boys. Which didn't turn out to be a problem, after all.

A distraught Tremayne met them at the door. "Get Doc Henry!"

"What?"

"Doc Henry. Hurry! Sabrina's in labor."

Blake ran the entire half-mile to the doctor's house,

arriving with lungs that felt frozen. "Sabrina needs you! The baby—"

Doc Henry gathered his bag and hustled out the door. "Tremayne said to hurry."

The old doctor chuckled. "She'll be fine. All she needed was a little time, and now she's had it. Tonight we'll have a baby." When they arrived at the house, he added, "I'll deliver the baby; you sit with the papa."

So Blake spent the next few hours with Tremayne, although it didn't involve much sitting. Tremayne paced. Blake made coffee. And the boys were quiet for a change.

The first time Sabrina cried out, their eyes popped open, and Tremayne headed for the door.

"Wait up," Blake felt obliged to say. "I think that's normal."

Tremayne turned a hardened glare on him. "Easy for you to say." He glanced anxiously at the closed door. "She's not your wife."

That gave Blake pause. Here he was contemplating marriage, and look what that meant for a woman. When he thought of Ket being in a room like that, wracked by wrenching pain, he wondered how a man could put the woman he loved through such torture.

He glanced at Luke, who was as ashen-faced as his father. "She survived it once," he reminded them.

"That doesn't make it easier. Do you know how many women die—"

"Shh," Blake advised, and Tremayne immediately gripped himself.

Then before they had time to worry much more, Doc Henry opened the door. "She's a cute one."

Tremayne bolted through the doorway as if he hadn't heard. "How's Sabrina?"

Luke was right behind him. "How's my mama?"

"She's fine, son. So's your sister."

"Sister?" Luke crept uncertainly through the door, followed closely by an obviously more uneasy Tres Robles.

"You can go in." The doctor stepped aside, grinning broadly at Blake. "You don't look all that good yourself, son."

"Me?" Blake swallowed the lump in his throat.

"It's all part of the scheme of things," Doc Henry told him jovially. "Part of what women must endure in this ol' world. The survival of humanity, and all that."

After a quick visit to offer congratulations, Blake slipped away into the cold night, his mind far from easy. The experience had rocked him. Just when he was thinking of marriage, he had been presented with a startling example of what marriage meant to women.

It put things into a completely different light. Children were one of the goals of marriage, yet how many men were confronted with the pains of childbirth on the night they intended to propose?

It didn't seem fair, somehow. At the same time, Doc Henry was right. It was the good Lord's way of ensuring the survival of humanity. Not the well-thought-out plan of a benevolent God, Blake decided.

Stopping by his new quarters, Blake changed into riding clothes, picked up a couple of warm blankets, and headed for Apache Wells. At least the boys would be preoccupied for the rest of this night.

When he rode away from Fort Davis in the chill of night, his thoughts turned from childbirth and children to the present, and precisely the difficulty he faced before any children were possible—persuading Ket to marry him.

By the time he arrived at Apache Wells, the sun had begun to rise. He sat atop the ridge, studying the valley, gathering his thoughts, deciding what words to use, how to persuade Ket . . .

A sudden flash of skepticism burst through him, taking him by surprise. Was this what he wanted for the rest of his life? He recalled his father's despicable words about his mother; had theirs been a marriage that should never have happened? He certainly didn't want to make the same mistake. He would be faithful to Ket, he knew that, given the example of a womanizing father. But would he be happy?

Then the scene below him came into full focus. Smoke rose from the chimney. The cabin door was ajar. Just before he panicked, he saw her.

She stood at the well, leaning over . . . Was she crying? While he watched, wondering what to do, she flung her head up and he saw her face.

Then he knew. He loved this woman. No doubt remained. Not one.

Now the question changed. Could he make her happy?

Ket's heart skittered at sight of Blake. She held him in her sights while he nudged his mount and descended the hill. She felt skittish, like a new colt. Yet, she felt anxious, too. Anxious to touch him, to kiss him, anxious to tell him about her dream, anxious to love him.

She felt as though she watched her future approach, and a glorious future it was. The mountains rose around them, protecting them from danger, secluding them from the harsh world outside this valley.

She awaited him eagerly. A fleeting sense of poignancy brought tears to her eyes for the second time today. While she stood here filled with dreams for her future, her people had been forced to flee to certain death in Mexico.

Yet, Blake was right. She had another people, and for the first time in her life she felt a kindling desire to belong to them, too. Watching Blake descend the mountain, she knew she was luckier than she would ever have imagined she could be to have found such a man to love.

Like her father had been lucky to have found Sabrina.

He had tried to tell her that, but she couldn't listen. Wha
she heard as rejection and abandonment had been hi
profession of finding such a love. Sabrina was the bes
thing that had happened to her father. Rather than stea
him away from Ket, Sabrina had healed the wound in he
father's heart made by the death of her mother. Ket wa
eager to tell him that at last she understood.

Yes, Sabrina was the best thing that had happened t
her father, and Blake Carmichael was the best thing tha
had happened to Ket, and she stood filled with anticipa
tion. Her sense of belonging with this man grew with eac
plod of his horse's hooves.

When he drew rein, they held their places for the longes
time, each silently questioning the other.

He slid from his horse beside the ancient well and
approached her with a determined stride. Ket knew ther
that it didn't matter whether the guardian confirmed it o
not, this was the right man for her.

He opened his coat and drew her inside, and it was a
long, long time before either of them thought of anything
except lips touching lips, cold bodies becoming heated
and fluid.

He was first to break the trance. "I'm damned tired o
chasing you all over this cockeyed country, Ket. You're
gonna have to marry me, so I can keep up with you."

She couldn't have pulled her gaze from his if she had
wanted to, and she certainly didn't want to. She felt los
in him and wanted to remain lost for the rest of their lives

"You can't keep me harnessed," she told him, speaking
words she knew were true. It was her greatest remaining
fear. "I can never give up my freedom. I'd die—"

"I may not know much about this country, like every
one's always telling me, but I'm not stupid, either. You
think I'd harness a wild horse? I won't try to tame you
Ket. I love you the way you are."

She smiled, suddenly shy. "I know." This time she initi

ated the kiss, which didn't end with lips on cold lips, but with hands groping, bodies pressing, questing, needing.

Again Blake pulled apart first. "It's awful cold out here to do what I think you might be ready to do."

He was right. She was ready. She took his hand and pulled him toward the cabin. "It's warm inside."

"Inside the cabin?"

She heard his surprise. "I spent the night there."

"You did? I thought—"

"I got rid of a lot of ghosts last night."

She walked with him while he hitched his horse beside hers at the old hitching rail.

"You'd better bring those blankets." She indicated the roll tied to his saddle. "There aren't any inside."

"No blankets? What did you . . . ?"

She snuggled closer into her furry robe and watched passion consume the last of his words. In the cabin they spread blankets on the stone floor and covered them with her fox pelts.

"It's perfect." She pulled him down beside her.

"Except for one thing."

"What?"

He took his time answering, holding her rapt attention the whole time. "I want to see your leg first."

She thought maybe her heart had stopped. "No. I mean . . . not . . . before . . . After—"

"First," he insisted.

She just stared at him, but he showed no sign of relenting.

"We've waited all this time to make love, Ket. When we do, I want it to be perfect."

"But—"

He was determined, though, and while she sat benumbed, he tugged off her moccasins and began to unlace her britches.

Resigned to the inevitable, she slapped his hand away.

"I'll do it myself," she told him crossly. "I should have known you'd be like this. Any man who would get himself caught by Comancheros and then sneak into an Apachería during a snowstorm . . ."

By this time she had discarded her britches; she sat on the pallet, legs stretched out in front of her, eyes averted. Her resignation had turned to apprehension and filled her up.

She knew Blake well enough by now to know he loved her. He wouldn't stop loving her, no matter what he thought about her leg. He wouldn't even show revulsion at the shriveled-up calf.

But she didn't want his pity, either.

"Damned!" he uttered. "May I touch it?"

Her eyes flew to his. She nodded, stiffly, and he ran his fingers up and down the scar. Then he took the largest part of the calf between his fingers and squeezed.

"Not much muscle left." He might have been examining a side of meat. "But what's there's hard as rock."

She didn't reply, and after another moment he took his hand from her calf, cupped her chin, and lifted her face to his.

"Guess that answers my question."

His reaction struck her as strange, at best. "What question?"

"Any woman who could make it through something that painful should do all right in childbirth."

"Childbirth?"

Blake knelt before her. The flames were behind him and cast him in silhouette. Although his features were shadowed, she could tell his thoughts were intense.

"Sabrina had the babe last night. I stayed with Tremayne. She screamed . . . and screamed . . ."

Ket absorbed his compassion. She reached for him, stroked the side of his face, then began to tug at his shirt. "Was she still screaming afterward?"

"No."

"Then what are you worried about?"

"Nothing."

By this time she had stripped his shirt over his head, and he had lifted hers. In a matter of seconds they lay in each other's arms, skin to heated skin.

"I've imagined this for so long." His mouth claimed hers; his body pressed hotly against her.

"I never imagined anything like it," she admitted. "Not before I met you."

His response was to trail his lips down her neck and over her chest. While his hands worked magic, his lips touched places they had never touched before.

She writhed in pleasure, anticipating the thrills she had already experienced from his touch, yet yearning for the culmination she had never been brave enough to allow.

Every touch of his hands and lips increased her fervor. When he moved his body, length matching length, over hers, she clung to him.

"I've wanted this so long," he whispered hoarsely into her mouth, "it won't last . . . I wanted . . . your first . . ."

Her heart thrashed in her chest. Her wildness surprised her. All her desire, all her attention, now centered on one place. She had longed for fulfillment, too. It was true, what he had told her that first day behind the steward's house. She wanted him.

Reaching between them, she guided him to the place that had wept for him all these months. "You said this was proof."

"Ah . . . Ket. It is." He sank into her, filling her with all of him—body, soul, and spirit.

She didn't need the guardian of the well. She had Blake. And he had her.

Then her head began to spin and all her thoughts merged together like threads of gold and red and black on a spinning wheel, until at the end the only color left was gold and it exploded in her head like the sun rising suddenly above a dark horizon.

She was sweaty afterwards, and he was, and they clung together on her robe of fox pelts, and she knew she was where she belonged.

"I know what love means," she told him.

When he questioned, she told him the story of Chi Caliente and Doré making love in the rain.

"Then you knew all about it," he teased.

"Not long after that they were murdered by soldiers. Emily was taken to the fort; then I fell into the fire and Papa brought Sabrina to heal me; then he left me for Sabrina . . . After all that I believed that to a white eyes love meant death or betrayal."

Blake kissed her face. "No wonder you had trouble believing in me."

"Last night I dreamed about my mother."

"You were brave to come here."

"Sabrina said to find my way in life I should return to my beginnings. She insisted I must have happy memories about Apache Wells, too. And she was right."

"I'm glad you listened to her."

They lay in each other's arms, holding tightly, damp skin to damp skin. She remembered his fear of childbirth, then she recalled the baby.

"What did Sabrina have?"

"A girl. With a full head of red hair."

"A sister." She thought of Emily, just buried, and a sister just born into this world.

"The wind is picking up," Blake said suddenly. "Hear it whistle through the chinks in the walls? Guess I'll have to patch—"

"That isn't the wind," she objected. "It's my heart."

When he chuckled, she explained. "Sabrina believes the guardian is a person's heart and that it laughs when it recognizes its own desire."

He kissed her tenderly. "Then I agree. It isn't the wind."

Later, he inquired, "You really got rid of all those ghosts last night?"

She nodded against him.

"Does that mean you're free to marry me?"

Now that she knew her own heart, she wasn't afraid to answer. "I can be married to you. I don't know about the marrying part."

"You mean a wedding?"

"I wouldn't like a . . . white-eyes wedding."

"How 'bout we ride into town and take out a marriage license at the courthouse and call ourselves married?"

"Would that be all right? Would you worry about . . . ?"

"Only thing I'm ever going to worry about, Ket, is if I can be as tough as my wife."

Epilogue

Two Months Later

"A party? I don't want a party. How could anyone think I would want a party?" Ket slipped the delicately beaded doeskin dress over her head, then slung her single braid across her shoulder. "I won't know how to act—"

Blake took her by the shoulders and planted a tender kiss on her lips. "Calm down, Ket. It's only family, a few friends. That's all."

Ket's anxiety had grown steadily since Tremayne rode out for a visit two weeks earlier. Blake had been away surveying the last couple of lots for his father.

"Leave it to J. J. Carmichael," he had commented upon receiving a curt message that he was expected to have those lots surveyed on time. "He's mad as all get-out at me, but business must go on."

Ket had been at the creek when she heard Tremayne's horse. By the time she reached the cabin, he had drawn up to the hitching rail.

At first he seemed awkward. He untied a bundle from behind his saddle and handed it to her.

Inside she found the doeskin dress. She handled it reverently. At first glance she could tell it was old.

"Belonged to your mama," he said in a hushed tone.

She fingered the soft tanned leather, then looked up to find his eyes upon her. Without a moment's thought she was in his arms.

She didn't cry. Long moments passed while she held him and he held her. Conversation had never come easily for either of them, so their silence was not uncomfortable.

"Where did you get it?" she asked at last. What she wondered was why she had never seen it.

"A trunk of her things was left here in the cabin," he told her simply. "I kept them for you. I'll bring the rest out later."

"Oh, Papa. This is so beautiful. Thank you."

He shrugged. "Thought you'd like to have it." He looked her up and down. "You're a bit taller, but it should fit."

"I'll treasure it."

She invited him in and offered him coffee. She could tell he was surprised that she would consider such a white-eyes act, but she could also tell he was pleased.

Truthfully, she had longed for such an occasion. She had many things to say to this man. Now that the opportunity was at hand, she was uncertain how to proceed, but she would not let it pass.

She motioned him to a chair at the small table, one of several pieces of furniture he and Nick Bourbon had brought out a week before.

"Did Sabrina tell you about our talk that last time I stayed with her?"

"Some of it," he acknowledged.

"She is very wise." She came to sit beside him at the table. "I'm sorry for all the hurt I caused you."

"Now, Ket, you didn't—"

"I didn't give you a chance to be my father," she said simply. "I regret that. I hated Sabrina, and I shouldn't have."

"You'd lost so much," he said. "How were you to know?"

"I didn't try."

"You were a child."

"I am no longer."

"That is true," he acknowledged with a grin. "You've made a beautiful woman, Keturah. Your mother would be very proud."

He left soon after, and she hugged him good-bye. "I want to be your daughter again."

"Now, Ket, you've always been my daughter. I never gave up—"

"I know. Sabrina told me. What I mean is, now I *want* to be part of your family."

He hugged her tightly, and she knew his emotions ran high. When he stepped into his saddle, she thanked him again for the dress.

He grinned. "Thought you might like to wear it to the party Sabrina and Lena are planning."

Now the party day had arrived. It was a beautiful sunshiny day, which everyone took to be the harbinger of spring.

"There's more than family," Ket worried, seeing their guests ride down the hill one after another.

"Just about the whole town," Blake agreed.

Except of course J. J. Carmichael. Ket felt bad about that, or she would have if Blake hadn't been so obviously happy.

With that thought, she decided she could endure a few hours being uncomfortable in the company of white eyes, for the sake of the man who had truly been disillusioned by the father he had wanted so badly to love.

Each woman who attended brought a layer for the stack

cake, which Sabrina and Lena assembled on the table the
had set up under the cottonwood tree.

While the women worked at getting the meal ready to
serve, the men set up extra tables constructed from saw
horses and planks.

Luke and Tres Robles were everywhere under foot
claiming credit for getting Blake and Ket together. Then
true boys their age, when serving time arrived, they were
off in the hills.

Ket found them tumbling about on the ledge above
the creek, arguing over their latest obsession: Luke's baby
sister, Penny.

"That's a strange name for a girl," Tres Robles argued

"Ain't neither," Luke replied. "Her hair's copper, so
she's named Penny. Makes more sense than your name.'

"What's wrong with my name?"

"Tres Robles? Who ever heard of a boy named Three
Hills?"

"That's not what it means."

"Is, too."

"At least I wasn't baptized in any ol' red well water."

"Penny wasn't baptized in that well."

"Can't tell by lookin'," Tres taunted. "If I had a baby
sister, I wouldn't let them baptize her in the well."

"If you *had* a sister."

Watching from the side, Ket saw Luke's mind change
directions.

" 'Course, since we're almost nearly brothers," Luke
told his friend charitably, "I reckon Penny's almost nearly
your sister."

Tres Robles stopped thrashing about, obviously thinking
this over. Ket felt proud. Then Luke added fuel to the
fight with a new taunt.

"Ha, ha, ha! You have a sister who had her head dunked
in the well."

Ket broke it up. "If you want cake you'd better wash

p.'' When they exchanged wily glances, she quickly added,
In the creek.''

Before the cake was cut, Tremayne broke out cham-
agne to toast his new son-in-law and his first-born daugh-
er. Instead of feeling uncomfortable, Ket felt only loved.

Then it was Blake's turn. He led Ket to the well, where
e surprised her by reciting the Legend of Apache Wells.

"Since Luke and Tres Robles splashed me with well
ater that first day we camped here," he told those gath-
red around, "don't reckon it'll be necessary again."

He kissed her in front of everybody there, then lifted
is glass in a toast.

"To Luke and Tres Robles. Without their help I'd proba-
ly never have lassoed Ket's wild heart."

Then he kissed her again and she knew at last that she
as standing in the place where she had always belonged—
n this mystical valley beside the legendary well surrounded
y friends and family and in the arms of the man she knew
he had been destined to love.

The Legend of Apache Wells

After the Great Spirit created the earth and the heaven, He hung the moon and flung a handful of stars into the ebony sky. In that single moment before the People were fashioned from the rock of the sacred mountain, an errant star slipped from the hand of the Great Spirit. Falling to the ground, it formed a crater that reached to the heart of our Mother Earth. From the depths of this crater sprang a pool so rich with the blood of life that only a man of great powers dared drink from it. And the word came down that he who drank of the water and lived would be chief of all he surveyed. Should this chief become lonely he had only to bathe in these sacred waters to find love everlasting. But for those who would bring harm to the People, the water would become fire and they would be consumed by it.

AUTHOR'S NOTE

Today the rugged region of Texas west of the Pecos River is known as the Trans-Pecos region. West of the Pecos indicates not only rugged territory, but rugged individuals.

In writing this story I have attempted to be true to this ruggedness—both the people and the land which has formed them.

The characters I portray here, especially the officers who served at Fort Davis, are entirely fictional and are in no way intended to reflect on the integrity of the dedicated men who served this post, which was considered the "Queen of the Frontier Posts" by many who served there.

Legends of the Fort Davis area are dear to the hearts of the citizens, and I have delighted in using some of them in these stories.

The story of Emily, the Apache child found on the battlefield and adopted by a Fort Davis officer and his wife, is based on one of the most beloved legends in the Fort Davis area. Indian Emily's story occurred basically as I have related it here and in my first Tremayne book, *Chance of a Lifetime*, (Zebra, 3/99).

The story of the sheepherder Manuel Ramériz follows another much loved local legend.

I have condensed a couple of important dates in order to fit events into the framework of this novel:

1. The great Apache war chief Victorio was killed along with most of his followers in the mountain stronghold of Tres Castillos in Northern Mexico on October 14, 1880.

2. *The last Indian battle in Texas was fought around Victorio Canyon in the Diablo Mountains on January 28, 1881, after their leader's death in Mexico.*

For anyone wishing to read earlier accounts of the Tr
maynes of Apache Wells and their friends and foes, *Chan
of a Lifetime* tells the story of Sabrina and Tremayne.